STOLEN
MOMENTS

ARIEL TACHNA

Dreamspinner Press

Published by
Dreamspinner Press
382 NE 191st Street #88329
Miami, FL 33179-3899, USA
http://www.dreamspinnerpress.com/

Stolen Moments

Cover Art by Reese Dante   http://www.reesedante.com

ISBN: 978-1-61372-270-1

Printed in the United States of America
First Edition
December 2011

eBook edition available
eBook ISBN: 978-1-61372-271-8

ARIEL TACHNA
Contemporary Romance at its Finest

Her Two Dads

"…one of the most emotionally rewarding and uplifting love stories that I have read in a long time." —Dark Diva Reviews

"This is one of the best books I have ever read."
—Judging the Book by Its Pages

"…a fast-paced story with a well developed storyline that will leave you begging for more. It's a story about overcoming hatred and bigotry, the joys of parenthood and discovering love when you least expect it."
—Literary Nymphs

"…a sweet and stirring novel about the power of love and family."
—Romance Junkies

Seducing C.C.

"…a great comfort read." —Blackraven Reviews

"…a seductively sexy and romantic story." —Night Owl Reviews

Out of the Fire

"This story tore at my heart." —TwoLips Recommended Read

"…something in it for just about everybody who has a kink…"
—The Romance Studio

Once in a Lifetime

"… a coming-of-age story that introduces heart-pounding firsts and nostalgic lasts." —¡Miraculous!

http://www.dreamspinnerpress.com

NOVELS BY ARIEL TACHNA

Her Two Dads
The Inventor's Companion
The Matelot
Once in a Lifetime
Overdrive
Out of the Fire
Seducing C.C.
A Summer Place

THE PARTNERSHIP IN BLOOD NOVELS
Alliance in Blood
Covenant in Blood
Conflict in Blood
Reparation in Blood
Perilous Partnership
Reluctant Partnerships

WITH NICKI BENNETT
All For One
Checkmate
Hot Cargo
Under the Skin

WITH MADELEINE URBAN
Sutcliffe Cove

NOVELLAS BY ARIEL TACHNA

Healing in His Wings
Rediscovery
Rose Among the Ruins
Why Nileas Loved the Sea

WITH NICKI BENNETT
Something About Harry
Tying the Knot
THE EXPLORING LIMITS SERIES
Book 1: Exploring Limits
Book 2: Stretching Limits
Book 3: Refining Limits
Book 4: Breaking Limits
Book 5: Transcending Limits
Book 6: No Limits

AVAILABLE AT DREAMSPINNER PRESS
http://www.dreamspinnerpress.com

To Nicki,
who goes on this journey with me
wherever it may lead.

[*1*]

WHEN the phone rang and Jacob Peters saw the name that flashed up on the caller ID, he almost didn't answer. He hadn't spoken with his former lover, Beau Braedon, in nearly a year, not since he'd called to tell Beau he was going to do the honorable thing and marry Melissa Winters because she was carrying his child. He wouldn't have answered if Melissa had been home or if Finn, their three-month-old son, had been awake, but Beau had picked the perfect time to call, the one moment when all the reasons not to talk to him were absent.

"Hello?"

"I need to see you," Beau said without preamble, the sound of his voice, the demand in his words bringing back all the reasons Jacob had broken things off between them a year ago. "It's been too long."

Jacob closed his eyes against the longing that challenged his determination to resist Beau's pleas. Yes, he had been the one to end things between them a year ago, but he hadn't actually expected it to work. He'd expected.... It didn't matter what he'd expected. He hadn't heard from Beau since his wedding, and now, out of the blue, the man he still loved despite everything wanted to see him again.

"I'll be in Prestonsburg next weekend for a teaching conference," Jacob said, the words out before he could stop them. He knew better than to agree to this. He knew what would happen if they met up again. The same thing that had happened every time they met up when they were still together. "What explanation are you going to make up this time if anyone asks what we're doing together?"

"You're married with a new baby. If anyone sees us, we're old friends catching up on the news," Beau said, the explanation too pat and too swift for Jacob to be comfortable with it. When they'd first met two years earlier, working on a Big Brothers Big Sisters summer program,

Beau had insisted they be discreet, always having an excuse for their "dates" so no one would guess they were a couple. It had created a world of tension between them as time went on. "We'll still be discreet, of course, so hopefully no one will even know we saw each other, but if they do, we'll have an explanation ready."

Discreet. Such an innocuous word to have caused so much havoc in Jacob's life for over two years. "You haven't changed your mind, then."

"We've talked about this."

"Yes, we have," Jacob said with a sigh, "and discretion was the path we decided to take. That's fine, but don't snap at me for the choices you made. You were the one who said we couldn't have a life together, so don't yell at me because all you got was the crumbs."

"I'm sorry, Jake. You're right," Beau said. "It's just been a long time, and I'm restless. Call me when you get to town. I'll feel better after I see you."

"I'll call you when I get to town Thursday night," Jacob promised, already regretting agreeing. "You can tell me where to meet you then."

JACOB navigated the country roads between Elliot and Prestonsburg with the ease of someone who had driven the route too many times to count. The familiarity allowed his thoughts to wander to the night ahead and back over the two years that had led them to this point. Sometimes he wondered how he'd ended up here in Elliot, closeted, married to a woman he didn't love, with a new baby he adored and a lover who only wanted him sometimes.

That wasn't fair to Beau. Jacob had no doubt Beau wanted him all the time, but the realities of life in a small southern town, the realities of their careers in such towns, made that difficult.

He'd sworn when he left home to go off to college that he was done with the South. He'd thought if he heard his mother's favorite expression, "That just isn't done," one more time, he'd scream. And yet he'd ended up in a different southern town, but just as conservative as the one he'd left. When he signed up for Teach For America, he'd expected to end up in an urban center, dealing with underserved kids there. He hadn't expected to end up in Elliot. He hadn't expected to fall in love with Elliot. Sure, it was the same southern conservatism as his childhood home, but the kids were so hungry for knowledge and so in awe of his experiences. When his two-year commitment was up, he'd stayed. He hadn't been able to remain in the same school because of funding cuts, but he'd gotten a job at the Elliot Christian Academy instead.

The kids there might be from slightly more well-off families since they had to be able to pay the tuition, but that didn't mean they were less in need of good teachers, and Jacob was good. He had been in Elliot for six years, and every kid he'd taught, in either school, had left his fourth-grade classroom either on grade level or at least two grade levels ahead of where they had been when they came to him. And many of them were well above grade level.

It was one of the reasons he'd gone along with Beau's crazy plan. If he came out, he'd lose his job at the Christian school for sure, and finding a job at a public school would be challenging given the financial problems that had led to so many schools cutting positions left and right in a desperate attempt to make ends meet. If he didn't even have a recommendation because of the reasons for his dismissal, it would probably be impossible. It was unusual enough to have a man in an elementary classroom. He doubted Elliot, or even Prestonsburg, was ready for a gay man in an elementary classroom.

He sighed. Beau. Beau's court schedule hadn't allowed him to be as involved in the Big Brothers Big Sisters project as Jacob was—Beau still had to hear cases at the county courthouse at least part of the day during the week—but he'd been around in the evenings and on the weekends, his crazy sense of humor endearing him to the kids and adults alike. Judge Braedon presided on the bench with all the dignity one would expect of a man in his position, but once the robes came off, Beau was a little kid, more than happy to play basketball with the boys and just as willing to have a tea party with the girls (even the ones who'd already kicked his ass at basketball).

Jacob had fallen a little in love the first time he'd seen Beau make the effort to draw out Jim, the artistic autistic boy who always sat in the corner and rarely replied to anyone. Beau had sat down next to Jim and started to draw in the sand with a stick. Jacob had stopped to watch, sensing, in the way only those who work with kids can, something miraculous about to happen. It had taken Jim a few minutes to look up from his own drawing, but when he did, he spoke for the first time Jacob had ever heard. "The head is crooked."

Beau handed the boy the stick. "Fix it for me."

Jim had taken the stick, erased Beau's drawing, and fixed it. The two had been fast friends for the rest of the summer. Beau had even managed to get Jim to put down his sketch pad and participate in some of the other group activities. Not all of them. Jim still refused to play basketball. But it was more than anyone else had been able to do.

It was the memories of moments like those that made it so hard for Jacob to end things with Beau. As screwed up as their relationship was, especially now, Jacob loved the man, and nothing seemed to be able to change that. Not the hiding, not the limited number of times they saw each other in the year they were together, not the anger and hurt at yet another canceled meeting that had led him to break things off with Beau, get drunk, and sleep with Melissa a year ago. Nothing.

Because no matter how angry or hurt or frustrated or sad he was at any given moment, he couldn't deny the existence of the man he fell in love with.

They'd had a week together, after the summer ended. Beau had a cruise planned for Thanksgiving, a vacation for himself, and there had been space available. Jacob had purchased a ticket as well, not mentioning his reasons for the trip to anyone else, simply citing his lack of vacations since moving to Elliot. He and Beau had spent hours on the phone planning all the things they could do at each of the stops: snorkeling, scuba diving, hiking, swimming.

They'd hardly left the cabin except to eat, too caught up in the total freedom to love each other to care about anything else.

It was the happiest Jacob could ever remember being. He was young and in love with a magnificent, marvelous man. Everything else had seemed unimportant.

Beau hadn't agreed, insisting they couldn't damn the torpedoes and simply come out when they got back. They had to be discreet. Neither Elliot nor Prestonsburg was ready for a gay couple living openly in its midst. It had been a huge risk on Beau's part to even approach Jacob the first time. If he had misread the situation and Jacob had made a stink, Beau would have lost all credibility on the bench and wouldn't have been reelected.

Beau hadn't misread the situation and Jacob had been eagerly receptive to his advances, but Jacob was bound by the morality clause in his contract, and while homosexuality wasn't specifically forbidden in so many words, he knew what the reaction of the board of directors would be. A colleague had been reprimanded for cussing at a city function not even associated with the school. It was a reprimand, not a dismissal, but Jacob knew better than to test his luck. If he came out, he'd have to change schools. He'd been willing to do that, to move to Prestonsburg or even to leave the area entirely, to be with Beau.

Beau nipped that idea in the bud. Prestonsburg was his home. He had a life and a career there, and he wasn't willing to give that up. Furthermore, his mother was in the late stages of Alzheimer's disease, and her doctors advised against moving her. Jacob should have walked away right then, but he hadn't. He'd agreed to Beau's plan to see each other every few weeks, when they could find a reason for Jacob to be in Prestonsburg and a plausible excuse for them to meet if anyone saw them.

Every few weeks had turned into every couple of months. And then Beau had canceled three meetings in a row.

After the third cancellation, Jacob had been determined to end things once and for all. He'd gone out, gotten drunk, and gone home with the first sweet thing to approach him. When she showed up on his doorstep a month later claiming to be pregnant with his baby, he'd looked at the empty wasteland of his life and jumped at the chance not to be alone anymore. He didn't love Melissa, and he had no illusions that she loved him, but he loved the baby. Even when it was no more than a bump in Melissa's belly, he'd loved the baby. Now, he could sit and hold Finn for hours.

Jacob had a lot of regrets as he drove toward Prestonsburg and, hopefully, Beau, but he would never regret having Finn: the one good and pure thing in his life.

JACOB slumped on the hotel bed, already missing Finn. He was exhausted from the sleepless nights, but he loved his son to distraction, more than enough to make up for a few interrupted dreams. He was tempted to take a nap before calling Beau, but he was afraid if he did, he wouldn't wake up, and he didn't want to complicate things any more than they already were. He could sleep late in the morning. The workshops for the annual school meeting didn't start until noon.

Steeling himself for whatever mood Beau might be in, he dialed the number.

"Hello?"

"Hi, Beau, I'm at the hotel."

"It'll look odd if I come there," Beau said. "I don't have any reason to visit a hotel in my hometown. Can you meet me at a friend's house? He's out of town and left me his key so I can water his plants. It would be a neutral spot, nothing to draw the attention of anyone who might see you."

"I thought you said no one would care about two old friends catching up to share news of one's new baby," Jacob reminded him. "They're far more likely to question us meeting at your friend's house than at yours."

"Only if they see us together," Beau said. "I can walk down the alley to his backyard. No one will see me going inside."

"Give me the address," Jacob said tiredly. He had reached the point of mostly not caring, other than the fact that Beau obviously cared whether people saw them together, but he wouldn't argue. They'd have precious little time together as it was. "I'll be there as soon as I get directions."

Jacob noted the address on the pad by the phone. He thought about taking a quick shower, but if he was honest with himself, he needed to see Beau too. He'd mostly stopped calling to arrange meetings before their breakup because Beau had an excuse to say no more often than he said yes, but that didn't mean the need for his lover's presence had lessened.

A quick search on MapQuest gave Jacob the directions he needed to get to Beau's friend's house. Jacob only hoped no one would see them, because the pretense of friends meeting up there would be far harder to defend than if they met at Beau's house or if Beau came to see Jacob at the hotel. This was Beau's game, though, and Jacob would play it his way. It had been too long since he'd last been fucked. Not since the last time he'd seen Beau, fifteen months ago.

The drive across Prestonsburg took all of twenty minutes at the height of rush hour traffic, and Jacob found the house, a 1920s brick Tudor, with ease. He parked his car down the street, not sure Beau would want him to park in the driveway where anyone passing by would see his car at that specific address. Beau's car wasn't in the driveway either, but he had said he would come up the back alley, so that was no surprise. Heart pounding in his chest as he walked toward the house in question, Jacob tried to act like he belonged there and had no reason to blush or worry about what the neighbors might say.

The door to the house stood ajar in silent welcome, but Jacob grimaced at the sight anyway, knowing Beau had opened it so he wouldn't have to answer the door—and be visible from the street—when Jacob came in. Jacob wondered why he put up with the charade, but when he closed the door behind him, hard arms closed around him, pulling him back against a body that should never be hidden beneath a judge's robes, and Jacob knew the answer.

Nobody made him feel like Beau made him feel.

He relaxed into Beau's embrace, not trying to turn or take control. If Beau could stay long enough for their hurried encounter to stretch into a second round, Jacob would press his own demands then, but for now, he ceded control to Beau as he had from the very beginning.

"I've missed you," Beau murmured in his ear, his breath teasing the hairs on Jacob's neck the same way his hands teased Jacob's skin through his clothes.

"I've missed you too," Jacob said, angling his head in hope of a kiss. It came almost immediately, Beau's lips closing over his, his tongue surging deep as he urged Jacob to turn in his arms.

Jacob moved willingly, wanting nothing more, now that he was here, than to find oblivion in Beau's arms for a few stolen hours. Reality would intrude again, but for now, he could pretend he was coming home to his partner's loving embrace from a few days away.

Beau's hands delved beneath Jacob's clothing, pushing down the casual jeans he'd donned, wanting to be comfortable before driving into Prestonsburg. Jacob moaned into the kiss as Beau squeezed his ass, massaging the muscles as he teased the crease. Another time, Jacob might have protested the lack of foreplay, but it had been over a year since they had been together, and Jacob was as eager as Beau was, sliding a hand between them to undo Beau's trousers as well, working his fingers around the thick girth of the shaft that would soon split him wide open.

He couldn't wait.

"Now," he begged, breaking the kiss. "Fuck me now."

Beau spun Jacob around and urged him into the parlor, dim with the curtains drawn, to kneel on the straight-back chair on one side of a gilt mirror. Jacob braced his arms on the back of the chair, pushing his ass out in blatant invitation. Seconds later, slick fingers breached him, working the slippery gel inside him. The stretch stung a little, his muscles not used to giving beneath a lover's penetration after the long drought, but Jacob panted through the pain until his guardian ring relaxed. He rocked back against the invading fingers, signaling his readiness for more. Beau didn't need any more than that, replacing his fingers with his sheathed cock faster than Jacob could blink. He moaned again as his body gave beneath the amorous onslaught, welcoming his lover back inside him. Back home.

Then the tip prodded his prostate, and all thought fled as he gave in to the erotic stimulation. He stroked himself in rhythm with Beau's thrusts, his climax already boiling deep in his gut. It wouldn't take much more and he'd lose it completely.

"I love you."

Beau's words shredded what remained of Jacob's control. He barely had the forethought to cup his hand over his erection to catch the outpouring so it wouldn't stain the chair and give them away. Seconds later, he felt Beau's hips stutter against him, a long, low groan proof of his own pleasure.

"I love you too," Jacob said when Beau pulled out and Jacob could turn again to face his lover. "It doesn't fix anything, but I love you too."

"Please, Jacob," Beau said, his voice tired. "I didn't arrange a meeting so we could fight."

"No, only so we could fuck," Jacob replied bitterly. "So pat me on the head and send me on my way like a good little trick."

Beau grabbed Jacob's upper arms, shaking him lightly. "Don't say that. Don't even think it. Whatever else you think of me, whatever abuse you want to pile on my head, that's fine, but don't ever demean yourself that way. You are *not* a trick to me."

"You couldn't prove it by the way you've acted this past year," Jacob insisted.

"I'm not the only one who screwed up," Beau retorted, "or have you forgotten which of us slept around behind the other's back?"

"That's a low blow," Jacob snarled. "If all you wanted to do was yell at me, you could have done it over the phone and saved me the trip.

And I didn't sleep around 'behind your back'. I told you before I did it what I was going to do. I don't know when you got the message, but I called and told you before I went out that night. All it would have taken was you calling me back and asking me not to do it, and I would never have gone through with it."

He wouldn't have Finn if he hadn't gone through with it, and he couldn't bring himself to regret that except for the distance it put between Beau and himself now, but he would never have touched Melissa if he'd thought for an instant he could have a life with Beau.

"You want things I can't give you," Beau said tiredly. "I told you that when we got back from Mexico."

"I want things you won't give me," Jacob corrected, "and that's a choice, not something that's set in stone. I'd hoped.... Never mind what I hoped, it's obviously not going to happen. So you tell me, what happens now?"

"I don't know," Beau said slowly. "I only know I'm not happy without you. Unfortunately change comes slowly to Prestonsburg."

"Change requires a catalyst," Jacob replied. "It's a basic tenet of elementary science. If you don't introduce something new into a static equation, it stays balanced. Introduce something new and a reaction will occur until a new balance is attained."

"You can't tell me you use that kind of terminology with your fourth graders."

"You're avoiding the point," Jacob said, pulling away and starting to pace. "You say change comes slowly to Prestonsburg, but you aren't willing to do anything to speed that change along."

"I'm hardly in a position to come out," Beau protested.

"You're in a perfect position to come out," Jacob shouted. "A respected member of the community, a judge with an impeccable record... they wouldn't be able to simply dismiss you as 'one of those people' because they already know you."

"You think any of that would matter?" Beau shouted back. "The respect, the record, all of it would be tarnished with the same black brush and they'd forget all the rest. The fact that I was a faggot would be all that mattered."

"Don't use that kind of language," Jacob snapped. "It demeans both of us. I don't let my students say it. I'm not about to let you get away with it."

"Fine," Beau huffed. "The fact that I'm gay would be all that mattered. Does that make you happier?"

"None of this makes me happy," Jacob said with a deep sigh, "and no choice of words will change that."

"Short of coming out, what would make you happy?" Beau asked, his voice returning to a more even tenor.

"I don't know," Jacob admitted. "I miss you like crazy, but it seems like all we do when we're together is fuck and then fight. As good as the sex makes me feel, I'm not sure it's worth the stripes we tear off each other when we're done."

"Oh, baby," Beau said, pulling Jacob back into his arms and kissing him softly, "I'm sorry. I really didn't bring you here to fight. I wanted us to have an evening together like a real couple, even if we have to hide that fact. I wanted to show you how sorry I am for not calling all this time and try to make it up to you. I wanted…. It doesn't matter what I wanted."

Jacob rested his head on Beau's shoulder, allowing himself the comfort of being held. "It does matter what you wanted," he said after a moment. "It matters that you want to do something special for us. I just don't know if I can live with this solution. I don't want to give you up, but I'm not sure I like what else I'm giving up to keep you."

"What do you want me to do?"

"Say you'll move to Atlanta with me," Jacob replied immediately. "You can work in a law firm there. I'll find a job teaching. Melissa won't fight a divorce. She'd probably be thrilled to give me custody of Finn."

"We've been through this. Prestonsburg is my home, and I can't leave my mother," Beau said.

Jacob sighed. He'd known Beau would say that. As much as he hated the situation, he even respected Beau for refusing to leave his mother in the nursing home without being close enough to visit her regularly. "Forget it. There isn't any more solution now than there was a year ago or two years ago. I should go."

"No, please," Beau said. "At least let me fix you dinner. I want to hear about Finn and see his pictures and be with you. Not fighting for once. And I want to make love to you again and then figure out when we can see each other. And not in another six months or a year. We can't come out, but I don't want to lose you."

Jacob wasn't sure that would work, but it was so much more than he'd expected to hear that his heart gave in and he nodded. "So what's for dinner?"

DINNER was surprisingly good and surprisingly relaxed, given their argument, much to Jacob's relief. He wanted to be with Beau outside of bed (or a chair), but he hated the fighting, and it seemed like that was what they did most. They ignored the elephant in the living room by conscious choice, but other than that, they could have been any couple having dinner together. Beau cooked as he'd promised, but he let Jacob help, stopping every so often to kiss him or nuzzle his neck.

Each time he did, the ice around Jacob's heart melted a little more, making him hope somehow this time could be different. He didn't really know how, since Beau still refused to come out, but they were both intelligent men. If they put their heads together, maybe they could concoct a cover people wouldn't see right through. Even in a town as small as Elliot, people carried on affairs without it getting out. Sure, it got out sometimes, but he knew affairs happened more than that. If he and Beau created a plausible cover for each meeting, no one would know what actually happened once the doors closed. They had worked together before. Perhaps they could find another organization to volunteer with, one that would give them the excuse of needing to meet to discuss it.

Or maybe Jacob could arrange a program at school that Beau could participate in, something to teach the students about the judicial system. They would have to meet before each of Beau's visits to his school so they could go over lesson plans. If those meetings took a little longer or became a little more intimate than necessary, no one else had to know.

If Beau really meant what he said about wanting them to see each other more often, they could find a way to make it work.

Jacob gave a passing thought to the fact that seeing Beau, sleeping with Beau, was cheating on Melissa, but since being with Melissa in the first place had been cheating on Beau, Jacob figured he was damned if he did and damned if he didn't. At least if he saw Beau more regularly, he'd be happier, and that had to be better for Finn, even if not for his marriage.

Best of all, Beau had seemed genuinely interested in seeing Finn's pictures and in hearing all about him.

"I miss my son," Beau admitted as Jacob put the pictures away.

"I didn't know you had a son," Jacob said, surprised to learn something new about his lover after all this time. "Where is he?"

"He lives with his mother," Beau said. "She left me on the grounds of emotional neglect when Harrison was two. I was trying to get my career off the ground. I thought she understood that, but apparently not. The ink was barely dry on the divorce settlement when she took Harrison and moved to upstate New York. She apparently met a man on the Internet and moved up there. I get to go see Harrison a couple of times a year, but I can't take him out of New York, so he hasn't been down here since he was two."

"That's awful," Jacob said, holding Finn's picture tight to his chest as if a tighter grip could keep that from ever happening to him. "Didn't you fight it?"

"I tried," Beau said, running his fingers through his blond hair, "but the court wasn't sympathetic. My ex-wife got full custody plus child support. When Harrison turns fifteen, the restrictions will lift a little and he'll hopefully be able to visit me here, but that's still three years away."

"You're welcome to come play with Finn any time," Jacob offered impulsively. "If that will help, I mean. If it reminds you too much of your own son, I understand."

Beau smiled. "That's a kind and generous offer. I might take you up on it someday. For tonight, though, I'm more interested in Finn's daddy than I am in Finn."

Jacob grinned. "I won't say no to that, although I wouldn't complain about a bed this time instead of a chair in the parlor."

"I don't know where my friend keeps the clean sheets," Beau admitted, "but how does the shower sound?"

It wasn't ideal, but Jacob bowed to the constraints of their reality. "A shower sounds wonderful."

If nothing else, he wouldn't have to worry about smelling like sex when he went back to his hotel tonight. Not that he really thought anyone would notice, but better safe than sorry.

Beau led him into a small bathroom off the kitchen. The shower stall had clearly been redone from the original, a large glass enclosure easily big enough for two, with dual showerheads. "It looks like we aren't the only ones who like to share a shower," Jacob said with a grin as Beau turned on the water.

Beau grinned back. "It's a pleasure I wouldn't say no to sharing more often."

Jacob bit back the offer to never shower alone again. He refused to spoil the evening by starting another argument. Instead he reached for the buttons on Beau's shirt, parting the fabric to reveal the mat of blond chest hair he could never get enough of running his fingers through. It had made Beau self-conscious at first, but Jacob loved a hairy chest and hadn't been shy about letting Beau know it.

Now Beau shrugged the shirt off quickly, letting Jacob take his time with the thick pelt, stroking and tangling his fingers in the light curly hairs. "Sometimes I think you like playing with my chest hair better than you like fucking," Beau teased.

Jacob tugged gently. "You're going to make me choose?"

"No," Beau said, the word turning to a moan as Jacob flicked his fingers over Beau's nipples. That was the other thing Jacob loved about Beau's chest. His lover's nipples were nearly as sensitive as his cock, and enough attention paid to them always ensured Jacob a long, hard ride. The round of sex in the parlor notwithstanding, far too much time had passed since they'd had sex for Jacob to want anything less than a thorough round now. Especially since he didn't know when they would meet again.

Replacing one of his hands with his mouth, Jacob used his now free hand to tug off his own shirt. The moment it hit the floor, he draped his arms around Beau's neck, rubbing his smooth skin back and forth against his lover's body. He groaned at the rasp of all that hair, every brush sensitizing his skin until even the flow of air from the shower added to his arousal.

Beau's hands settled on his hips, guiding him so that their cocks nestled together through their clothes as they swayed back and forth, increasing the erotic friction of their upper bodies. "Sometimes I think I could come just from looking at you," Beau whispered, nipping at Jacob's ear. "All hard muscles and smooth skin."

One hand slid between their bodies to tweak Jacob's dark nipple. It pebbled beneath the teasing touch, already half-hard from the brush of Beau's skin. The added stimulation went straight to Jacob's groin, his cock hardening even more in eager sympathy.

"Maybe we should finish getting undressed and get in the shower before we waste all the hot water," Jacob said hoarsely.

"Maybe we should turn off the water and make love on the floor instead," Beau said.

Jacob shook his head. "I am not lying down on that cold floor. If you want my ass, it'll be against the shower wall since a bed isn't an option."

"I was hoping you'd want my ass instead." Beau bit the juncture of Jacob's neck and shoulder, the spot guaranteed to make him weak in the knees, as if the thought of turning the tables on his usually dominant lover wasn't already enough to knock him off balance.

"Really?" Jacob groaned.

"Really," Beau said, lifting his head and kissing Jacob tenderly. "It's been too long. I know that's my fault, but I want to make it up to you."

"I don't mind bottoming," Jacob said. "I love feeling you inside me."

"I know that," Beau replied, "but I want tonight to be special. I'm turning over a new leaf, and this is part of it. I can't give you everything you want, but I can give you this."

"As long as you still fuck me sometimes," Jacob said, "because I really do love feeling you inside me."

"Don't worry. It's not a pleasure I plan on giving up any time soon," Beau said, "but we can be a little more balanced about it."

"Deal," Jacob said, pulling away and dropping his pants as he toed off his shoes. He reached for Beau's trousers the moment he was undressed. "So let's see this ass I'm getting to fuck tonight."

Beau chuckled. "What a mouth for an elementary teacher!"

"I'm not in class right now," Jacob retorted, pushing Beau's pants and underwear down to his ankles. Beau stepped out of them and turned to open the shower door, giving Jacob a prime view of his backside. If it wasn't a classic bubble butt, it was still firm and as smooth as a baby's bottom, in lovely contrast to Beau's chest. Jacob crowded into the shower behind Beau, his cock slotting into the crease as he rubbed against the hard muscle.

Beau turned his head so they could kiss as the hot water ran over them and between them, slicking their skin. Fortunately they were close enough to the same height not to make the kiss too awkward. Jacob combed his fingers through Beau's chest hair again before sliding them down over his lover's taut belly to circle his hardening shaft. Beau groaned through their kiss, the sound reverberating in Jacob's mouth.

Jacob stroked Beau a few times before cupping his balls, rolling them in his palm. Beau's head fell back on Jacob's shoulder. "That's it," Jacob purred. "Relax and let me make you feel good."

"You do," Beau said, his voice husky with desire. "Everything you do to me makes me feel good."

Jacob grinned. "Then you'll really like this. Hands on the wall and don't move."

Beau shifted his weight, taking up the position Jacob had indicated. Jacob angled the showerheads so he wouldn't get a face full of water and then kissed his way down Beau's back, lingering over each vertebra until he reached the top of his crevice.

As if anticipating Jacob's course of action, Beau spread his legs wider. Jacob nipped at the curve of muscle. Beau jumped slightly, bringing a grin to Jacob's face as he parted the cheeks with his thumbs, scenting musk and sweat despite the fall of water over their bodies. Nuzzling closer, he lingered on the preliminaries, wanting to wallow in the freedom to love the other man this way. Beau so rarely gave over control, much less this completely, that Jacob intended to take full advantage of it. He didn't know when he might next have the opportunity.

"Don't tease," Beau pleaded above him, turning to look over his shoulder.

Jacob looked up into the darkened blue eyes and knew he wouldn't ever be able to resist a plea in that soft, urgent voice. With a slow nod, he turned his attention back to what he was doing, his tongue darting out to lick over the tight iris. Beau moaned above him, sending another shot of arousal through Jacob at the thought that he could reduce his articulate lover to moans and sighs.

Before long, Beau started pushing back against Jacob's mouth, urging him to work his tongue inside the guardian ring. The muscle didn't give easily, but Jacob kept licking and sucking and pushing at it with his tongue until finally it opened for him, letting him reach inside.

Not far enough. Never far enough. Jacob thought he could climb all the way inside Beau and still not be deep enough, close enough. He would have to settle for what he could get, extending his tongue as far as it would go and then sliding a finger in next to it when he couldn't go any deeper.

"Oh, fuck," Beau gasped when Jacob found his prostate. Jacob grinned, but he didn't pause to chide Beau for his language. He had more important things to concentrate on, like driving his lover so wild with need that he'd fuck himself on Jacob's cock just to get relief when the time came. Not that Jacob doubted the sincerity of Beau's offer, but he didn't want his lover to balk at the final hurdle. Not now when he finally had a chance to be inside the other man again after so long.

"S-stop," Beau said. "I'm going to come."

"Why is that supposed to discourage me?" Jacob asked, lifting his head but not pausing in his teasing of Beau's gland.

"Because I want to come with you inside me."

They'd already come once before dinner, and Beau wasn't twenty anymore. He was barely in his thirties. Another night, Jacob might have teased him about his recovery time, but not tonight. Tonight he needed the sense of togetherness that came from a shared climax. Relenting, he rose to his feet. "Condoms?" he asked, realizing they didn't have any in the shower.

"In my trouser pocket," Beau said. "There's lube as well."

"I didn't get you wet enough?" Jacob teased as he opened the door to retrieve the necessary items.

"Probably, but it's been a while," Beau said.

It had been. Nearly two years. Jacob had topped a few times on their cruise, but not during any of their furtive meetings since then. There had never been time, and Jacob had learned early on that Beau had to relax into the idea of bottoming. It made the offer tonight all the more precious.

He rolled the condom on quickly and coated his fingers with the slippery gel, working it inside Beau's passage carefully. His patience was nearing an end with the prospect of fucking his lover again after so long finally at hand, but he didn't want to hurt Beau accidentally. It might make him change his mind about letting Jacob top again in the near future.

When Beau was rocking eagerly back into his hand, Jacob pulled his fingers free. "Ready?"

Beau grunted an affirmative, the sound so needy it nearly brought Jacob undone right then, but that wouldn't give Beau what he wanted. He shifted until his cock brushed Beau's entrance, holding himself steady so Beau could push back and impale himself at his own pace. Jacob knew his control wouldn't last for long, but hopefully he could hold out long enough for that first penetration.

To Jacob's surprise, Beau bucked back against him hard, impaling himself in one long thrust. Jacob bit his lip to hold back a moan as he fought for some semblance of control.

"Do it now," Beau ordered, ending that attempt on Jacob's part. He let go, driving hard into his lover's body, his fingers digging mercilessly into Beau's hipbones.

"Yes," Beau hissed, arching his back to change the angle of Jacob's penetration. "Just like that."

Jacob pounded into his lover, all finesse gone in the flurry of mindless need. He was sure he'd regret this later, but for now it felt too damn good to stop. He reached around to enclose Beau's cock in his fist, the loose skin moving with his grip as he strove for Beau's release. Only then could he let himself go.

It only took a few strokes, much to his relief, because he doubted he'd have lasted much longer. The moment he felt the heat of Beau's release mingling with the hot water still raining down on them, he stopped trying to hold back his own climax, his hips stuttering hard as he came in great rolling waves.

He collapsed against Beau's back, needing the support of his lover's body. Fortunately Beau seemed steadier on his feet than Jacob was. He pulled out and tossed the condom in the corner where it wouldn't get drawn into the drain. He'd deal with it later, but for now he needed Beau's arms around him.

Beau obliged, pulling him into a tight embrace and kissing him passionately. "You know I don't let anybody but you love me that way."

"I hope you don't let anybody but me love you any way," Jacob said, too sated to inject much heat into his words. He wanted to demand exclusivity, but he could hardly justify it when he was married to someone else.

"No, but even if I went to Atlanta or Birmingham to find relief, it wouldn't be that way," Beau said.

"If you need 'relief', you call me," Jacob said, possessiveness surging inside him. "I don't want anyone touching you but me." So much for justifications.

"And does that apply to you as well?" Beau asked, his voice far calmer than Jacob had expected it to be.

"All you have to do is say the word and I'll file for divorce tomorrow," Jacob replied immediately, "but I don't see any reason to do that to Melissa or Finn if I'm not going to see you again for six months or more."

The sudden chill in the water interrupted their conversation. "Let's dry off and get dressed," Beau said, "and then we'll talk. Really talk instead of yelling at each other. Maybe we can find a compromise we can both live with."

Jacob had no idea what that would be, but for once, Beau was willing to talk instead of simply dictating the way things would be. He wouldn't look a gift horse in the mouth.

[2]

"SO WHAT are you offering?" Jacob asked seriously when they were dried and dressed and once again sitting at the kitchen table.

"You remember Jim from our Big Brothers Big Sisters summer?" Beau asked.

"Of course I remember him," Jacob said. "I fell in love with you watching you work with him."

"Well, Jim's mother called me the other day," Beau said. "She's very active with the Autism Society, and they're planning a summer program. She was hoping I'd be willing to sit on the steering committee since I'd done so well with Jim before. I told her I'd think about it, but I also asked her if she needed other volunteers. She sounded desperate for help when she said yes."

"So we steer this program together," Jacob said. "That gives us an excuse to see each other in public occasionally."

"They'll have monthly meetings for the full committee," Beau said, "but there will be subcommittees. You know how that goes. If we're the extent of our subcommittee, we can meet as often as we need to under the guise of working on our responsibilities. As long as we've actually made progress at each monthly meeting, no one will question how often we meet in order to get it done."

"An open-ended opportunity to meet as often as we want," Jacob said slowly. "I'd have to see what the actual time commitment would be because of Finn, or else I'd have to bring him with me sometimes."

"I wouldn't mind if you bring him with you sometimes," Beau said. "He's part of your life, which makes him part of mine now."

Jacob wanted to shake his fists at the heavens and demand why Beau hadn't had this attitude a year ago. If he had, Jacob might not have gotten drunk and ended up married to Melissa. He wouldn't have Finn, but his life would be a whole lot less complicated.

"So you've arranged a chance for us to meet regularly," Jacob said, not ready to throw all caution to the wind despite his words in the shower. "What do you want from me in return?"

"Give me six months," Beau requested. "Six months to convince you we can make a relationship work even if we have to hide portions of it. At the end of that six months, if I've convinced you, I hope you'll make good on the offer of divorcing Melissa."

"Meet me for dinner tomorrow night," Jacob said. "You can pick the restaurant, but we have to go out. Bring the information on the program so I can look at the actual time commitment and make a decision. I want the chance to be together, but I won't sneak around when we have a legitimate reason to meet. If people get used to seeing us together when we have a reason, they're less likely to question it should they see us together when we don't have one. They'll assume they know what we're doing and go about their business."

Jacob could see Beau start to refuse and then stop himself. "Why is this so important to you?" Beau asked. Jacob started to get up, but Beau caught his hand, stopping him. "I'm not refusing. I'm trying to understand."

"I feel like your dirty secret," Jacob said after a moment. "I feel like you're ashamed of your feelings for me. I understand the reasons for not telling people that we're gay or together, but sneaking around doesn't help. If someone sees us together now, hiding inside your friend's house, it's far more damning than someone seeing us eating out at a restaurant, especially if we have the Autism Society material on the table between us. I don't particularly care what fiction we create, but I don't want to still be sneaking around to meet you forty years from now."

"I can't do anything while Mama's still alive," Beau said, "but she won't live forever. It may be a few years, but she's seventy-five, and her Alzheimer's isn't her only health issue. She was lucid last week when I went to see her, for the first time in months. Do you know what she was worried about?"

"What?" Jacob asked softly.

"She was worried about me spending all my time alone and not having anyone when she's gone," Beau replied. "She all but ordered me to find myself a wife so she wouldn't have to worry about me anymore. I don't want a wife. I did that once and it was disastrous, but she's right about not wasting time. She made me see how empty my life has been without you."

"I should send her a thank-you note," Jacob said, his voice breaking a little. "She sounds like a wonderful lady."

"She is," Beau agreed, "but chances are, she won't remember our conversation the next time I go to see her, and she wouldn't understand the note even if she remembered the conversation. She doesn't know about me either."

That didn't surprise Jacob. As far as he could tell, he was the only person in Prestonsburg who did. "Will you meet me for dinner tomorrow night?"

"We can have dinner at Third Street Bistro," Beau said after a moment. "That's where most of the business dinners in town take place. It won't be like any of the meals we had on the cruise, but it's probably the best food in town."

"It's not *where* we go that matters," Jacob replied, taking Beau's hand and stroking his thumb over his knuckles. "We could go to McDonald's for all I care. It's the fact that we're going at all. I finish my sessions at six tomorrow, and it isn't one of the evenings that includes dinner. We could meet at seven?"

"Yes, that will give me time to finish up at the courthouse and get home to change," Beau said. "No need to dress up. We're discussing business, but it isn't a business meeting."

"You mean you don't want to see me in a tie?" Jacob teased.

"If you come to dinner in a tie, I won't be able to keep my hands to myself," Beau said, "and that isn't an option while we're in public."

"Maybe I should wear one so you'll take me somewhere private when dinner's over," Jacob said, grin widening. In the time they'd been apart, he'd imagined all kinds of scenarios, including one in which Beau no longer desired him. That fear, at least, had been put to rest by their evening together.

"I thought that was understood," Beau replied.

Jacob squeezed Beau's hand. "I was just teasing, but it's a good point. We let things be 'understood' when we tried this before, and that didn't go so well. Maybe we should lay some ground rules this time so we don't end up with misunderstandings."

"Like what?" Beau asked warily.

"I don't know," Jacob said. "Like how often we want to see each other. Like what we expect from each other when we aren't together. Like how we know whether this experiment is a success at the end of six months."

"How often do you think would be reasonable to see each other?" Beau asked.

Every day, Jacob thought, but he didn't say it aloud. "At least once every two weeks," Jacob said. "I know stuff comes up, and with the baby, it'll come up for me as well, but if one of us has to cancel a meeting, we reschedule it then so we don't go more than two weeks without seeing each other. And the full board meetings for the Autism Society don't count. If you and I discuss our responsibilities while we're together, that's one thing, but if the whole meeting is in public and business-related, that doesn't count."

"That sounds fair," Beau said after a moment. "Could you get away for a weekend now and then? Not every month or anything, but once or twice? Would… your wife agree to that?"

Jacob heard the bitterness in Beau's voice. He had to bite back the reminder that he only had a wife because Beau had pushed him away once too often. They were trying to move forward, not cast blame for the past. "We'd need an excuse," Jacob said. "I could see about finding some other conferences, farther away. I don't need the professional development hours, but she doesn't keep track of things like that. It would give me an excuse to be gone, and if it was in Birmingham or Atlanta, we could disappear into the crowd."

"Atlanta would be better," Beau said. "I'm not unknown in Birmingham."

"I wasn't planning on leaving the hotel room," Jacob quipped. "I want to ask you not to sleep with anyone else, but it feels a little hypocritical when I can't make the same promise."

"Your wife," Beau said again.

"At the moment, I think she'd give me a divorce and even custody of Finn without much argument," Jacob said. "I don't want to give her a reason to be vindictive. I can promise not to initiate anything with her, but if she comes to me, I can only make so many excuses before she gets suspicious."

"Does she… often?"

"She isn't in love with me any more than I'm in love with her," Jacob said, "but she obviously found me attractive enough to sleep with, or we wouldn't have Finn. She isn't after me for sex every night, but once, sometimes twice a week. I don't want her if I can have you, but I can't lose Finn. If sleeping with her occasionally means I get to keep my son when I do file for a divorce, it's a price I'm willing to pay. Is that a deal breaker for you?"

"Just don't tell me about it," Beau said after a moment's pause. "That probably won't stop me from thinking about you with her, but if I don't know, I can pretend you found an excuse this week."

"Are you really okay with that?" Jacob asked.

"No," Beau admitted, "but I figure it's part of my punishment for being stupid enough to let you get away the first time. I'll live with it until you're ready to change it."

Jacob wanted to say he was ready now, but while his heart was eager to pick up where they left off, his mind was more guarded. Beau had made promises he'd been unwilling or unable to keep in the past. While Jacob would turn his life upside down willingly if Beau really meant it this time, he had to be sure. He couldn't risk losing his son for nothing in return. He didn't think Melissa would fight him for custody, but he needed a reason to take that chance in case he was wrong.

"Give me six months like you said, and then hopefully I'll be ready," Jacob said. "Can you think of anything else?"

"Not right now," Beau said, "but if either of us thinks of something, we can always discuss it or adjust things later. It's not like we're drawing up a contract. Now you have to decide what constitutes success."

"I don't really know," Jacob admitted. "You know what my ideal would be, but I know how you feel about that. If we can't shoot for that, then the answer is more nebulous. I have to feel like I'm getting the emotional connection I need along with the physical gratification, because I can live without the physical side if I have to, but not without the emotional side. I don't want to have an affair even though that's what it will look like to everyone else. I want to have the kind of relationship that lasts a lifetime, even if we have to hide it from everyone else for a while longer."

EVERY sound seemed magnified once Jacob left: the dishes clanking together as Beau washed them, his footsteps on the tile floor as he tidied up and put the dishes away, the creak of the shower door as he opened it to dispose of the condom Jacob had tossed to the side after they'd finished making love.

Jacob.

A deep sigh escaped as Beau lifted Jacob's towel to his face, hoping to catch the lingering scent of his lover's body. Jacob had looked good tonight. A little tired, like he wasn't getting enough sleep, but Beau figured he probably wasn't with a new baby in the house. His hair was longer than Beau remembered, too, not that it had ever been short. He kept it pulled back in a messy ponytail that always made Beau want to pull the band free and bury his hands in the nearly black strands. He rarely did because they rarely had time for that. That was one of the things he intended to change.

He'd gotten Jacob's message the night he went out and slept with Melissa. He'd brushed it off, telling himself Jacob wouldn't go that far, wouldn't really end their affair because he'd canceled another meeting. He'd been wrong. Not that Jacob had intended to get Melissa pregnant, but intentions hadn't changed the facts. Beau had wondered at first if she'd used that as an excuse to trap him into marriage, if she'd seen him as the best prospect without actually knowing who the father was, but he could see Jacob in Finn's face and eyes and the slightly olive cast to his skin. Melissa was far too fair, despite her dark hair, for that to have come from her. He still suspected she was looking for an easy life, and he was jealous as hell that the lucky bitch got to share Jacob's life the way Beau wished he could, but he no longer doubted the baby's paternity.

It galled Beau to admit it, but this whole imbroglio was his fault. He'd had his reasons for the decisions he'd made, and he still stood by those reasons, but he hadn't been willing to work harder to find a compromise. He'd believed Jacob accepted their situation and could live with it just as Beau could. He hadn't counted on the impetuousness of youth.

In retrospect, he should have known. Jacob had always been impetuous. It was one of the things that had attracted Beau to him in the first place.

His court schedule had kept Beau from spending as much time volunteering at the Big Brothers Big Sisters summer program as he would have liked, but he'd ended up spending more time than he'd planned because he'd walked into the first meeting, taken one look at Jacob, and wanted more. The "experienced" volunteers made suggestion after suggestion, all of which Jacob ignored because his experience with kids had already given him a different perspective. Instead of the twenty-year-old self-esteem workshops, he had organized activities centered around the kids, educational but fun. He'd taken them on nature walks and shown them a new way to look at the world around them. He'd taken them to the local dump to help them understand the importance of recycling. Beau missed most of those trips because they took place during the weekdays when he was in court, but the kids were full of news when he arrived in the evenings to give the day volunteers a break. The kids couldn't stop talking about Mr. Jacob, and Beau couldn't stop thinking about him.

On impulse, Beau had invited Jacob back to his house for dinner one Saturday night after the kids had all gone home. They had the day off on Sunday, and Beau had convinced Jacob he could take a few hours and relax in adult company. Jacob had been ridiculously grateful.

The evening had been cool by summer standards, a storm the night before having chased away the humidity for a few hours, so Beau had fired up the grill and they'd sat on the screened-in porch, had a few beers, and talked. Beau couldn't remember exactly what they'd talked about now because it hadn't been anything important or life changing. Just two friends shooting the breeze after a long day.

The fence around Beau's backyard and the bougainvillea that climbed it created the illusion of privacy, and as the sun set and darkness fell, it had seemed to Beau they were the only two people in the world and his garden was the only place in the universe. The porch swing creaked as they swung gently back and forth. The crickets chirped over the whir of the cicadas, and fireflies danced beneath the overhanging branches of the southern live oak trees. It had been the perfect evening, the sense of intimacy so strong that Beau's resolve to ignore his growing attraction to the man beside him had shattered. He'd leaned over suddenly and kissed Jacob.

Thinking about it now, it had been a huge risk. If Jacob had rebuffed him, he could have made a huge stink and ruined Beau's career. At the time, though, it had seemed like the most natural thing in the world.

He'd taken the band from Jacob's hair that night, as they sat on the porch swing and made out like teenagers. He'd pulled it free and run his fingers through the messy fall of hair over and over until he knew every curve of Jacob's scalp by touch, just as he knew every corner of Jacob's mouth by taste.

They hadn't made love that night. They hadn't even discussed it. Darkness had fallen as they sat there, kissing, breaking apart to talk a little, and then kissing some more. They'd both recognized it as too special to rush.

Beau kicked himself regularly for having lost sight of that feeling of specialness when they were apart and all the stresses of being discreet pressed in on him.

The blame for their current situation lay firmly at his feet. He knew that. He hated it, but he knew it. Jacob would have come out in a heartbeat when they got back from their cruise to Mexico, having gone from being occasional lovers to admitting they were in love. It wasn't that easy, though. Beau had his mother to think of. Even if she hadn't been aware of the scandal that would have ensued, Beau had to think about her medical bills. Medicaid only covered a small fraction of her expenses. Beau paid the rest from his pocket. Some days when he visited her, she didn't know him. Some days when he visited, she wasn't even aware of anyone being there, but she still had good days, too, like the one last week that had led to him calling Jacob and trying to mend fences. He didn't want to miss the good days, or even the bad days, she had left.

Jacob had talked about change not coming without a catalyst, but Beau lived in Prestonsburg. He listened to the conversations in the grocery store and at the local diner each time a new state approved gay marriage or civil unions, when DADT was repealed, when California's Proposition 8 was all over the news. Each new victory for gay rights led to another round of wringing hands and demands to know what this world was coming to. Jacob was sure that knowing Beau as they did would change their opinions, but Beau had lived in Prestonsburg his whole life. He knew the people and their attitudes. It would take far more than Beau coming out to change things.

If it were just him, Beau would have considered moving, even if it meant giving up his bench and returning to practicing law, but the doctors insisted moving his mother at this stage would hasten her decline, and Beau simply could not do that to her. If he moved to Atlanta, he could drive to see her most weekends, depending on his case load and whether he could get time, but living in town, he could visit her almost every day. There were other towns closer than Atlanta, but they would be no different than Prestonsburg in their attitudes, he was quite sure, and he wouldn't even have the advantage of being a known quantity there. No, as much as he hated the corner he'd painted himself into, as long as his mother lived, he didn't see as he had any choice.

Then Paula Hodges had called him, asking if he would be willing to help with the Autism Society's new summer program. It had seemed like a sign, and so he'd called Jacob to meet again after not having seen him in a year. Although he and Jacob had talked a few times since breaking off their affair a year ago, the conversations had always degenerated into shouting matches and slamming phones, and even those had stopped after Jacob had told Beau Melissa was pregnant and he was going to do the honorable thing and marry her.

Even then, Beau suspected he could have stopped it if he'd asked Jacob not to go through with the marriage, but he was too shocked, too hurt by hearing his lover had slept with someone else to speak then, and when he was finally ready to say something, it was too late. Melissa was the new Mrs. Peters and Jacob was in love with his baby.

It was a feeling Beau understood wholeheartedly. Beau's feelings toward his ex-wife might range from annoyance to disgust to flat-out hatred at times, but his feelings for his son hadn't changed since the first time he'd held Harrison in his arms. He'd taken one look at the scrunched-up little face and fallen irrevocably in love, so he understood Jacob's need now not to do anything that would give Melissa a reason to fight him for custody. Beau hadn't asked why Jacob was so sure she wouldn't fight it, but they could discuss that another time, when Beau was more certain he could convince Jacob of his sincerity.

Finished with the tidying up, Beau folded the towels into a bundle to carry home and wash. He could return them tomorrow when he watered the plants again. Turning off the lights, he walked out the back door and down the alley to his house. In the honest silence of his thoughts, he could admit he was nervous about his dinner date with Jacob tomorrow. Even with the Autism Society papers on the table between them, he worried he would give something away in the way he looked at Jacob or in the way they talked to each other. He wouldn't refuse—he'd asked Jacob to compromise in so many ways that this seemed like a small thing to give in return—but he knew he'd be on edge the entire time they were at the restaurant.

BEAU left the courthouse as early as he could justify it on Friday, going home and cleaning his house before taking a shower. He didn't know if he'd work up the nerve to invite Jacob back after dinner, but this way he could if he chose to. It seemed odd to think about Jacob here. He had not been in Beau's house since the night they first kissed. After that, after they were together, it hadn't seemed safe to meet there, as if everyone would equate Jacob's presence with them having an affair.

Jacob had accused Beau of treating him like a dirty little secret. Beau had denied it at first, but he was coming to realize Jacob was right. All the reasons not to come out still applied, but this time around Beau would find a better way to balance discretion with his need to see Jacob. This time around, he would find a way to make Jacob feel like he was a central part of Beau's life, even if they couldn't share a house and a life the way Jacob would like.

Gathering the materials on the Autism Society from Paula Hodges, Beau checked his appearance once more in the front hall mirror, making sure his hair was neat and his tie straight. He left the jacket on its hanger since this wasn't really a business meeting, but he didn't feel comfortable going more casual than that. Not on a workday when he was ostensibly meeting with a contact to discuss business of a sort.

Third Street Bistro passed for fine dining in Prestonsburg, but Beau knew it wouldn't qualify anywhere else. Not that the food was bad, because it was really fairly good, but it was simple, unimaginative fare, nothing like what he could find at a fine restaurant in Birmingham or Atlanta. Still, it was the best choice for dinner with Jacob since the whole point was to be out where people would see them together.

Patty, the owner and hostess, greeted him at the door with a friendly smile. "Judge Braedon, how nice to see you!"

"Hello, Patty," Beau said. "I'm meeting an old acquaintance for dinner and to discuss some volunteer work. Do you have a quiet table where we won't be in the way if we stay for a couple of hours to go over all this?" He held up the packet of papers in his hand as he spoke.

"Of course," Patty said. "Come back this way. We'll put you over here where you won't be disturbed by people walking past you all the time." She led Beau to the table in the front corner of the restaurant, just beyond the large bank of windows. They would be visible to anyone who came inside, but someone walking by on the street would not be able to see them. It was the exact mixture of public and private Beau preferred for true business meetings. He didn't know what Jacob would think of it, but it suited Beau to a tee.

"This is perfect," he said with a smile. "And I can keep an eye out for my friend from here as well so you don't have to worry about me."

"Do you want a bottle of wine or a beer or anything?" Patty asked.

"I think I'll wait and see what my friend wants," Beau said. "If he isn't drinking, I certainly don't need a whole bottle of wine."

He stifled the memory of sharing a bottle of wine with Jacob on their cruise, drinking half of it at dinner, and taking the rest back to their cabin, where they had tasted it from each other's mouths and skin. The last thing he needed was for Patty to notice his discomfiture.

"I'll just bring you some water until he gets here, then," Patty said. "Specials are on the board like always."

Beau thanked her and opened up the packet from the Autism Society detailing the work it did in the area as well as the budget and the current shortfall, pretending to study the figures while he waited for Jacob to arrive. A few minutes later, the door to the restaurant opened again and Jacob came in, looking windblown and positively edible in his polo shirt with his hair coming loose from its queue as if a lover's fingers had been tugging at it. Beau shifted uncomfortably on the chair as his body reacted to the image of combing the stray tendrils back from Jacob's face. He lifted a hand to draw Jacob's attention his way, his breath catching in his throat at the smile that lit Jacob's eyes from within, little lines appearing around his mouth and eyes. The expression hit Beau in the gut. He hadn't seen Jacob smile like that since they had returned from Mexico, and now he seemed so happy, all because of one measly business dinner.

Jacob joined him at the table, and Patty appeared with a glass of water for each of them moments later. "Welcome to Third Street Bistro," she said. "I don't think I've seen you here before."

"No, this is my first time here," Jacob said. "I'm in town for the teaching conference and ran into the judge, who wanted to discuss some volunteer work. He suggested we come here, with the conference being just down the street. So tell me what's good."

"Everything," Patty said with a laugh, "but the specials are on the board over there. Mark does wonders with gumbo."

"Mark is Patty's husband and the chef here," Beau added. "And she's right. The gumbo is very good. So is the venison when it's in season."

"Fortunately for me it is," Jacob said with a grin. "What are you having? Maybe we can split a bottle of wine."

"I'll have the venison too," Beau decided, "and we'll have a bottle of that Ménage à Trois. It should go well with the meal."

"I'll get the orders in and bring your wine right out," Patty said.

Looking back at Jacob, Beau saw the smile had faded. "What's wrong?" he asked softly.

"Not the wine I would have picked," Jacob replied equally as softly, glancing around to make sure no one was close enough to overhear them. "Not under the circumstances."

It took Beau a moment to follow Jacob's train of thought. Ménage à trois. Melissa. "I didn't even think about that," Beau said. "I was thinking about a wine I knew Patty had that would go with the meal. I'm sorry, Jake. I can call her back and order something else."

"No, don't do that," Jacob said. "It will only draw attention to us. It's a bottle of wine, and I'm sure it's a good one if you chose it." He summoned a smile. "Let's talk about something else. How was your day at court?"

"Same as always," Beau replied. "Mostly parking tickets and civil disputes. We don't get a lot of crime in Prestonsburg. How was the conference today? Did you learn anything worthwhile?"

"There were a couple of interesting sessions," Jacob replied, "although the ones I'm really looking forward to are tomorrow."

"Which ones are those?" Beau asked. Jacob's answer would undoubtedly go over his head, but it wasn't as much about the answer as it was about him asking the questions. That's what couples did. They asked.

Jacob started talking animatedly about centers and self-directed learning and Montessori theories. As he'd known it would, the vernacular lost Beau almost immediately, but the joy on Jacob's face as he talked made understanding unimportant. He could ask for explanations another time. For now, he simply basked in the presence of his lover.

"You're beautiful when you get all passionate like that," Beau murmured, glancing around to make sure no one was close enough to hear him. "You should always be this excited about life."

Jacob flushed, reaching for his glass of water and sipping it nervously. "I'm sorry. You invited me to dinner so we could talk about the Autism Society, and all I've done is rattle on about my conference."

Beau wished they were alone so he could reach for Jacob's hand or, better yet, kiss his lover to stop the self-deprecation, but the setting precluded that. Instead he slid his foot against Jacob's under the table, hoping Jacob would understand.

Just as their feet touched, Parker Nicholson, a lawyer Beau often saw in court, came over to the table. "Beau, what are you doing here?"

"Hello, Parker," Beau said, drawing his foot back slowly though he doubted the man could see it with the shadows from the table. "I'm having dinner, of course. What are you doing here?"

"Touché," Parker said. "We just don't see you out all that often."

"I don't know if you've met Jacob Peters," Beau said. "He's a teacher down in Elliot. We met a couple of years ago on a volunteer project, and I'm trying to rope him into another one."

Parker nodded in Jacob's direction. "Will we see you at the Oaks this weekend?"

"I don't know," Beau said. He maintained a membership at the exclusive country club because it was expected of him and because it was a good way to campaign subtly without having to do much more than attend the occasional function, but he hoped to spend as much time as possible with Jacob while he was in town. "I hadn't really made any plans."

"You should come out tomorrow," Parker said. "Ken Dickerson challenged Aaron Waters to a grudge match on the tennis courts. It'll be quite the sight to see."

"I'm sure it will be," Beau agreed. "They've been trying to kill each other on the courts for years. I'll have to see what I can get done in the morning. I've been neglecting my yard and it shows."

"You really should hire a lawn service and be done with it," Parker said. "There's no reason to do all that yourself."

"I enjoy it," Beau said. "Now, I hate to be rude, but Jacob and I have business to discuss, and I know he's on a tight schedule. I'll look for you tomorrow if I make it out to the Oaks."

"They're starting at three," Parker said with another nod for Jacob.

"I'm sorry about that," Beau said when Parker was out of earshot. "The man lives for that country club."

"It's fine," Jacob said. "I know you don't exist in a vacuum. I don't mind meeting your friends."

"I wouldn't call him a friend," Beau said. "A colleague and a constituent, but I wouldn't socialize with him by choice."

Patty reappeared with their wine. "Here you go, gentlemen," she said. "I've put your order in, but it'll be a few minutes. Are you sure you don't want something while you wait?"

"Do you have any of those fried green tomatoes in the back?" Beau asked. "Those are always a nice appetizer."

"We sure do," Patty said. "I'll bring them right out."

"We can discuss business after we eat," Beau said. "If you have time to linger a little."

"I don't have anywhere to be until eight o'clock tomorrow morning," Jacob said. "There's a keynote speaker with breakfast, but tonight is just for socializing and networking. The idea is that we'll make contacts at these kinds of gatherings to share ideas with later. Sometimes it's more successful than others."

"That's what the country club is for me," Beau said. "A necessary evil. So tell me more about the baby."

Jacob's face took on such a dreamy expression that Beau slid his foot across the space between them again, resting his ankle against Jacob's. "He's amazing," Jacob said with a proud smile. "I'm sure every parent feels that way about their children, but I just want to hold him and watch him all the time. He astounds me regularly."

"I remember when Harrison was that age," Beau said wistfully. "Not that he's less amazing now. I just don't get to share it as often."

"I meant it when I said—"

"Fried green tomatoes as requested," Patty said, setting the platter on the table between them. Beau felt Jacob pull his foot back reflexively at her arrival. "And I included the spicy sauce you like, Beau, as well as some of the regular sauce in case your friend doesn't care for the spicy one."

"Thank you," Jacob said. "I like spicy food, but it's nice to have the choice."

"Anything else I can get you?" Patty asked.

"No, I think we're fine," Beau said, trying to hide his impatience with all the interruptions. He wanted a quiet night out with his lover and instead the world seemed to be conspiring against him. "Just our meals when they're ready."

"Just holler if you need anything," Patty said, leaving again.

"You were saying?" Beau asked.

Jacob shook his head. "Nothing important. Tell me more about what Paula has in mind."

Beau stifled a sigh at the loss of intimacy. He left the folder of papers closed but accepted the change of conversation and described the summer program Paula had outlined for him. "They need help in two ways," Beau said. "They need people to organize the program ahead of time, to line up activities and events for the kids, and then they need people to run the program when it actually takes place. All of the organization will be done by volunteers. They're hoping to do some fundraisers and be able to actually pay some of the staff during the summer, at least a director and a couple of counselors."

"That sounds like a lot of work," Jacob said. "Lots of meetings and all."

"Definitely," Beau agreed, hoping he read Jacob's enthusiasm correctly. "But hopefully very rewarding as well."

Jacob's grin made it clear he had followed Beau's train of thought. "I'm sure it will be. So how often does the full society meet?"

"They have monthly board meetings," Beau said, "but we wouldn't both have to attend those. I could take a few hours away from court to report on the work we've done if the time doesn't suit you to attend. From what Paula said, it sounds like a lot of the board meetings take place during the day, which wouldn't work for you."

"No, that would be hard," Jacob agreed. "I'd need evenings or weekends to be able to attend."

"I can list you as a member of my subcommittee and report on the work we've done," Beau said. "Paula asked if I'd help with the activities for the kids since I worked so well with Jim, and your educational background would be useful in that regard as well."

"Are you spoiling my cooking with business talk?" Patty asked, appearing at the table again. "You've barely touched those tomatoes and now your dinner's ready."

"Leave them," Jacob said. "We'll be good and eat them. I promise."

Beau hid a smile as Jacob charmed Patty as thoroughly as he charmed everyone he met. Not for the first time, Beau thought Jacob would be a great asset during campaigns if Prestonsburg were less homophobic.

"I didn't know you enjoyed gardening," Jacob said as they started to eat.

Beau didn't reply right away, taking a moment to savor the venison. "It's my R & R," he said after he'd swallowed. "The flowers don't expect anything of me except my attention. They don't want the judge's favor or the weight of his approval. A few hours a week with a watering hose and a trowel and they're happy."

Jacob smiled. "I remember being impressed by it the one time I visited."

"You should come see it again," Beau said. "It's not at its best at the moment, with winter coming on, but I've still got some things blooming. The chrysanthemums are riotous at the moment."

"I'd love to see it," Jacob said. "If you think we can."

"I show off my garden to anyone who will look at it," Beau said, feeling his cheeks heat a little. "The neighbors won't be surprised to see me showing it to someone else. And you're about to be a frequent visitor as we work on the Autism Society program, so they may as well get used to seeing you now."

Jacob's smile widened. "I like the sound of that."

[*3*]

"IT IS a beautiful garden," Jacob said, looking around the yard in front of Beau's Victorian-style house. The clapboard siding was freshly painted a lovely dusty gray with brilliant white trim that reflected the setting sun. The front porch wasn't screened like the one in the back, but it ran the length of the house and around onto one side, wicker rocking chairs completing the image of southern comfort. For a moment, Beau allowed himself the fantasy of coming home from the courthouse to find Jacob waiting for him in one of those chairs. The rose bushes were no longer covered in flowers, but the chrysanthemums in front of them burst in rust and yellow, pink and white, a wash of color designed to brighten the darkening fall days. "Show me the rest?"

Beau opened the gate to the backyard, letting Jacob pass through before following him in. As soon as the latch snicked shut, he pulled Jacob into his arms. "I've wanted to kiss you since you walked into the restaurant tonight."

"What are you waiting for?" Jacob asked, nuzzling Beau's jaw. "An invitation?"

"Just a little privacy," Beau replied, catching Jacob's chin with his hand and guiding their lips together.

Beau half expected the kiss to turn wild, as their kisses so often did, but Jacob seemed content to stand quietly in his arms, exchanging tender brushes of lips in the deepening twilight. The cicadas whirred softly, the fragrant night air surrounding them as Jacob's lips parted beneath Beau's, inviting an increase in intimacy. Beau lingered still, tasting the wine they'd had with dinner on Jacob's lips as he delved into his lover's mouth, exploring his palate as if it were the first time they had kissed that way.

"You kissed me for the first time on a night not so different than this one," Jacob said softly, breaking the contact.

"It was a little warmer and there were a few more flowers blooming," Beau agreed, "but yes, it was very much like this one apart from that. I've done a lot of things I regret since then, but I have never regretted kissing you that night."

"I think we both have done a few things to regret," Jacob said. "How about we declare tonight amnesty night? We made mistakes. We admit it. That's done now and we're turning over a new leaf. No more apologies, no more recriminations for what we did wrong. If we have to talk about them, we do so neutrally."

"Deal," Beau said, knowing he was getting off easily with that offer. "Now we just have to seal the deal."

"And how should we do that?" Jacob asked with a grin.

"I thought we might go inside and make love in my bed," Beau proposed. "If that's all right by you."

"All right?" Jacob repeated. "I've been waiting to be invited into your bed since the first time you kissed me. The cabin on the cruise ship doesn't count."

"It's just a bed," Beau said, "nothing special."

Jacob shook his head. "It's your bed and that makes it very special. It could be a mattress on the floor and I wouldn't care. What matters is you've invited me there."

If things were different, Beau wouldn't let him leave his bed, but they weren't, so instead of speaking his thoughts, Beau pulled Jacob close again and kissed him tenderly. They had time tonight, for once, and Beau intended to savor every moment of it, starting with Jacob's mouth. He could feel the hint of stubble against his lips, an erotic rasp on his recently shaved skin. When Jacob deepened the kiss this time, Beau ceded control, giving himself over to his lover. "Tonight is for you," Beau whispered. "Whatever you want, however you want to make love, you decide."

"Let's go inside," Jacob said, kissing Beau softly. "That's a discussion best suited for the privacy of a bedroom."

Beau nodded and led Jacob inside, not bothering with lights as they passed through the kitchen and up the stairs to his bedroom. Making sure the shades were drawn, he flipped on a lamp, bathing the room in a soft glow. "Now," he said, pulling Jacob into his arms again, "what do you want tonight?"

Jacob smiled. "I want you to make love to me," he replied, "like you're never going to let me go. Make me feel like I'm the center of your world."

You are, Beau thought as he kissed Jacob tenderly. He wished he could say the words aloud, but as long as his mother was alive, he couldn't make good on promises like that, and he didn't want Jacob to doubt his sincerity again, not when he had only barely begun to win his way back into his lover's good graces.

His hands roamed slowly as they kissed, the contact still languid despite the growing passion between them, as if they had agreed without words to hold back as long as they could. Always before, Beau would have sought skin by now, his awareness of their limited time together pushing him to hurry their encounter, but no one expected Jacob back at a particular time tonight. They could linger and love as they had on the cruise, taking their time to savor each other. Beau took a step forward, nudging Jacob back toward the four-poster bed in the center of his bedroom. When Jacob bumped the edge of the mattress, he broke their kiss, smiling shyly as he toed his shoes off and lay down across the slate comforter.

Beau's breath caught in his throat at the sight of the younger man sprawled across his bed. He had always resisted bringing Jacob here, knowing that if he did, he wouldn't ever be able to forget the sight. Now that he had Jacob in his bed, a night wouldn't be enough. It was the same reason he had started canceling meetings before, this sense of needing Jacob more than his reality would allow, but he refused to go back to that. As hard as it would be to sleep here alone after having made love with Jacob in this bed, letting the opportunity pass was no longer an option. He had lived in hell over the past year. Anything had to be better than that.

He took off his own shoes and loosened his tie, tossing it onto the chair behind him. Jacob sat up and undid the top two buttons of Beau's shirt. "Now you look more comfortable."

Beau laughed and stretched out on the bed next to Jacob. "I wear them so much I don't even notice anymore."

"Mmm... maybe I should leave your tie on next time," Jacob said, his voice husky. "I rather like the image of you in a tie and nothing else."

"I can put it back on," Beau offered, conscious of his offer to fulfill any fantasy Jacob had tonight.

"Not tonight. All I want tonight is your skin against mine."

"Then let's see about making that wish come true," Beau said huskily, reaching for the buttons on Jacob's shirt. He kissed his way down the center of Jacob's chest as he went, licking and nipping at the smooth skin. He could smell the cologne Jacob had applied earlier in the day as well as a hint of sweat, the combined scents arousing him intensely. He paused for a moment, his lips resting against Jacob's navel as he wrestled with the words that pressed against his silence.

"I love you," he whispered finally, tracing the letters onto Jacob's skin. If they were not the words he wished he could offer, they would have to do for now.

Jacob's fingers stroked across his scalp in silent answer, the tender caress as clear as if Jacob had shouted his feelings from the housetops. Beau lifted his head, meeting Jacob's eyes. "I can't believe you're actually here with me."

The moment the words left his mouth, he wished he could call them back, not because they were false—they couldn't have been any truer—but because he saw the change in Jacob's expression. Beau had kept this situation from occurring before now. Jacob didn't have to say the words aloud for Beau to know he was thinking them. Determined to make up for every time he'd canceled, for every night Jacob had spent alone and in doubt, Beau lowered his head again, nuzzling the smooth skin. Jacob shifted restlessly beneath him, but Beau stilled him with gentle hands. It would be so easy to rush, to let passion sweep them away and steal their senses once again, but Beau wanted more than that. More importantly, Jacob deserved better than that. He deserved to feel he was loved beyond any question. It would take time for him to trust that feeling, but Beau intended to start tonight. He only had six months to convince Jacob to leave Melissa for a half life that would last as long as Beau's mother lived. He had to make every moment count.

To that end, he left Jacob's pants in place for the moment, focusing on cherishing him rather than arousing him. He licked and nibbled his way across the smooth skin that had rivaled that of the much younger boys when they played shirts and skins basketball two years before. Unlike those boys, though, Jacob had a man's body with a man's strength, something Beau found incredibly alluring. He lingered on the upper curve of Jacob's shoulder, appreciating the breadth of his chest and the harnessed power beneath the soft skin. "Do you have any idea how much your strength turns me on?" he murmured against the rise of Jacob's collarbone. "I lie in bed sometimes and think of you shirtless. I don't even have to imagine the rest to get hard."

Jacob chuckled above him. "And here I was thinking you were the one with the great body."

Beau flushed, not comfortable with the compliment to his physique. He was in decent shape, especially compared to many of his former classmates, but he was ten years older than Jacob, and those years showed. He wasn't heavy by any means, but he wasn't nearly as trim around the waist and hips as Jacob was, his wiry muscles not given to the elegant V that defined Jacob's body.

Beau slid down to the chocolate-drop nipples on each side of Jacob's chest, preferring to distract his lover rather than have Jacob decide to convince him of his own attractiveness. Tonight was about Jacob. Beau had learned early on how sensitive Jacob's nipples were, how attention paid to them could reduce his usually glib lover to a mass of babbling nonsense. Beau needed that tonight. He needed to know he could rouse Jacob to those heights, even after a year apart. Their encounter last night had been passionate but rushed, as much about the anger that never seemed to leave them as it was about the love in Beau's heart. Tonight would be different. Tonight was all about Jacob's pleasure.

"Don't tease," Jacob gasped when Beau tweaked one nipple lightly.

"I'm not teasing," Beau promised, lowering his head to lick one bud quickly. "Tell me what you want and it's yours, or lie back and let me lavish pleasure on you like never before. It's your choice."

Jacob's hand cupped the back of Beau's skull, guiding his head down so his lips closed over one nipple. Taking that as his cue, Beau drew the crinkled bud into his mouth, sucking gently on the slightly salty flesh. Jacob cried out almost immediately, the sound going straight to Beau's cock. He ignored the demands of his own body in favor of Jacob's, sucking harder in response to the increasing pressure of his lover's fingers. Another ragged gasp sounded above him as he nipped at the peaked nipple hard enough to send a jolt through Jacob's body.

Rolling Jacob toward him, he replaced his mouth with his fingers and turned his attention to the other side, showering that areola with the same loving attention its mate had received. Jacob ground against Beau's hip, his cock tenting the front of his pants.

"Take your shirt off," Jacob demanded, tugging ineffectually at the collar of Beau's shirt, all he could reach in their current positions.

Beau sat up for a moment, releasing the rest of the buttons and tossing his shirt aside. He leaned back over Jacob, intending to resume his task, but Jacob had other ideas, pulling him up instead so their lips met at the same time their chests did. "Yesss," Jacob hissed, dragging his chest back and forth against Beau's.

Beau chuckled and caught Jacob's shoulders with his hands, stopping his movement. "Lie still," he ordered. "I'll give you what you want."

Jacob looked like he might argue until Beau undulated above him, rubbing his lightly furred chest deliberately against Jacob's nipples. Jacob gasped and lifted his head blindly, seeking more contact. Beau gave it to him, mating their lips and tongues as he continued to move, determined to leave Jacob mindless. He could feel Jacob's hips beginning to rock in time with his movements, their cocks bumping together through the fabric separating them, but Beau refused to rush, even if it meant taking time to recover before starting round two. He would not take the chance of Jacob feeling like this was another fuck-and-run encounter.

Beneath him, Jacob's movements grew more frantic. Beau almost pulled away to give them a moment to calm before undressing the rest of the way and continuing, but it felt too good to pull back, and Jacob showed no sign of complaining. Beau shifted so his hips settled more fully between Jacob's legs, riding him hard now, the frottage between them as intense as any fucking they had ever done.

Jacob obviously felt it, too, his head falling back as he moaned long and low before collapsing onto the bed in a boneless heap. Beau was so close it hurt, but he stopped moving, letting the passion bubble within him without coming to fruition. Jacob would rouse faster a second time than Beau would. This way they wouldn't have to wait.

Before long, Jacob stirred beneath him. Beau rolled to the side, keeping Jacob close but giving him space to breathe. It took a gratifyingly long time before the limpid eyes opened. "That was... incredible."

"I'm glad," Beau said with a smile. "I wanted to make you feel good."

"You did," Jacob said. "I feel a bit selfish at the moment."

"Don't," Beau said quickly. "The night's young. I'm hoping I can interest you in a second round."

"I'm not averse to the idea," Jacob replied, a smile dancing around his lips, "as long as you let me take care of you this time."

"We'll take care of each other," Beau agreed, stroking Jacob's hair back from his face. "Just as soon as you've recovered."

"In that case," Jacob said, "we're overdressed." He tugged on Beau's belt, undoing it and his pants so he could push them down.

Deciding he could rouse Jacob again faster if they were undressed, Beau stripped Jacob's pants and boxers off as well, the smell of sex strong now.

"You'll have to lend me a pair of shorts," Jacob joked, "or the whole hotel will know what I've been up to."

"We can't have that," Beau replied, his voice light despite the reminder of the risk they were taking. They could share a shower before Jacob left, and if Jacob put on a clean pair of boxers on, no one would be any the wiser. He licked the sticky skin, lapping up some of the cooling fluid. "I bet I can think of a way to clean you up."

"I bet you can," Jacob said hoarsely as Beau nuzzled his quiescent cock.

"Not to mention getting you ready for round two faster."

Jacob groaned and bumped his burgeoning erection against Beau's lips in invitation. Beau didn't hesitate, taking the head in his mouth and sucking lightly as Jacob moaned again and tightened his grip on Beau's skull. Beau chuckled at his lover's eagerness, knowing the vibrations would carry over to Jacob. "Hand me the lube," he said, tipping his head toward the bed stand. "I'm in the mood to multitask."

"Fuck, yes," Jacob gasped, passing the bottle to Beau and spreading his legs so Beau could move between them. Beau took a moment to get settled before returning to licking and sucking at Jacob's cock like it was his favorite treat. He didn't immediately slick his fingers to prepare Jacob. They didn't have to rush, and Beau rather enjoyed the litany of curses falling from Jacob's lips at the moment. His lover was usually so careful about how he spoke. Beau loved that he could make Jacob lose all control this way.

He probed the slit with the tip of his tongue, the salty flavor of a fresh spurt of fluid his reward. Deciding he had waited long enough, he coated his fingers and circled Jacob's entrance, determined to take his time now as he had before. Jacob was getting hard again, but he wasn't completely ready for a second round, and Beau wanted to take Jacob with him when he climaxed this time.

Jacob had other ideas, though, planting his feet on the bed and pressing his hips up into Beau's fingers. "Prepare me already."

Beau did as Jacob ordered, pressing inside with two fingers. Jacob spread his legs wider, welcoming the intimacy. Beau timed his caresses with the movements of his tongue, tickling Jacob's sweet spot at the same moment he pushed his head down, swallowing Jacob deep.

"Oh, fuck!"

The warble of a cell phone broke into the moment. Beau ignored it since it wasn't his ringtone, but Jacob struggled to pull away.

"Ignore it," Beau said, licking the tip of Jacob's cock again.

"I can't," Jacob said, resisting Beau's caress. "It's Melissa."

"What does she want?"

"I don't know," Jacob said, digging through the pile of clothes to find his cell phone on his belt. "Hello?"

Beau guessed Melissa was nagging, given the way Jacob rolled his eyes.

"I'm in the middle of something," Jacob said shortly. "What's going on?"

Beau suppressed a chuckle, leaning over to lick Jacob's skin lightly. He had no idea what the bitch wanted, but Jacob was his for tonight, and he intended to remind his lover of that fact every chance he got.

"What's wrong with him?" Jacob said, brushing away Beau's attentions and rising from the bed.

Beau's stomach fell. He could fight Melissa, but he couldn't fight Finn. He'd lose that battle the moment he engaged it because even if he won tonight, he'd lose Jacob in the end because of it.

"All right. I was in a meeting with an old friend about a new project he thought I'd be interested in. I'll have to go back to the hotel and get my stuff, but I'll be home as soon as I can."

Jacob hung up the phone and turned to face Beau. "I'm sorry, but Melissa says Finn is sick. He's been crying for hours and nothing seems to help."

"Babies cry sometimes," Beau said, feeling Jacob slipping away from him.

"Finn fusses a little when he's hungry or needs his diaper changed, but he doesn't cry," Jacob said, "not really. I could hear him screaming in the background. And Melissa says he's been like that for hours. I don't know what's wrong, but something is. If nothing else, he should have exhausted himself by now, if he's really been crying as long as Melissa said."

Beau nodded, conceding defeat. "Go take care of him. Call me to let me know he's okay?"

Jacob pulled his clothes back on. "I'll call when I get a chance. It may be a couple of days, though. If Finn really is sick, I won't have a lot of time between work and taking care of him. Melissa's a sweet girl, but, well, she's not a natural as a mother."

Beau rose from the bed as Jacob finished dressing. "I know you have to go," he said slowly. "I would never try to keep you from your son, but we made promises to each other as well, promises I want to keep."

"I already said I'd call you," Jacob snapped. "I wasn't the one guilty of not calling before. I won't be now either."

Beau nearly snapped back, but he bit back the sharp retort. They had agreed to let the past stay in the past, and he wouldn't violate that agreement simply because Jacob had. Jacob might be the one leaving tonight, but Beau had made his share of mistakes and canceled his share of meetings in the past. Dragging all of that back out wouldn't help either of them. He caught Jacob's hand instead, kissing him hard and fast before releasing him. "Drive safely. Getting in an accident on the way home won't help anyone, least of all Finn."

"I'll at least send a text when I get there," Jacob said, his expression softening. "I really am sorry about this, but he's never been sick before and—"

"Go," Beau said. "I don't need explanations. I love you."

"I love you too," Jacob said, rushing out the door before Beau could say anything else.

He slumped back down on the bed, his hard-on fading slowly now that the enticement of Jacob's body was gone. If Jacob walked back in, Beau had no doubt it would return immediately, but the scare of the phone call and the tension of the near-argument had killed any desire to take care of himself. With a frustrated sigh, he gathered the scattered clothes and headed for the bathroom to take a shower. The hot water would hopefully unknot some of his muscles so he could sleep.

Standing under the pounding spray, he faced up to the jealousy eating at him. Jacob didn't love Melissa, but she had a claim on his time and attention that Beau didn't have. That was his own fucking fault, but that thought didn't change the reality of Jacob walking out the door, summoned home by the demands of a wife and child.

"This is how Jacob felt when you put propriety and position before him," Beau muttered. "No wonder he got fed up with waiting."

Beau wouldn't get fed up. He had found a way forward now, and he would stay the course until he convinced Jacob it was worth the risk to divorce Melissa in order to be with him, however secretly. Until that time, he'd have to live with the mess of his own making and not make it worse.

THE drive home was a nightmare for Jacob, the sound of Finn screaming in the background of his phone call with Melissa haunting him. He told himself babies got sick all the time and that Finn would be fine. He told himself Melissa was probably overreacting and Finn just had a tummy ache, but all the telling in the world couldn't stop his heart from pounding faster with each minute that passed as he navigated the roads in the dark, eyes searching the verge for the telltale reflections of an animal's eyes. He'd seen what happened when a car hit a deer. He couldn't afford to have that happen tonight.

His conscience ate at him as he drove, all his mother's lectures about cheating spouses replaying in his mind. It didn't matter that he didn't love Melissa, that he'd only married her because of the baby. It didn't matter that she'd lied to him first about her age, then about being on the pill the night they'd slept together. He'd stood before a justice of the peace and made certain promises, promises he'd broken last night and tonight with Beau. Promises he had gone to Prestonsburg knowing he would break. Promises he had agreed to keep breaking until Beau convinced him to divorce Melissa and exchange one set of lies for another.

"Fuck," he muttered, slowing down as he neared the outskirts of Elliot. "This can't possibly be a good idea."

Reaching his house, he sent Beau a quick text saying he'd made it home. He switched the phone off when he was done, not wanting to deal with any replies tonight. He needed to focus on Finn. Everything else could wait.

Melissa met him at the door, all but throwing Finn into his arms. "He's been screaming like that for hours," she said, her voice cracking. "I don't know what else to do!"

"Go take a bath," Jacob said. "Close the door, turn on some music so you can't hear him, and forget about it for a few minutes. You're tired and stressed, and that carries over to him on top of whatever's wrong with him."

Melissa looked so ridiculously grateful that Jacob felt sorry for her. He rocked Finn against him, checking his forehead to see if it felt hot. Finn turned into his touch, his screams quieting to hiccupping sobs. "You aren't sick, are you, baby?" Jacob asked, stroking the smooth curve of Finn's skull with its downy covering of fine hair. "You're tired and scared and probably hungry, and your mom didn't know what to do with you, did she? It's all right. Daddy's home now and we'll make everything better."

He walked into the kitchen, rocking Finn carefully in his arms, continuing the crooning babble. It took a few minutes to prepare a bottle, but by the time it was ready, Finn had settled, the sobs coming only rarely now instead of constantly. Jacob slid the nipple into Finn's mouth and smiled as he sucked hungrily on it.

He could tell from the empty bottles in the sink that Melissa had tried to feed Finn, but as upset as he was, he probably hadn't wanted to eat, and even if he had, he'd probably ended up with an upset stomach from all the tears. It hadn't happened to Finn before, but Jacob had listened to his colleagues talk about their children, as they reminisced and as they gave him advice, and they all warned him about babies getting so worked up they couldn't settle. Usually it had happened with an unfamiliar babysitter rather than with one of the parents, but Melissa didn't spend a lot of time caring for Finn, preferring to leave that to Jacob. Jacob hadn't ever complained about it because he wanted to spend as much time as he could with his son, but now he wondered if it had been such a good idea.

Or maybe you could use it if it comes to a custody battle, the devil on Jacob's shoulder whispered. If Melissa couldn't even take care of Finn when Jacob was gone for a weekend, how could she take care of him permanently?

He snuggled Finn closer. "Don't worry, Finn," he whispered. "I won't let anyone take you away from me."

"He stopped crying."

"He got himself so worked up he couldn't settle down," Jacob said. "The more he screamed, the more frustrated you got, and that tensed him up even more. He'll sleep tonight and you'll both be fine tomorrow. I'll come home after the end of the sessions instead of staying in Prestonsburg. That way you'll have a break. It's not like it's that far a drive."

"He hates me," Melissa said with a pout.

"He doesn't hate you," Jacob said. "He's three months old. He's too young to hate anyone."

"Then why did he settle down for you and not for me?" Melissa demanded petulantly, reminding Jacob once again of just how young she really was. Despite the ID that had proclaimed her to be twenty-two when they first met, she had yet to turn twenty-one, and it showed in her occasional lack of maturity.

"Because I wasn't as tense and stressed as he was," Jacob replied. "The girls at work talk about colicky babies all the time. All you can do is rock them and switch caregivers occasionally to save the sanity of the person watching the baby. And sometimes that change is enough to calm the baby too, for a while, anyway."

"Which means he'll be like this again all day tomorrow while you're gone," Melissa said. "How am I supposed to write my term paper with him screaming?"

"I told you I'd come home after the sessions end," Jacob said, trying to hold on to his patience. He wanted to snap that if she spent more time with Finn, he wouldn't react this way when she did take care of him, but she hadn't heard him any of the other times he'd said it. She wouldn't hear him now. "I'll be here by six since I won't have dinner tomorrow night. And the sessions end at two on Sunday, so I'll be home by three. That'll give you tomorrow evening and Sunday afternoon and evening to work on your paper. It's getting late, but you could even work on it for an hour or two tonight if you wanted."

"And here I was, hoping we could spend a little time together now that Finn has settled down."

Jacob's stomach fell. "If you're that worried about your class, you should take advantage of this time," he reminded her, hoping he sounded like a responsible adult and not like a guilty husband. "We can spend time together after you've finished it."

Melissa's pout grew more pronounced, a distinctly unattractive expression as far as Jacob was concerned, although he thought someone must find it attractive since he saw it on a number of models and ads that were supposed to be sexy. All it did for him was to make him think of his fourth-graders, and while he loved teaching them and gained great satisfaction from watching them thrive under his tutelage, he was also grateful to leave them behind when he went home at the end of the day. Having to deal with the same childishness from a purported adult strained his patience.

"Oh, and while I'm thinking about it," he said, "you'll have one evening next week free as well. I ran into Judge Braedon tonight, and he asked if I'd help with the planning for the Autism Society summer program. He doesn't mind if I take Finn with me, so you can study that night while we're gone. I'll have to call him tomorrow to see what evening he wants to meet since you called before we could finalize a schedule."

Finn finished the bottle and cooed up at Jacob.

"I'll put Finn to bed and let you work on your paper," Jacob continued, not at all above using the baby as an excuse to avoid Melissa until she fell asleep. It wouldn't work every time, but he'd have one hell of a time getting hard with her when he'd been with Beau earlier in the evening. She was pretty enough in her own way, but she wasn't Beau, and tonight that was all that mattered.

"Fine," Melissa huffed, storming into the other room.

"You ready for bed?" Jacob asked Finn, burping him as he walked toward the nursery. "I'll sit and rock you for a while until I'm sure your mommy's gone to sleep. Or maybe I'll sleep in here with you tonight."

He had put a daybed in Finn's room, thinking to make it easier for Melissa to nurse him at night, but her milk hadn't come in right, and so Jacob used the daybed far more often than she did, feeding Finn during the night so she could get a few more hours' sleep before going to class during the day. Being a college student was hard enough without adding the demands of motherhood on top of it. Jacob could have taken the high road and said it was her fault for telling him she was on the pill when she wasn't, but that served no purpose, and he didn't mind getting up with Finn. His students were energetic enough to keep him awake during the day, and Jacob dozed when Finn did in the evenings and through the night. Melissa might not be much of a mother, but she liked cooking and she kept the house clean in exchange for not having to deal with Finn except on the rare occasions when Jacob had a meeting or conference like the one this weekend.

Juggling Finn and his blankets to get comfortable in the rocking chair, Jacob kissed the top of Finn's head. "Let's get some sleep, okay? Daddy's tired tonight, and since I came home to take care of you, I have to get up extra early tomorrow so I don't miss the keynote speaker, so this would be a good night to take your bottle and go right back to sleep."

Finn gurgled softly, his eyes already heavy. Jacob smiled and rested his head against the back of the rocking chair, the smooth motion relaxing him as well, his mind drifting back over the evening with Beau. Dinner had gone well, far better than he'd expected. They had handled the occasional intrusion and question with ease, the Autism Society project giving them legitimacy. Parker Nicholson and his ilk might not understand the impulse that led Beau to volunteer his time that way, but they couldn't criticize it.

Once they were alone, the evening had progressed far better than Jacob had hoped. He'd visited Beau's house once, the night they first kissed, before Beau fell into the trap of thinking that being seen together at all was sure to damn them to the whole world, but he'd never been upstairs until tonight. The house was lovely, although not as meticulously tended as the gardens, but that wasn't the attraction. No, the attraction had definitely been the look in Beau's eyes as he'd made love to Jacob.

He'd looked at Jacob the same way he'd done on their cruise, before everything had gotten tense between them, before the arguments started. He'd looked at Jacob like he loved him.

Jacob didn't want that to matter. Beau had more than a few mistakes to make up for, but it had touched him despite his best intentions. Beau had been more demonstrative tonight, both at the restaurant as they played footsie and at his house, than he'd ever been, even on the cruise where no one knew them and no one cared. It gave Jacob hope that this time would be different. Jacob understood the need for discretion even if he hated it, but for him, discretion was different than avoidance. They could live discreetly and still be together, and he would be fine with it, at least for as long as Beau's responsibility to his mother kept him in Prestonsburg, but he'd given up hope of that happening. Now Beau seemed to be offering him what he'd wanted all along.

If the offer was genuine, Jacob would be the happiest man in town.

Melissa appeared in the doorway in a slinky nightgown obviously intended to entice him to join her. "I'm going to bed," she whispered.

Jacob waved her on toward the bedroom without speaking. She could interpret that however she wanted. He had no intention of moving from Finn's side before morning.

FORTUNATELY, Finn slept fairly well during the night, only waking Jacob twice and falling back asleep immediately. Melissa's pout continued the next morning when Jacob woke her to tell her he was leaving, but he ignored it the same way he ignored his students when they looked at him that way. As soon as he turned the corner out of sight of the house, he pulled into a parking lot and texted Beau.

On the road back to Prestonsburg. Call me if you have time to talk.

Moments later, his phone rang.

"How's Finn?"

"He's fine," Jacob said, "and good morning to you too."

"Sorry," Beau said. "I was worried about him during the night."

"He really is fine," Jacob promised. "He was colicky and fussy, which got Melissa all worked up, which worked him up more in turn. He settled down once I got home, but I promised her I'd come home after the last session tonight in case he was fussy again today. She has a paper due for a class she's taking, and that's got her stressed out."

"Sounds to me like she's taking advantage of you," Beau said.

"She probably is," Jacob agreed, leaving Elliot and heading for Prestonsburg, "but I don't mind spending the time with Finn. I told her about the Autism Society project last night and that I'd have to come to Prestonsburg one night next week to meet with you. I'll have Finn with me, but you said you wouldn't mind."

"Of course I don't mind," Beau replied, his voice warm. "It's been a long time since I last held an infant for more than a photo op."

Jacob chuckled. "Finn loves to be held. He'll snuggle up in my arms and not move for hours, although he doesn't do that for Melissa much."

"We'll hope I have better luck than she does," Beau said drolly.

"You got luckier than she did last night," Jacob joked.

"Really?" Beau asked, his voice soft. "Is that why she called for you to come home?

"No, Finn really was crying," Jacob said, "although he wasn't sick after all, but once I got him calmed down, she came parading into his room in some excuse for a nightgown. I slept in Finn's room."

"Thank you," Beau said. "I know you won't be able to put her off forever, but it means something to me that you didn't go straight from my bed to sleeping with her."

"I wasn't going to get into this now," Jacob said. "I wanted to wait until we were together and I could convince you of my sincerity, but I think I owe you the whole story about Melissa."

"What more is there to say?" Beau asked. "You slept with her, she turned up pregnant, you married her."

"That's it," Jacob said, "but that's my point. That's it. I married her out of a sense of duty to the baby. To her, too, to a small extent, although that's mostly gone now. I went to that bar looking to get laid, nothing more. By the time she approached me, I was way too drunk to have any business going off with anyone, but while she was young, she wasn't shy or inexperienced, and she had me half naked and aching for release before I knew what hit me. You weren't there, and she was. I didn't see any reason to fight it. It was stupid, but I was too drunk and too hurt to care at the time."

"Are you sure Finn is yours?" Beau asked, Jacob's revelations bringing back doubts he had put aside upon seeing Jacob in Finn's coloring. He had only seen Melissa once, but her hair was nearly as dark as Jacob's. "Not to be indelicate, but if she was that forward with you, you might not have been the only one."

"I'm sure," Jacob replied. "He has the same birthmark on his shoulder that I do. It runs in my family and has for generations. My mother always said you could tell a Peters the moment you saw him because of it. I don't know if all four of my uncles have it, but I know at least two of them do besides my dad. That's not the important part, though. The important part is Melissa herself. I picked her because she was completely opposite of you. Dark where you're fair, short where you're tall, female, the whole nine yards. I'm only human. Touch me the right way and my body's going to react. But thinking about her objectively does nothing for me. I don't fantasize about her the way I do about you. I don't look at her and wonder how soon I can get her in bed, even knowing I could pretty much any time. You're the only one who does that to me. Hell, half the time when I do have sex with her now, I have to think about you to get off, and that's when we were estranged. Now that we're back together, it'll be even more true."

"I'm not sure if that makes me feel better or worse," Beau admitted, making Jacob wish he could see his lover's face.

"Better I can see, since I'm thinking about you even when I'm with her, but why worse?" Jacob asked.

"Because if I hadn't been so stubborn before, we might not be in this situation," Beau said, "and because it bothers me to think about you with her at all. Knowing you're thinking about me while you're touching her seems… dirty, I guess."

"This whole situation is distressingly sordid," Jacob agreed. "I don't see any way out of it other than what we're already trying, though. What does your week look like? Other than a faculty meeting on Wednesday, I don't have any specific plans. We could order a pizza and start brainstorming for the summer program. I have a couple of journal articles on autism that could be useful as well."

"You are planning on letting me make love to you while you're here too, right?" Beau teased.

"No," Jacob retorted. "I'm planning on making love *with* you. But for the cover story to hold, we really will have to work on the project too."

"We will," Beau promised. "I wouldn't do that to Paula and Jim, not that I could stand to make that kind of commitment and not follow through even with strangers. Bring your articles. We'll start researching and planning over dinner. But before and after, I want the lover, not the teacher."

"As long as you can deal with the father as well as the lover, you can have as much of the lover as you want," Jacob said. "And I'm getting into Prestonsburg, so I should hang up soon. I don't want to cause an accident. What night do you want to meet?"

"Thursday," Beau said. "If that suits."

"I'll be there by six," Jacob said. "It may be a little earlier, depending on how quickly I can get my papers checked and get on the road, but it won't be any later."

"I'll be home a little after five," Beau replied, "so whenever you get here is fine. I love you."

"I love you too."

Switching off his Bluetooth, Jacob rubbed at his eyes, refusing to acknowledge the prickling of tears behind his lids.

[4]

JACOB juggled his school bag and Finn's diaper bag as he bent to free Finn from his car seat. "Come on, baby," he said as the school bag slipped off his shoulder and nearly knocked him over.

"Do you need help?"

"Yes," Jacob said, his voice betraying his gratitude. "I seem to be one hand short."

Beau came down the sidewalk and took both bags from Jacob's shoulder. "You get the baby. I'll take care of the bags."

Jacob leaned back into the car, unfastening Finn easily now that his hands weren't tangled up with bags. Finn gurgled happily at him. Charmed as always, Jacob kissed Finn's forehead as he lifted the baby out of the car. "Let's go inside so you can meet Beau."

Seeing one of Beau's neighbors in the yard next door looking at them oddly, Jacob called after Beau, "I found that article on coping with autism I told you about. I skimmed it before I left school today. It should be very useful when we start thinking about activities for the summer program."

"Good," Beau called back as Jacob walked toward the house.

The moment they were inside and the door shut behind them, Beau pulled Jacob into his arms, Finn and all, kissing him hard. "I missed you."

"It's only been a few days," Jacob said, warmed by Beau's words despite his protest.

"A few days too many," Beau agreed. "So can I hold Finn?"

"Sure," Jacob said, setting his son in Beau's arms. His hands hovered for a moment until it became clear Beau remembered how to hold a baby. "It's almost time for a bottle anyway, so I'll get that ready while you have him, and then we can work until he falls asleep."

"And once he's asleep?" Beau asked, following Jacob into the kitchen.

Jacob grinned back at Beau over his shoulder. "Once he's asleep, I'm going to finish what we started Friday night."

"I like the sound of that," Beau said, his voice raspy with desire.

Jacob mixed the formula and set the bottle in the refrigerator so it would be ready when Finn was. Then he pulled the journal out of his school bag. Beau took one look at it and pushed it aside. "We'll work, I promise, but not yet. How's your week going?"

"Very well," Jacob said. "I took some of the things I learned on Saturday and started using them in my classroom. I've still got some bugs to work out, but the kids seem really engaged. I've always used a somewhat self-directed approach to their education since every kid is different and working with that instead of against it yields better results, but this is going one step further and really putting control in the kids' hands. Some of them aren't quite sure what to do with that yet, but they'll get used to it. I just have to keep guiding them until they do."

"How do you make sure they get everything they need that way?" Beau asked. "Or that they progress?"

"They have goals I help them set in all the areas we're supposed to be studying," Jacob explained, "and I monitor to make sure they're working on activities that will help them meet those goals. And we still have group sessions where we discuss things as a whole class so I can introduce new concepts."

Beau shook his head. "That's a long way from when I was in school and we sat in straight lines and did everything at the same time as everyone else."

"We know a little more about learning styles now than we did then," Jacob replied. Finn kicked restlessly in Beau's arms. "He's getting hungry. Do you want to feed him?"

"Go ahead," Beau said. "I'll enjoy watching you instead."

Jacob fetched the bottle, running it under hot water until it reached room temperature, and then took Finn back from Beau, settling the baby comfortably in the crook of his arm and offering the bottle. Finn grabbed for the nipple as Jacob guided it to his mouth. "Now that I've babbled about my week, tell me about yours," Jacob said once Finn was settled.

"It's actually been fairly quiet," Beau said. "It'll pick up a bit as it gets closer to Halloween, with adolescent pranks and the rest, but at the moment, I don't have much of a docket. It's nice. I've used the time to catch up on some work in the garden. I want everything ready for winter."

"Have you told Paula we'll help with the summer program?" Jacob asked as he lifted Finn to his shoulder to burp him before letting him finish the bottle. "I don't want her to be surprised if your neighbor says something after my comment outside today."

"I told her on Monday," Beau said. "I mentioned seeing you last week and convincing you over dinner so everything lines up. She was thrilled to hear it and offered whatever resources we need as well, so if we end up with questions your journals can't answer, she might be able to find things out for us."

"Did she say exactly what she wanted us to work on?"

"The actual programming," Beau replied. "The activities and outings for the kids. She assured me she has plenty of people capable of organizing fundraisers and all that, but they haven't been able to find a coordinator to handle the day-to-day organization of the summer program. I told her we couldn't commit to that, what with my court schedule and you having Finn. She said they're looking for someone they can hire to run the program, but they'd like to have at least some things in place in case they don't find anyone until the last minute."

"We should also maybe think about some kind of introductory package for volunteers," Jacob mused. "Paula probably has plenty of materials, but we should decide what to give the volunteers to help them cope with the autistic kids. As you discovered working with Jim, it's not the same as working with other kids."

"No, it isn't," Beau agreed, "and while I think the personal approach is always best, having some general information ahead of time is a good idea. Hold on a second. Since we're talking about this now, let me get a notepad so I can jot down our ideas for later."

THEY brainstormed for an hour, passing Finn back and forth between them so they could eat as they worked, until Finn finally fell asleep in Jacob's arms. "Is there somewhere he can sleep?" Jacob asked.

"I don't have a baby bed."

Jacob chuckled. "A nest of blankets on the floor will be plenty. He isn't mobile yet, so as long as he's safe and comfortable where we put him, he'll be safe and comfortable when we come back to him."

"I can handle that," Beau said. "We can put him in the room next to mine so we'll hear him if he wakes up."

"That will work," Jacob said, following Beau upstairs and into the spare bedroom. They pulled the blanket off the bed and formed it into a nest for Finn, leaving him sleeping soundly. "Now," Jacob purred. "Where were we?"

"Discussing the summer project."

Jacob shook his head, taking Beau's hand and leading him into the bedroom. "Not tonight. Friday night," he explained, stripping his shirt over his head and letting his pants and underwear fall to the floor.

Beau simply stared, his gaze flying over Jacob's body in a silent caress.

"Don't tell me you've forgotten Friday night already," Jacob teased, pulling Beau's shirt off as well. "We were lying in bed together, your mouth driving me wild as you fucked me with your fingers. Ring any bells?"

Beau groaned and stripped the rest of his clothes off. "Maybe," he said, pushing Jacob backward onto the bed. "Keep talking."

Jacob grinned, lying back on the pillows and stroking himself a couple of times. "You'd just made me come in my pants," he continued, "although maybe we'll skip that tonight. I don't want to wait that long to have you inside me." He passed Beau the lube. "Put your fingers in me, just like on Friday."

Beau coated his fingers and slid one of them between Jacob's buttocks, finding the tight hole. It relaxed immediately under his touch, assuring Beau of his welcome despite the lack of foreplay.

"That wasn't all I was doing on Friday," Beau said as he slid one finger past the constricting muscle. "At least not if I remember correctly." He lowered his head and licked at Jacob's balls. "Or did I remember wrong?"

"You remember just fine," Jacob said, his voice cracking with need. "Suck me already, damn it."

Beau grinned and did as Jacob ordered, wrapping his lips around the tip of Jacob's cock at the same time he found his lover's prostate.

Jacob was fully hard and thrashing beneath him in seconds. Beau lingered only long enough to prepare Jacob properly. He had no idea how long Finn would sleep, and he didn't want to be interrupted again. They could snuggle together afterward and continue the intimacy for as long as Finn would let them.

Jacob seemed of the same mind, pressing a condom into Beau's hand within moments of landing in bed. "Now."

Beau didn't need more incentive than that, sheathing himself in the latex and forging his way into Jacob's body. Jacob arched into the contact, his hips rising to meet Beau's inward thrust. Matching groans escaped as they moved together, their bodies fighting for release.

Beau wanted to hold back, but his need got the better of him. Fortunately, Jacob's did the same, his climax hitting seconds after Beau's did, leaving them both panting and sweaty on the comforter. Beau dealt with the condom and snuggled Jacob against him. "It still doesn't feel entirely real having you here."

"It doesn't feel real being here," Jacob agreed. "It's the stuff of dreams, us in bed together with Finn sleeping in the next room." He lifted his hand to look at his the wedding ring still on his finger. "If I can get rid of this in a few months, we'll be one step closer to making it real."

Beau kissed Jacob's dark, messy curls gently, not mentioning that a divorce wouldn't be enough because they'd still have to be discreet. Jacob might be able to spend more time at Beau's, but he wouldn't be able to move in permanently. He'd worry about that later. He had to convince Jacob he was sincere first, and he suspected he had a long way to go. Still, Jacob was considering it, and that was a start. Time and deliberate care would take care of the rest.

SMILING more than he had in what felt like months, Jacob unfastened Finn's seat belt and carried him inside. The school bag could stay in the car since he'd graded all his papers before he left to meet with Beau. Finn gurgled up at him before scrunching up his face. "Are you getting hungry again? Let me get inside and I'll make you another bottle."

Melissa met him inside the door. "How was your day?" she asked, taking the diaper bag from his shoulder and leaning up to kiss him. He let her because he saw no graceful way to stop it, but he didn't linger either, not that he ever really did except when she wanted sex.

"Long," Jacob replied, feeling guilty at how put-upon he felt at her acting like a good wife tonight, "but good. The kids are really enjoying the new activities. How was your day?"

He made himself ask. He didn't hate her, after all. He asked his colleagues how their days were. The least he could do was ask his wife.

"Great," Melissa said. "I finished my paper this morning and got it turned in. And I got another one back with a good grade."

"Good for you," Jacob said, the disconnect between her world and his so vivid in that moment. He remembered being in college and worrying about what grade he'd get on his next paper, but it seemed so long ago. Before Teach For America, before Beau.

"Have you had dinner?"

"Yes, I ate with Beau while we worked," Jacob said. "Did I not tell you I was going to?"

"You said you probably would," Melissa replied, "but I wanted to make sure. I know I'm not that great of a mother, but I'm trying to be a good wife at least."

"You're doing fine," Jacob said, his conscience eating at him even more. She wasn't a bad wife, if that had been what he'd wanted, and if he loved her, he suspected they could find a way to be happy together, even with the difference in their ages. She would graduate eventually and their lives would overlap more. It wasn't her fault he loved someone else.

"If you can get Finn settled while I take a quick shower and get things ready for tomorrow, I'll make Friday night up to you," he offered on impulse. He'd close his eyes and think of Beau.

HALFWAY home from work the next day, Jacob pulled over into a parking lot and picked up his cell phone. He'd spent the entire day with his stomach tied up in knots. In the course of one evening, he'd cheated on his wife and then he'd cheated on the man he loved. He had to talk to someone.

"Hello?"

"Hey, Billy, it's Jacob. Do you have a few minutes?"

"Hey, Jacob. I always have a few minutes for you. What's up?"

Just the sound of his best friend's voice helped settle Jacob. "I fucked up," he said, "and I don't know what to do about it."

"Always a good reason to call your best friend," Billy said with a chuckle.

"This isn't a laughing matter," Jacob said. "I don't know what to do. You want to come to Elliot for a weekend?"

"Why don't you come to Atlanta?" Billy proposed. "Oh, wait... the baby. I forgot."

"I could bring him with me," Jacob said, "although that would limit what we could do while I was there. It would be easier if you could come visit."

"Why don't you tell me what's going on?" Billy said. "That's the real issue here."

"I told you about Beau and getting Melissa pregnant and all of that," Jacob began.

"Yeah, I remember."

"He called me last week. He wants another chance."

"Fuck that," Billy said. "He had his chance and blew it."

"Things are different this time," Jacob insisted.

"Where have I heard that before?" Billy muttered. "Wait, you said are. Have you seen him?"

"Three times," Jacob replied. "The first time started exactly like it always did, sneaking around someplace 'safe', fighting as much as we fucked, but instead of getting fed up and storming out, he had a proposition."

"I don't think I like the sound of this."

"Just shut up and listen, please," Jacob said, exasperated. "You know we met on a volunteer project. There's another project we could work on together. It's a reason to meet, a way to be together openly without anyone guessing why we're really together. We went out to dinner on Friday night. Out to a real restaurant in Prestonsburg, and the sky didn't fall. And last night I went to his house for dinner. I parked in front of his house, walked inside as openly as you please, and spent several hours there. We worked on the project because it's a good project and we want to help, but we also spent time together, something we didn't really do much before."

"You let him fuck you."

"We made love," Jacob retorted, "and don't tell me it's semantics. There's a difference, and having done both in the past week, I recognize it when I see it."

"So you did let him fuck you."

"No, I mean, yes, but that's not the problem," Jacob said with a sigh. "I got home last night, and Melissa was doing her best to be a good wife, and I felt guilty for cheating on her and took her to bed."

"Oh."

"That's it?" Jacob asked. "Not helping here, Bills."

"What do you want me to say?" Billy retorted. "Either way you look at it, you're cheating on someone."

"I'm aware of that fact," Jacob said. "Why do you think I called?"

"So tell me this," Billy said. "What do you want? If you could wave a wand and fix all of this right now, what would it look like?"

"Beau, Finn, and me, making a life together somewhere," Jacob replied immediately. "I don't care where, just together."

"And what's stopping that from happening?" Billy asked.

"Beau won't leave his mother. She's in a nursing home with Alzheimer's. As long as she's alive, he won't leave Prestonsburg, and he's convinced we can't have that life together here," Jacob answered.

"Do you agree?"

"I think we'd end up sacrificing some things if we came out," Jacob said slowly. "I might have to change schools. Beau thinks he'd lose the next election and that people wouldn't come to his law practice if they knew he was gay. And I don't know how the courts would feel about giving me custody of Finn, even joint custody, if I was living with Beau openly."

"Not exactly easily surmountable problems there," Billy commented. "What's the next best case scenario?"

"I divorce Melissa and get custody of Finn, and Beau and I keep finding acceptable ways to be together to cover up our relationship," Jacob said, "but I don't want to live that way forever."

"His mother won't live forever," Billy reminded him. "If she's already in a nursing home, it could be just another couple of years until she dies. The average survival rate is only something like six years with the disease."

"That's the average," Jacob agreed, "but it can be as many as twenty. I don't know when she was diagnosed, but I don't want to still be living this way when I'm nearly fifty. And I don't want Finn to grow up that way."

"You can try an ultimatum, but you know those always backfire," Billy warned. "I guess you have to decide which is better: living with Melissa or living alone with Beau on the side. Unless you think living with Melissa with Beau on the side is an option?"

"Not in the long term," Jacob said. "Beau asked for six months to convince me he was serious about finding a way to have a life together discreetly. If, at the end of that time, I feel like I can live with his solution, I'll divorce Melissa and we'd go from there."

"So what's the problem?" Billy asked.

"How to live with myself for the next six months," Jacob admitted. "It hasn't even been a week, and the thought of what I'm doing is making me sick."

"Is there a reason to wait six months?" Billy asked. "I know you don't love Melissa, so you wouldn't lose anything except a little respectability by divorcing her tomorrow. She's still a cover if you need one should someone accuse you of being gay. You might be divorced, but you were obviously into her enough to get her pregnant."

"Only barely," Jacob said.

"But they don't know that," Billy countered. "You were married, you fathered a child. That's pretty much proof of at least some level of heterosexuality, no matter who you were thinking about when you slept with her. Give me one good reason not to file for divorce tomorrow morning."

"Finn," Jacob said immediately. "I don't want him to grow up in a broken home for no reason."

"Jacob, sweetheart," Billy said, his voice indulgent, "he's already growing up in a broken home. There isn't anything about your relationship with Melissa that's healthy for anyone involved. Whether things work out with Beau or not, you'll be far happier without the guilt and without the sham of a marriage because even without Beau, it wouldn't last long. If you loved her, all the differences wouldn't be as important, but you don't love her. You won't ever be happy living a lie even if Beau isn't part of your life. And if he is part of your life, then it's all the more important to end the fiction sooner rather than later. It's only been a week, and your guilt is already eating at you."

"My guilt has been eating me alive since the first time I slept with her," Jacob said hoarsely. "Yes, Beau and I were having problems. Yes, I called him and told him I was going to do it if he didn't give me a reason not to, but the reality is that I cheated on him. We might still be having problems if I hadn't, but I wouldn't be a cheating bastard in both the eyes of the law and in my heart."

"Then you already know what you need to do."

JACOB spent the next few days researching divorce laws for the state of Alabama. He could have gotten the answers he needed with a quick phone call to Beau, but he didn't want Beau involved in this if he could help it. If he went forward with this now, he would be doing it for himself and for Finn, not for Beau. He wasn't ready yet to assume that would all work out, but Billy was right. No matter what happened with Beau, Jacob would never be happy living a lie.

If he could convince Melissa to sit down and negotiate with him and an arbitrator, the divorce could be finalized within thirty days of filing. He'd have to find the right way to break it to her, to convince her it would be best for both of them without revealing his real reasons for wanting to be free, but a little careful wording would take care of that. Getting full custody of Finn might be harder, but as long as he had physical custody, he didn't really mind sharing legal custody with Melissa or giving her visitation rights. Finn was her son, after all, even if he was an even bigger oops for her than he was for Jacob.

First, though, he had to get through his evening with Beau without telling his lover things he wouldn't want to hear, and he wouldn't even have Finn to distract him. For reasons of her own, Melissa had offered to keep Finn this evening while Jacob went to his meeting. Not that Jacob was complaining. He appreciated the chance to have a break, however small, but without Finn to occupy part of their time and attention, he wondered if he would be able to avoid mentioning the divorce and sleeping with Melissa last week.

He spent the entire drive into Prestonsburg planning how to start the conversation, how to avoid acting guilty around Beau, and what to say if Beau should ask him what was wrong. With each passing mile, the weight of dread in the pit of his stomach increased until he thought he'd be sick with it. He considered calling Beau and cancelling, but that was what had led to their estrangement in the first place. They were so close now. He didn't want anything to knock them off track again.

Driving into Prestonsburg, he parked in front of Beau's house, waved to the neighbor across the street as he pulled his briefcase from the back seat of his car, and walked up the sidewalk to knock at the door. He had no idea if Beau had mentioned the Autism Society project to any or all of his neighbors, but Jacob had decided that acting furtive or guilty would be far more damning than acting like his arrival was nothing special at all. He only hoped it worked. The neighbor waved back, giving him hope their secret was still safe.

He rang the bell and waited for Beau to answer even though Beau had told him more than once to simply open the door and come in. Jacob yearned for that level of intimacy, but he felt the eyes of the entire neighborhood on his back as he stood on Beau's porch. Rationally, he knew that was a function of his own guilt rather than because anyone was actually paying attention, but he still waited on the porch like a guest rather than walking in like he lived there.

Beau came to the door a few seconds later.

"It was unlocked," he reminded Jacob as he came inside and set his briefcase down on the table in the hall.

"I know it was," Jacob replied, "but your neighbor across the street was out mowing the yard. I thought discretion was in order."

Beau nodded and pulled Jacob into an embrace. "The door's closed now, and I see you don't have Finn with you today. We can be as indiscreet as we want." He lowered his head and nuzzled Jacob's neck, the hint of a five o'clock shadow working its magic on Jacob's body, which only added to the guilt roiling within him.

"I slept with Melissa last week," Jacob blurted out before he could censor his words.

"You weren't supposed to tell me that," Beau said with a groan, pulling back to look at Jacob.

"I know," Jacob replied, tightening his hold so Beau couldn't pull away any more than he already had, "but the guilt is eating me alive. Our plan isn't going to work, Beau. I can't do this."

"Can't do what?" Beau asked warily.

"I can't be with her when it's cheating on you, and yet being with you is cheating on her," Jacob explained, his voice desperate. "Something has to give."

"And have you decided what that is?" Beau asked.

Jacob could practically feel his lover withdrawing even though Beau had not moved. "I'm going to ask her for a divorce this weekend," he said. "If I wait six months like we talked about, it'll fail because I'll wind up feeling so guilty that I'll screw things up with you and maybe with her, and then the divorce will be more complicated, and I might not get custody of Finn, and—"

"And I get it," Beau said gently. "I'm certainly not going to argue with a plan that gets her out of your life that much sooner. I hate the thought that you go home to her every night, that you sleep next to her even if you don't touch her most nights. Knowing that she's the one with the right to roll over and touch you, kiss you, during the night, that she's the one who sees you adorably rumpled from sleep in the morning, drives me insane at night alone in my bed. I want to be the one there with you, even knowing I can't be."

You could be, Jacob thought, but he kept the words to himself.

"I can't just kick her out," Jacob said. "I have to give her time to figure out where to go, but I'll sleep in Finn's room until she moves out. I won't touch her again. I swear."

Beau nodded and cupped Jacob's cheeks with his palms. "Do what you have to do to make the divorce go smoothly and to get custody of Finn."

"Even if that means sleeping with her again?" Jacob asked.

Beau flinched. "Are you trying to start another fight? Because if you are, you're doing a damn good job, and if you aren't, you need to stop now or you'll have one anyway."

When he pulled away this time, Jacob let him go. "I'm sorry," he said. "That was uncalled for. I told you guilt was making me stupid. Maybe I should just go. It might be easier if we didn't see each other again until she's out of my life. That would take away one of the clubs we use to batter each other."

"We've gotten better about that," Beau reminded him. "We haven't had a fight since we started the Autism Society project."

"Until tonight," Jacob said. "That's only been two weeks, which might not be bad if we saw each other every day, but we've only seen each other three times, and we nearly fought tonight."

"We have a lot of hurt built up inside. It's going to take time and care for all of that to go away. That's why I asked for six months to convince you. I still want those six months."

That relieved one of Jacob's fears. Beau did not see Jacob's divorce as tacit agreement to carrying on a secret affair. He understood the jury was still out on their lives together. Jacob must have waited too long to reply because Beau pulled him into an embrace again. "Please stay. Even if all we do is the work we have for Paula, don't go yet."

"I don't want to go at all," Jacob said finally. "I want to go get Finn and come back here and never leave, but I can't do that, and we both know it, so I'm trying to figure out how to be satisfied with what I can have without rehashing old arguments. This hasn't been a very good week for me."

"What can I do to make it better?" Beau asked.

"Can we just go sit on your porch?" Jacob asked in reply. "I know we have work to do. I know we have decisions to make, but what I really want is to just be together for a few hours and pretend the rest of the world doesn't exist."

"Come on," Beau said, taking Jacob's hand and leading him through the house to the back porch. He sat down on the chaise longue and pulled Jacob onto the cushion in front of him. Jacob leaned back against Beau's chest, letting himself be held and comforted.

Time passed in silence broken only by the wind in the trees. The occasional patter of raindrops started after a time, enclosing them in a dim, damp cocoon.

"It's hard to end a marriage," Beau said into the deepening twilight. "Even when it was a bad choice from the beginning, a way to prove something to someone else or a choice you felt you had to make, it feels like you've failed when you have to go before a judge and say the marriage is over. An agreed divorce settlement makes it faster, but nothing can completely negate that sense of loss when it's done."

"I shouldn't feel like I'm losing anything," Jacob said, Beau's words resonating through him. "There's nothing to lose. She was a one-night stand with unintended consequences. I don't love her, she doesn't love me. The marriage was a sham from the moment we said our vows."

"But you said your vows anyway," Beau continued. "You don't have to explain it to me, Jake. I married my wife at a time when I was trying to pretend I wasn't gay. I liked her well enough, but I didn't love her the way a wife deserves to be loved. We bumped along together until Harrison was two, and then she left me. She was right to do so, honestly. Other than her taking Harrison, I'm far happier without her than I was with her because I'm not pretending to be someone I'm not."

"Does it get easier, thinking about your ex-wife?" Jacob asked. "Or will I always think of her with this sinking dread I feel right now?"

"My divorce was not amicable," Beau replied. "I don't hate her, if that's what you're asking, but I still dread dealing with her. I call Harrison when I know she won't be home, or I wait for him to call me. I brace myself for a fight when it comes to making arrangements to see him. She has to let me see him, but she doesn't have to make it easy or be nice about it. Hopefully you won't have that with Melissa and so can avoid a lot of that. It doesn't hurt the way it did then, but I can't say it's gotten easier."

Jacob nodded. "I guess I have to hope for the best and brace for the worst."

Beau pressed a kiss to his temple. "Tonight you don't have to do either. Tonight you relax in my arms and let me help you forget about everything else for a little while."

"If only it were that easy," Jacob said with a sigh.

"It can be," Beau said, kneading the muscles in Jacob's shoulders. Jacob hummed his pleasure at the feeling. Beau shifted out from behind Jacob and reclined the back of the lounger to a completely recumbent position. "Lie down on your stomach," he urged.

Jacob moved as Beau directed, pillowing his head on his crossed arms and stretching out fully on the chaise. At first, Beau's hands moved over his shoulders and back through the fabric of his shirt, but before long, they slid lower, pushing the fabric toward Jacob's shoulders. "I could take it off," Jacob offered softly. "With the rain, no one's going to see us lying here."

"You do that," Beau said. "I'll be right back."

He disappeared into the house as Jacob pulled his T-shirt over his head and tossed it on the swing where he and Beau usually sat. He had barely gotten settled again when Beau returned, straddling Jacob's thighs. "Let me know if this is too cold," he said as he smeared lotion across the small of Jacob's back.

"Are you a masseur now?" Jacob teased, uncomfortable with the sudden intimacy of the situation. He and Beau fucked. Sometimes they even made love, but they had never really acted like a couple before, taking care of each other outside the sexual plane.

"Hush," Beau said. "You're radiating tension. I'm no professional, but surely I can figure out how to help you relax."

Jacob shifted on the lounger, pressing his ass back against Beau. "I'm sure we could think of something."

"Something that won't send you home feeling guilty for cheating on your wife," Beau retorted, continuing to slide his hands along the sides of Jacob's spine with constant pressure. "Now stop talking and let me take care of you."

Jacob didn't say this kind of tenderness was a far greater betrayal of the spirit of his marriage vows than the sex because it implied a far more intense emotional connection than the sex that could be passed off as physical release. Taking a deep breath as Beau's hands pressed on a particularly tender spot, he pushed all thought but the feeling of his lover's touch from his mind and let himself sink deeper into the cushions as Beau worked. The tension seeped slowly from his limbs, chased away by Beau's curling fingers.

"May I?" Beau asked, his hands resting on the waistband of Jacob's sweatpants. "I can't get to your lower back."

Jacob lifted up slightly in tacit permission as Beau slid the elastic down across the swell of his ass. He shivered a little in the coolness of the night air, but Beau's hands made no move to take advantage of him, returning instead to the soothing, relaxing massage.

When Jacob's entire body felt as limp as a wet noodle, Beau finally stopped, stretching the full length of his body along Jacob's, covering him completely, and Jacob felt the bulge of the older man's erection. "Please," he whispered.

Beau's weight disappeared for a moment, and then Jacob felt a tug on his pants and heard a condom wrapper tear. He shifted enough for Beau to get them off, but more movement than that was beyond him. Beau's weight returned immediately, his slick shaft slotting into Jacob's crease. It might have stung another night, but Jacob was so relaxed from the massage that his ring gave and Beau slipped inside him, joining their bodies, undulating against him so that the lovemaking became a mellow extension of the massage, soothing as much as arousing, until they both climaxed in rapid succession.

"How late can you stay?" Beau asked when their breathing returned to normal.

"Melissa's expecting me home by ten."

"Then we have time," Beau said, his arms tightening around Jacob once more.

"WE NEED to talk, Melissa."

"Can it wait? I have a test on Monday," Melissa said.

"No, it really can't," Jacob said.

She gave a very put-out sigh and closed her books. "Well, what is it?"

"I think we should get a divorce," Jacob said. "We made a mistake when we got married. You've given up so much that you shouldn't have had to give up because of what was essentially a one-night stand."

"What… what does that mean?" Melissa asked.

"We hooked up at a bar," Jacob reminded her. "Yes, you're a beautiful young woman, but I wasn't in love with you and you weren't in love with me. We got married because it seemed like the right thing to do for Finn, but he doesn't deserve to grow up with parents who make each other unhappy."

"Do I really make you that unhappy?" Melissa asked.

"I was thinking more that I made you unhappy," Jacob replied. "If you didn't have to worry about me and Finn, you could go back to school full time, you could finish your degree and get a good job. You could meet a man who loves you the way you deserve. You could have all the things you dreamed of that you gave up because of Finn and me."

"You make it sound like I don't love Finn," Melissa protested.

"Of course you do," Jacob said, though sometimes he wondered, "but he's a responsibility you didn't ask for. I'm not saying you should just forget about him, but caring for him is a hardship for you. Think about the days I was gone for the conference. And that's when he's still an infant and can't go anywhere. It's only going to get harder when he's mobile and into everything. You can still come see him whenever you want, but you wouldn't have to fret over how you're going to get your papers done or get ready for a test because you have to watch him. You could have your life back."

"It has been hard this year. I hadn't exactly planned to get pregnant, but I don't want Finn to think I abandoned him," she said slowly.

"You aren't abandoning him," Jacob promised. "You're taking care of yourself so you'll be able to contribute to his life later. We'll set it up so you don't have to contribute child support until you have a job, and like I said, you can come visit him whenever you want. I'm not planning on moving away since I have a job here, so it's not like we won't run into each other in town sometimes."

"As long as I get to see him sometimes," she agreed. "He usually is happier with you anyway. I guess this means I have to find somewhere else to live."

Jacob stifled the urge to shout with relief. "Not right this minute," he said. "I'm not going to kick you out on the street, but within a week or two, you should probably have somewhere to go."

"So how will this work?" Melissa asked.

"We'll have to meet with an attorney and outline the terms," Jacob explained. "As long as we both agree, we simply appear in court to file for divorce and then go back a month later to have it finalized. If we can't agree on terms, that's what would drag it out."

Melissa nodded. "I have class on Tuesday evenings, but we can go any other evening that suits you and the attorney."

"I'll make the appointment next week," Jacob said. "I'm going to take Finn for a walk so we're out of your hair. That way you'll ace your exam."

"Thank you," Melissa replied. "For everything."

Her gratitude twisted the knife in Jacob's gut as he bundled Finn up against the October wind and strapped him into his stroller. Checking to make sure he had his phone as well, Jacob left the house to walk down the street, the limbs from the live oak trees meeting above his head. When he was far enough from the house that he felt safe pulling out his phone, he sent Beau a quick text.

She said yes.

Within moments, his phone buzzed in reply.

Good. I don't think we should see each other until the divorce is final.

Jacob read the text, then read it again. More than a little confused, he dialed Beau's number. "What do you mean we shouldn't see each other?" he demanded when Beau answered.

"If she's going to give you the divorce without fighting it, we shouldn't do anything that might jeopardize that," Beau said. "If she finds out about us, there goes your easy divorce."

"We have responsibilities to the Autism Society," Jacob insisted, feeling his one source of sanity slipping through his fingers. "We can't just drop that indefinitely."

"Then we'll meet at Third Street Bistro or at the library or somewhere equally safe," Beau replied. "It's not just the absence of impropriety that matters. It's the appearance of it as well."

"So you'll mess around with me when I'm married, but not now?"

"Jacob," Beau snapped. "Stop trying to pick a fight. You know what they say about a woman scorned. Right now, Melissa just knows you're leaving her, but if she finds out you're leaving her *for* someone, suddenly she's the injured party. She could start demanding the house, custody of Finn, anything, because it's no longer a no-fault divorce. You don't want that to happen, believe me. I've seen how quickly a divorce can get nasty. I will meet you at the library or at a restaurant, and we'll work. Weren't you the one who wanted to go out more anyway?"

"Yes, but somehow I don't think you're going to take me home afterward and make love to me," Jacob muttered. "Not what I intended when I talked about going out."

"You know it's not a question of desire," Beau insisted. "I can't keep my hands off you when we're alone. It'll just be for a few weeks, and then you'll be free of her for good, and you can start coming over here again. Maybe we'll even go away for a weekend to celebrate."

"Really?"

"Really," Beau promised. "Once you have the date from the judge, let me know and I'll plan something."

"No way," Jacob said. "I want to help you plan it. If we're celebrating our new life together, I want a say in it too."

"Our new life, baby?"

Jacob flushed, glad Beau couldn't see him. He hadn't intended to say anything so soon. "That's what I said. I'm sure we're not done compromising yet, but I want to give it a try, and waiting until March to say that doesn't do anything except keep us from relaxing and enjoying those six months fully."

"Then we'll have two reasons to celebrate," Beau said. "When does your passport expire?"

"I haven't the slightest idea. Where are you planning on taking me?"

"Probably only to Atlanta this time," Beau said, "but you should check and get one for Finn, too, just in case we want to go somewhere next summer."

"I like the sound of that." He wished Beau had felt this way a year ago or two years ago so they could have avoided all the heartbreak in the interim, but at least his lover felt that way now.

"I know this place in Canada, north of Toronto. Acres of forest, miles of hiking trails, three beautiful lakes," Beau said. "I've gone there a couple of times on my own. I'd love to go with you."

"It sounds wonderful," Jacob said with a smile. "We'll go there next summer when it's a hundred degrees here and only eighty up there."

"It's a date," Beau said, bringing a wistful smile to Jacob's face. "And in the meantime, I'll see you next Thursday at Third Street Bistro for dinner and Autism Society work."

"I wish I could see you sooner," Jacob said softly.

"I know, baby, but until your divorce goes through, we have to be extra careful. It'll only be for a month or two, and once Melissa moves out, we can talk every night if you want. I'll bet we could have some pretty creative phone sex."

Jacob laughed. "I bet we could. I love you."

"I love you too, Jake."

[5]

"THIS is getting really old, seeing you and not being able to touch you."

"I know it is, baby," Beau said, stretching out on the couch and kicking his shoes off, "but the divorce petition is before the court, so we only have a month more to wait."

"After three weeks of waiting already," Jacob said, his voice so frustrated Beau could practically see his pout through the phone.

"If I were there, I'd bite that lower lip that's sticking out past your nose," Beau teased. "I can see it from here."

"Fucker."

"Not tonight," Beau said with a laugh, "but I promise to make it up to you when your divorce is final. Where should we go? It'll be the first week of December."

"Somewhere warm," Jacob said, "and friendly, where we don't have to pretend for a few days."

"We could go to Key West," Beau suggested, in the mood to indulge Jacob's whims. His lover wasn't the only one suffering from their temporary hiatus. "It's as gay friendly as we're likely to find somewhere warm and close at this time of year. I'd have to check with Sean and see if he'll let me use his plane or else we'll never get there just for a weekend."

"You have a pilot's license?" Jacob squawked. "Why didn't you tell me this before?"

"It hasn't exactly come up," Beau reminded him, the familiar, unwelcome feelings of guilt at how little he had let the man he claimed to love into his life coming back. "And I don't have a plane myself, so it's not like we could have gone flying without Sean asking questions."

"I told my friend Billy who lives in Atlanta," Jacob admitted. "I had to talk to someone, and it's not like he's going to call up the busybodies here and say anything."

Beau flinched at hearing that anyone knew about them, but he suppressed the urge to take Jacob to task for it. "I trust you, baby. If you think it's safe to tell your friend, that's your call. Do you have your computer handy? We can look up bed and breakfasts online and decide where we're going to stay."

"We could," Jacob said, "or we can take advantage of the fact that Finn is asleep at the moment."

Beau's body reacted predictably to the purr in Jacob's voice. He shifted to a more comfortable position on the couch. "And how do you suggest we do that?"

"That depends on what you're wearing," Jacob replied.

"I'm wearing whatever you want me to be wearing," Beau teased, getting up quickly to close the curtains. He could go upstairs, but he liked the idea of sitting on the couch and imagining Jacob was there with him, not only in his bed, but in his house, like a couple rather than like secret lovers.

"If I had what I really wanted, you'd be in bed next to me, completely naked," Jacob said, "but since that isn't happening for another month or more, I'll settle for having you naked on the other end of the phone."

"Then undress me," Beau said, turning the phone to speaker so he'd have his hands free. "I'm wearing a T-shirt and jeans."

"Take your shirt off," Jacob said. "We'll start there."

Beau stripped his shirt over his head, content to give Jacob control for now. He didn't cede easily when they were together, but alone like this, with the phone between them, he could loosen his grip and let Jacob guide their interactions. "Should I keep going?"

"Not yet," Jacob said. "We have time. There's no need to rush."

The erection already straining against the placket of Beau's jeans seemed like a pretty good reason to him, but he kept that thought to himself. "Take your shirt off too."

"I'm already way ahead of you, lover," Jacob replied. "I've been waiting for this since I picked up the phone."

The image of Jacob sprawled naked in his room or on the couch flashed through Beau's mind. The light would cast shadows on the fading tan of his skin, highlighting the dips and curves of his muscles. Under Beau's gaze, Jacob would flush and preen, stroking a hand over his smooth chest or perhaps down to his erection, drawing Beau's attention and touch. "I thought you said not to rush."

"I did," Jacob replied. "I want to spend some quality time with your chest before I move south."

Beau ran a hand across his chest, imagining it was Jacob's hand instead. His lover reveled in the differences in their bodies.

"Close your eyes," Jacob instructed across the phone line. "That's my hand running through your chest hair and tweaking your nipples."

Beau had no problem imagining that caress as he touched himself according to Jacob's directions. When they had taken their cruise and had time to explore, Jacob had spent hours simply touching Beau this way. He doubted he'd have the patience for it tonight, alone on his couch.

"I love the way you touch me," Beau said huskily. "You make me feel like I'm Hercules and David and Apollo all rolled up into one."

"You are," Jacob replied, "at least to me. If I were there, I'd suck on your nipples until you were hard as a rock and begging for me to fuck you."

"You don't need to be here to make me that hard," Beau assured him, pressing down on his erection as if he could keep it under control that way. "Just hearing your voice is enough to do that."

"Get rid of your jeans."

Beau shucked off his jeans as fast as he could, sighing in relief at the release of pressure on his cock. "They're gone," Beau said. "I'm naked and waiting for you."

"Naughty man," Jacob teased, "going commando."

"What are you going to do about it?" Beau goaded.

"Fuck you all night long," Jacob promised.

Beau groaned. He knew Jacob wanted to top more often than he did, but he so rarely said anything that Beau didn't think about it most nights until it was too late. "I'm all yours, baby. Do whatever you want."

"Do you have lube?" Jacob asked. "I know how tight you get. You'll need it tonight as I pound into you like there's no tomorrow."

"There is no tomorrow," Beau agreed. "There's just tonight and making love until we can't stand it anymore."

"I'm squeezing lube on my fingers," Jacob said, "spreading it all over your ass, getting you ready for me."

Beau hissed at the cold lube as he rubbed his fingers around his entrance, waiting for Jacob's directive. "It feels so good," he rasped, "but it's not enough."

"It's never enough," Jacob replied, "not even when I put my fingers inside you, but we aren't rushing tonight, so it's just one finger at first."

Beau slid a finger past his entrance up to the first knuckle. "Are you touching yourself, baby? Stroking your cock until it's hard for me?"

"Not yet," Jacob said. "If I start that now, I won't last long enough to give you the long pounding I promised. Right now, I'm just enjoying the thought of you with your fingers up your ass because I said I wanted them there. Add a second finger. Stretch yourself wide for me. So wide I'll slip inside like I belong there."

"You do," Beau said, adding a second finger and scissoring them as wide as he could. Even if he wouldn't get to feel Jacob's cock inside him tonight, he could imagine it. "Touch my trigger, baby, please."

"Not yet," Jacob insisted. "If I do that, you'll come, and I'm not ready for this to be over."

Beau groaned in protest, but he resisted touching his sensitive gland. "I'm wide open for you," he said instead, hoping to speed things along. "Just waiting for you to fuck me."

"You're rushing again," Jacob chided. "What happened to me being the impatient one?"

"You don't have two fingers up your ass!"

"Yes, I do," Jacob said. "This is phone sex. I can imagine fucking you and having you inside me at the same time. I've got two fingers inside me in imitation of your cock and a hand wrapped around my dick in imitation of your tight ass."

"Jacob!" Beau moaned. "You can't say things like that and expect me to do anything other than come on the spot."

"Stroke yourself," Jacob said. "Imagine it's my hand on you, teasing you as I start to move inside you. I've found your sweet spot with my dick and I'm rubbing against it with every pass. I'm playing you like a violin, lover, hitting every note perfectly, teasing the slit just the way you like until it's leaking like crazy for me. I'd lean down and lick you clean, but that would mean pulling out, and your ass is too amazing to let go of, even to suck your cock. And that's saying something because you know how much I like to suck your cock. Are you close? Are you ready to come with me?"

"Yes," Beau said, his voice cracking.

"Then do it. Come all over your hand and your stomach. Show me how good I make you feel."

Beau pressed hard on his prostate as he pulled on his cock one last time, the proof of his pleasure spooling out of him to puddle on his belly.

"If I were there, I'd lick you clean," Jacob whispered. "All the way from the base of your balls to the tip of your chin, every last drop of sweat and come."

"I'd be ready for round two if you did that," Beau said, still trying to catch his breath.

"I'll remember that," Jacob said. "I might want to do this again sometime."

"Any time you want."

BEAU smiled and waved as Jacob came into Third Street Bistro for their weekly dinner to work on the Autism Society projects. Patty had gotten so used to seeing them that she left their table empty for them and simply waved to them when they arrived. A few minutes later, a plate of fried green tomatoes would appear on the table without them even having to order it. Jacob had Finn with him tonight, Beau noticed as his lover juggled the diaper bag and baby through the door. Patty swooped down on them the minute the door swung shut, cooing over Finn and shooing Jacob toward the table as she disappeared into the back with Finn in her arms.

"Should I be worried?" Jacob said with a smile as he joined Beau at the table.

Beau laughed, hoping his amusement hid the need to kiss Jacob. It had been four weeks since they had been alone together, and phone sex, while relieving the physical ache, did nothing for the need for intimacy. "She wants grandkids so bad she can taste it," Beau explained. "Until her kids decide to oblige, she fills the need with every baby she can get her hands on. She'll bring him back eventually."

"Then we should work fast while he isn't here to distract us," Jacob said.

"In a minute," Beau replied. "How are you doing?"

Jacob shrugged. "Okay, I guess. Everyone at school has been very supportive. Of course most of them want to make Melissa the villain in this even though I keep insisting it was a mutual decision. It doesn't help that Finn is staying with me. Honestly, it's getting old. I don't want to talk about it all the time. How are you?"

"I'm fine," Beau said. Lowering his voice, he added, "I miss you."

"Don't say things like that," Jacob whispered. "It's hard enough sitting here with you without you making me want things I know we can't have."

"Come away with me this weekend," Beau said impulsively.

"I can't," Jacob replied. "I promised to supervise a Thanksgiving program at school on Saturday. I can't back out now. Besides, I thought you said we shouldn't do anything that might give Melissa a reason to contest the divorce."

"I know what I said," Beau muttered, "but I didn't expect it to be this hard. Seeing you, being with you and yet not, is hell."

Jacob nodded. "It's just a few more weeks, and then we have the weekend in Key West to look forward to. Melissa has Finn one weekend a month as per our custody agreement, and that's her weekend, so I don't even have to figure out someone to watch him while we're gone."

"That's good," Beau agreed. "I can't wait to get there and sink—"

Jacob kicked him beneath the table, drawing Beau's attention to Patty's approach. "I'm just going to keep this darling boy with me all evening," she told them, kissing Finn's forehead. "What do you two want to eat?"

They placed their order quickly.

"Are you trying to out us?" Jacob asked when Patty was gone. "Because if you are, that's fine with me, but if you aren't, you need to be careful what you say where we can be overheard."

"Sorry," Beau apologized. "I don't know what's wrong with me tonight." He did, though. He was suffering from withdrawal. Thinking of living discreetly, of hiding in plain sight, had been easy, but the reality of it was far more difficult than Beau had intended. "Let's get our work done so we can enjoy our dinner when it gets here."

They spent the next thirty minutes going through the list of activities they had brainstormed the week before and figuring out the resources they would need for each one. Patty brought their dinner, took a bottle for Finn from Jacob, and disappeared again. "Maybe I should ask her if she wants to babysit whenever we plan a meeting," Jacob said with a shake of his head.

"You'll have to think about babysitters," Beau agreed, "unless you think Melissa will watch him some nights for you."

"She might," Jacob said, "but I don't want to impose too much or cause her to question our arrangement. It's probably better to stick with a regular babysitter unless it's a night or weekend that's part of Melissa's visitation schedule. It won't be an issue until the next full committee meeting for the summer program, and that's still a month from now."

Beau didn't repeat his request for a weekend away. They already had the trip to Key West planned for December, and Thanksgiving was coming up, so Jacob and Finn would probably spend most of that week with Jacob's family in Vicksburg. He could be patient for three more weeks.

"HEY, Sean, can I borrow your plane the second weekend of December?"

"Hello, Beau. I'm fine, thanks for asking, how are you?" Sean replied sarcastically.

"I'm fine," Beau said with a roll of his eyes at the not-so-subtle criticism. Sean was a stickler for certain things, and he had no tolerance for those who didn't share his pickiness. Beau could either play by the rules or not get an answer. "How are Marlene and the kids?"

"They're all doing well," Sean replied. "They'd love to see you. You should come for a visit."

"I've been busy," Beau apologized, not that he was really sorry given how much of his time had been spent with Jacob, either in person or on the phone now that Melissa had moved out and they didn't have to worry about her overhearing a phone conversation. "Can I borrow your plane the second weekend of December?"

"We don't have anything planned that weekend," Sean said. "I don't see why not. Got a hot date?"

"A friend's going through a divorce," Beau began. "I thought he could use a weekend away. I could take him down to Florida, get him out of town for a bit."

"That's downright generous of you," Sean said. "Anyone I know?"

"No," Beau said. "A teacher in Elliot. We met a couple of years ago on a volunteer project. We've kept in touch since then." The lie roiled in Beau's stomach. He might not be ready to come out to all of Prestonsburg, but this was Sean, his best friend. If he couldn't trust Sean, he couldn't trust anyone. "I fell in love with him."

"That's... wait. What? You fell in love with *him*?"

"Yeah, so?" Beau said, bile rising in his throat as he waited for Sean's rejection.

"Fuck, man, you've seen me naked!"

"I'm gay, not a sex maniac," Beau retorted, the words coming more easily than he expected them to. "I *am* capable of self-control."

"I know that. It's just... shit, I can't quite...." Sean stopped and took a breath that was audible even across the phone line. "When did you figure this out?"

"About the same time Christine left me."

"Then why the hell am I just now hearing about it?" Sean demanded. "I'm your best friend, and there's this whole part of your life I knew nothing about. Not cool, Beau. Not cool at all."

"I don't live in a big city, Sean," Beau protested. "I don't have the luxury of being more open about things."

"Since when is telling me something being open about it?" Sean replied. "And if you're so closed about it that you didn't even tell me, how did you manage to snag a lover anyway?"

"I got lucky," Beau said, knowing how true the words really were. "Luckier than I deserve, probably, but since he puts up with me, I'm not going to look a gift horse in the mouth."

"I want to meet him," Sean declared. "If he's that important to you, I want to have a face to go with the name."

"That'll be up to Jacob," Beau replied. "Not that I expect him to say no, but I don't want to make decisions for him since that's one of the things Christine accused me of when she filed for divorce."

"Learning from your mistakes is good," Sean said, "but so is remembering that Jacob is a different person. He won't want or expect the same things Christine did. Don't give him what Christine needed. Give him what he needs."

Beau chuckled. "Did Marlene teach you that?"

"Somebody had to," Sean muttered. Beau laughed louder. Sean's first two marriages had been disastrous, but he seemed to have finally met his match with his third wife. She barely reached his shoulder, but Beau had no doubt who wore the pants in that family, and it wasn't Sean. He'd never seen his friend happier.

"So, can I borrow the plane? Jacob is so stressed over the divorce and what it will do to his job and his future. I thought I'd take him down to the Keys for a weekend to give him a breather."

"Why is he married if you're together?" Sean asked.

Beau sighed. "Because I fucked up."

"Details would be helpful."

Rolling his eyes, Beau tried to decide how to explain the situation to Sean. "Neither of us is open about being gay. We can't afford to be in our professions. We had to be discreet about our meetings, and I got scared. I cancelled a couple of dates. Okay, more than a couple. We hadn't seen each other in months, and Jacob got tired of it. He went out, got drunk, and got a girl pregnant. He did the honorable thing and married her, only he doesn't love her and she doesn't love him."

"Sounds like he's the one who fucked up, not you," Sean observed.

"We both did," Beau allowed, "but we've gotten over it. That's in the past, and we're doing better this time around. The courts have given him custody of the baby, so he won't have to go through what I did with Harrison, which is good. It's a no-fault divorce, so it's just a matter of waiting for the judge to sign the paperwork, but we haven't seen each other since he asked his wife for the divorce because I didn't want to take the risk of her finding out about us and deciding to make his life difficult."

"So you're borrowing my plane to go somewhere discreet and fuck each other's brains out for the weekend," Sean deduced. "If you weren't my best friend, that would be way too much information, but since you are, I guess I'll have to get used to it."

"There's nothing wrong with having a healthy sex life," Beau reminded him, smiling finally with the knowledge that Sean had accepted his revelations. He wouldn't be teasing Beau this way if he hadn't.

"Doesn't mean I want to hear about it," Sean said.

"Since when?" Beau challenged, remembering more than one occasion when he and Sean had exchanged blow-by-blow accounts of their hookups.

"Since you told me you were fucking a guy," Sean replied, "or does he fuck you? Don't answer that question. I don't want to know."

Beau couldn't stop the laughter at the horrified tone of Sean's voice. Deciding to return a little of his friend's razzing, he replied, "I'm an equal opportunity kind of guy."

"I said don't answer that question," Sean protested. "I really don't need the image of some guy with his dick up your ass in my head, okay?"

"But it's such a nice dick," Beau said. "Long and—"

"Hanging up now."

"I'm sorry, Sean," Beau apologized. "I'll stop. I promise. I'm hoping I can persuade Jacob to take Friday off work so we can leave Thursday night and have three days down there, but I'll have to let you know for sure. He takes his responsibilities to his students very seriously."

"That's not a bad thing."

"Not at all," Beau said. "It's a wonderful thing, but it might mean he won't feel comfortable leaving until Friday night and coming back on Sunday. That just isn't a very long break for him."

"What about for you?" Sean asked.

"I'm not the one having to deal with a divorce and everyone either pretending to be sympathetic while whispering behind their hands or being openly snarky about it," Beau said. "For me, it's life as usual, other than not getting to see him as often."

"Just take care of yourself while you're taking care of him, okay?"

JACOB tucked his Bluetooth into his ear and hit the speed dial for Beau's number as he neared town after the six-hour drive home from his parents' house. His parents had not been openly critical of his divorce—his mother's good breeding would not allow her to say anything directly—but he had felt the weight of their censure in their silence and the notably empty seat where, last year, Melissa had sat. He was tempted to tell them about Beau, just to get it all out in the open, but he decided against it. The divorce wouldn't be final for another ten days, and he didn't want a lecture on infidelity on top of the veiled comments about marriage and divorce.

"Hi, baby. Are you home?" Beau asked as soon as he picked up the phone.

"Not yet," Jacob replied, "but I'm getting close. With Finn and everything, I figured if I didn't call now, I wouldn't get a chance for several more hours."

"How was your visit?"

"Awful," Jacob said. "My mother kept making comments about Melissa or about the sanctity of marriage. I spent the whole weekend biting my tongue. Is it time to go to Key West yet? I need a break."

"Stop here on your way home," Beau suggested. "We missed our meeting this week because of the holiday. Maybe I can make it up to you a little."

"I thought you said we shouldn't do anything to raise suspicion," Jacob said, although his protest sounded weak even to his own ears.

"I know I did, but it's been too long since I've had a chance to hold you," Beau replied. "Please, Jake. Come by the house."

Jacob started to say no before realizing that Beau was offering him exactly what he wanted instead of pulling the discretion card the way he usually did. "I'll be there as soon as I can."

What had seemed like only a few minutes' drive home before he called Beau suddenly seemed interminable. Fortunately Finn gurgled happily in his car seat as Jacob took the exit for Prestonsburg and drove through town to Beau's house. He debated where to park, but his car had been a frequent enough fixture in Beau's driveway that he decided not to worry about it now. He was here at Beau's invitation. Getting Finn out, he walked up the sidewalk to the porch. Beau opened the door before Jacob could even knock.

"Hey there, buddy," he said, taking Finn from Jacob's arms and kissing the crown of his head. "I hear your daddy had a rough few days with your grandma. You think maybe we can cheer him up a bit?"

Jacob couldn't help but smile, watching his lover coo over his son. "I swear you're his favorite person. He doesn't even go to my parents the way he goes to you."

"No, you're his favorite person," Beau said, "but I don't mind being his second favorite person." He juggled Finn onto one hip and reached for Jacob with his free arm, pulling him into a loving embrace. "I'm sorry it was such a rough week for you."

Jacob turned his head for a kiss, leaning into the caress with all the neediness of over a month of separation. After a moment, he rested his head on Beau's shoulder, that contact nearly as much a balm to his battered spirit as the kiss had been. "Can we sit on your couch and snuggle for a couple of hours?"

"We can do whatever you want, baby," Beau said.

Jacob didn't challenge that statement or ask to stay the way he really wanted to. It was enough that Beau had invited him over without pretense tonight and that they could be together for a few hours. He could imagine they were a family relaxing after the busy holiday weekend, even if it was an illusion that would be shattered when he had to leave to go home.

He set Finn's bag down by the door and walked with Beau into the den, sitting down and pulling the afghan off the back of the couch. It was not particularly cold outside, but he felt chilled inside. He had not expected his parents to be happy about his divorce, but he had hoped they would circle the wagons and support his decision. In fairness to them, he hadn't told them the whole story, so they probably saw the divorce as the same kind of rash decision the wedding had been, but until he had more to tell them about Beau and their relationship, Jacob would keep that to himself. They had accepted that he was gay when he came out in college, although they had been thrilled to be able to change that label to bisexual after he married Melissa. He had no idea how they would react to hearing his new lover was male, but he would cross that bridge later.

"Penny for your thoughts," Beau said, squeezing Jacob a little tighter. "You're awfully quiet."

"Just wondering how my parents will react when I tell them about you," Jacob replied honestly. "They know I'm gay, although I think they were more comfortable when they could say I was bi and married, but they've never had to meet a guy I was serious about before. There wasn't really anyone serious in college, not anyone I was ready to take home to Mama anyway, and then I moved here and ended up back in the closet. There's a big difference between having your son say he's gay and having him bring a man over for Christmas dinner."

"They'll react however they react," Beau said. "Worrying about it now won't change anything."

"Does that mean you'll come home to meet them at some point?" Jacob asked, afraid to get his hopes up.

"If you decide you want me to," Beau agreed. "We can't come out to the whole town, but your parents aren't likely to call the Board of Directors and tell them something that could get you fired. You told your friend. I told my friend Sean when I asked him about borrowing his plane in a couple of weeks. I don't want us to be a complete secret. I just want us to be discreet in the places where it could hurt us."

"You came out to your friend?"

Beau nodded, pressing a kiss to Jacob's forehead. "I was explaining how I had this friend who was getting divorced and needed a break, and I couldn't make myself lie to him again. It was bad enough lying by omission all this time, but to actually relegate you to the position of a friend I was helping out felt wrong."

"I'm glad you told him," Jacob replied, snuggling closer and turning his head for a real kiss. "How did he take it?"

"He demanded to know why I hadn't told him sooner," Beau admitted. "And then he said he wanted to meet you."

Jacob's heart thudded hard at the thought. "Is that good or bad?"

"Good," Beau assured him. "He's a little thrown by the whole situation, but he wouldn't have asked to meet you if he couldn't handle it. He has a gruff exterior, all brash and brawn and cusses and crude, but he has a heart of gold underneath all that."

"Then he's okay with you being gay?" Jacob asked.

"I don't know if okay is the right word," Beau said, "but he isn't rejecting me because of it. He agreed to let me use his plane, so now all we have to do is find a place to stay."

"We can do that later," Jacob decided. "I don't want to move right now."

"We don't have to move," Beau promised. "We can sit here until it's time for you to leave."

"I don't want to leave," Jacob admitted softly. "I wish I could stay here with you."

"I do, too, baby, but Prestonsburg isn't ready for you and Finn to have a sleepover."

Jacob was too tired to argue. "Someday can we live in a place that is ready for it?" he asked instead, his longing to stay making him desperate for reassurance.

"Someday, baby," Beau promised. "Where would you want to go? Key West, Atlanta, Houston? Or maybe somewhere that would let us get married?"

"You want to get married?"

"I know we can't right now, with Mom and everything, and I know you haven't decided what you want to do about us, but yes, someday I would love to marry you if you'll have me."

Jacob wanted to say yes, to throw himself in Beau's arms and start planning their wedding, but he held back. His divorce wasn't final yet, and even once it was, they had so much to figure out, so many details to work out, that he was afraid to commit to anything. "I want it more than anything, but I'm almost afraid to even say that aloud."

"Why?"

"Because the last time I admitted to wanting more, we had such a big fight I ended up married to Melissa," Jacob explained. "I don't want to fight any more."

"We aren't fighting, and you didn't bring it up," Beau reminded him. "I did. Things are different this time, remember? We've turned over a new leaf."

They had done better than Jacob expected in that respect. They hadn't had a real argument since they started working with the Autism Society project. "What happens when the summer is over and we don't have the excuse of our volunteer work to give us a cover for our meetings?"

"I don't know," Beau admitted, "but it's only November. We have until June for the program to start and until August before it ends to figure something out. Anything could happen between now and then."

"I suppose," Jacob agreed, "but it feels a little like living from paycheck to paycheck. At some point I want to get ahead, to plan ahead."

"We can start making plans," Beau said. "We can start looking now for other projects to work on, other—"

"But that's just it," Jacob interrupted. "It's exhausting. I want to come home to you at night and curl up in bed with you. I want to share Finn's milestones with you instead of telling you about them later. I want a life with you, and it doesn't feel like we can have one. As glad as I am to have the time with you that I do, it isn't enough. I don't know if it can be enough."

He rose from the couch, taking Finn from Beau's arms. "I should go because, the mood I'm in, if I stay, we'll end up fighting again, and I don't want that. I'll call you in a few days when I'm feeling a little less raw from seeing my parents, and we can make plans for our trip."

Beau let him go, walking with him to the door but not trying to stop him, for which Jacob was grateful. Short of a complete change of heart about coming out, nothing good could come of any further conversation this evening. He kissed Beau before he opened the door, hoping that would soften his abrupt departure. It was no surprise when Beau did not follow him out to the car.

BEAU watched Jacob drive away from behind the sheer curtains that covered the windows of his formal parlor. He hated seeing the taillights disappearing into the winter night, taking Jacob away from him. He recognized a strategic retreat when he saw one, but calling Jacob on it served no purpose, not when Beau had nothing helpful to add to the conversation. He wondered sometimes if he hadn't set them both up for more heartbreak, barging back into Jacob's life with his crazy proposition, but he hadn't been able to stay away any longer. The evenings they'd spent together in the past two months had been happier than he could have imagined, even after they stopped meeting in private because of Jacob's divorce.

The time apart had been hard, but not as miserable as the year they hadn't spoken at all. At least this time he had the real assurance of another meeting in the near future to tide him over when the nights seemed interminable, and now that Melissa had moved out, he could pick up the phone and hear Jacob's voice without worrying about who might answer the phone or who might overhear.

The problem was what to do now. Beau had so much more than he had ever imagined they could have that he could accept the limitations of their situation, but Jacob had always wanted more. Beau could understand that, but he didn't know how to give Jacob what he needed. They had to find a compromise somehow. He'd hoped planning for the future would assuage Jacob's need, but tonight it seemed only to have exacerbated it.

Beau sighed and picked up a rattle that had fallen out of Finn's bag. He loved having a baby in the house and looked forward to watching him grow up. The thought reminded him that he needed to call Christine and see when he would get to see Harrison over the holidays. He didn't want to have to cancel plans with Jacob because Christine decided to make last-minute plans.

Before he could call Christine, his phone rang, and Jacob's number popped up on the display. "Are you all right, baby?"

"I'm fine," Jacob said. "I wanted to apologize. I was in a mood tonight, and it wasn't fair to take it out on you."

"You didn't take it out on me," Beau said. "And everyone has bad moods. Dealing with them is part of any relationship. I'm just sorry you decided to leave instead of staying and actually dealing with your mood. Are you home yet?"

"I just got in," Jacob said. "Finn fell asleep in the car, so I put him in bed. He'll sleep for a couple of hours before he wants a bottle. I was thinking maybe we could find a place to stay in Key West. I know I didn't act like it tonight, but I really am excited about the chance to get away for a weekend with you."

"We can do that," Beau said. "Let me boot my computer up."

"I have to dig my laptop out of my bag too," Jacob said. "I'll do that while we talk. What were you thinking about in terms of a place to stay?"

"I tend to stay in bed and breakfasts when I can," Beau said, moving into his office and powering up his computer. "I like the personal touches you get in a small place. And Key West is gay friendly enough that we don't have to worry about the reaction we'd get to sharing a room. It's been long enough since I was in Key West that I don't have a favorite to recommend, but in Savannah and New Orleans, places I go somewhat regularly, I know the owners and even some of the staff by name."

"I like the sound of that," Jacob said. "I like the thought of going with you to some of these places even better."

"If you can get away for a weekend, say the word and we'll take a trip," Beau promised. "I need a few weeks' notice to clear my docket, but Fridays are slow days anyway, and if Sean lets us borrow his plane, we can be in Savannah in an hour and a half, and New Orleans is only two hours away."

"Melissa hasn't decided what weekends she wants Finn beyond the end of the year yet," Jacob said, "but I can push her to make those decisions. Any weekend I don't have him could work. Not that I think we should travel every month, since we're trying to be discreet, but it would let us plan ahead. I've never been to Savannah."

"It's a wonderful old city," Beau said. "Okay, my computer is ready. Do you have your laptop going?"

"Ready when you are," Jacob said.

"I'm always ready for you, baby," Beau teased.

"Oh, are we having phone sex?" Jacob teased back. "I have a web cam on my computer."

"I thought we were planning our trip," Beau replied, his body reacting to the inviting tone of Jacob's voice. *Why couldn't you have been in this mood when you were here?* He didn't give voice to his thoughts, not wanting to bring back the tension between them.

"We are," Jacob said. "We're planning what we're going to do when we're alone together without a pending divorce between us."

"After we find a place to stay," Beau said hoarsely. He could think of all kinds of things to do to and with Jacob once they checked into a room in Key West. He only wished they could do them sooner. He typed in a search for Key West bed and breakfasts and clicked on the first link that came up. "Here, check out Knowles House. It looks interesting."

They spent half an hour browsing through the web sites of the bed and breakfasts in Key West, picking out the room they wanted and making their reservations. The hour after that, they spent searching web sites for things to do in and around Key West, making plans for how to spend their days and deciding which restaurants they wanted to try. Their list was far too long for a weekend, but Beau didn't point that out. Jacob's voice was carefree again rather than weighed down by whatever snide comments he had endured over his Thanksgiving trip. When they finally hung up (without cyber sex, much to Beau's disappointment), Beau finally felt like they were back on track again after the rather large bump in the road that was Jacob's divorce. Now all he had to do was wait out the next two weeks and hope nothing happened to put a wrench in their plans.

$$[\ 6\ ]$$

"IT'S official. I'm now a divorcé."

Beau knew that already. He'd seen Jacob's name on the docket earlier that week, but he hadn't said anything, not wanting Jacob to think Beau was stalking him. He remembered all too well the sensation of everyone staring at him during his own divorce. He didn't want to contribute to that feeling for Jacob. Since he couldn't see his lover's face on the other end of the phone line, he settled for a safer approach. "How are you feeling?"

"Mostly relieved, I think," Jacob said slowly. "It's over. I still have to deal with her as far as arranging visitation and stuff, but I don't have any legal responsibility to her anymore."

"Where is she living now? Is it a safe environment for Finn?" Beau asked.

"She moved back in with her parents," Jacob replied. "They weren't thrilled about it until Melissa reminded them it was guaranteed time with Finn every month. I suspect they'll end up taking care of him more than she will, but at least I won't have to worry about him."

"That's good," Beau said. "And she has him next weekend, right?"

"It's all set up," Jacob said. "I'll drop him off at day care Friday morning, and she'll pick him up from there and keep him until Monday morning, so it doesn't matter how late we get back Sunday night, other than me having to get up to teach Monday morning."

"I'm looking forward to a weekend alone with you," Beau admitted. "As much as I love having Finn around, it'll be nice not to have to worry about him waking up and interrupting us while we're making love."

"He's sleeping for longer periods of time at night now," Jacob said. "It won't be long before he's sleeping through the night, I bet."

For all the good that did them, with Jacob in Elliot and Beau in Prestonsburg. Beau kept that thought to himself. He wasn't at a point where he could do anything to change that reality, and he didn't want to spark another fight. "I'm glad. I remember how hard it was when Harrison was still little and we were getting up every few hours to feed him. It was bad enough with two of us. I can't even imagine how tired you must be, having to do it all yourself."

"It's not too bad," Jacob insisted. "Better than being married to a woman I don't love."

"That's undoubtedly true," Beau agreed. "You aren't feeling down about this, are you?"

"A little," Jacob said softly. "I married her for all the wrong reasons, but I *did* marry her, and I don't like failing at things."

"You didn't fail," Beau insisted. "You fixed a mistake you made."

"That doesn't make me feel any better," Jacob replied. "How am I supposed to tell Finn his mother and I are divorced because having him was a mistake?"

"You don't," Beau said, heart clenching at the thought of ever saying such a thing to a child. "You tell him marrying Melissa was a mistake because you love someone else, but that you don't regret having him."

"You realize it's going to get harder to keep things a secret when he gets older and can start talking," Jacob said. "He'll know we're together, and kids don't always keep secrets well."

"Maybe by the time we have to worry about what he's saying, it won't be an issue anymore," Beau said, thinking of his visit with the doctors earlier in the week. "My mother is getting worse. The doctors don't know what triggered the decline, but she's less responsive on the whole and is having fewer and fewer moments of lucidity."

"I don't even know what to say," Jacob said. "I'm sorry she's doing worse. Do the doctors hold out any hope that she'll improve again?"

"Not really," Beau said. "Alzheimer's isn't a linear or predictable disease, but it is irreversible. She may have moments of lucidity right up until she dies, but she isn't going to be well again. It's more a matter of making her as comfortable and her days as rich as possible in the meantime. It's a waiting game."

One that had their lives on hold until it was over. Beau knew it and acknowledged the inherent unfairness of it, but he didn't have a solution now any more than he'd had one when they first met two years ago.

"Is it okay for you to be gone next weekend?" Jacob asked.

"Oh, yes," Beau said. "I didn't mean to suggest I was changing our plans. She's doing worse, but they don't think anything will happen that quickly. They were just updating me on her overall condition. I wouldn't miss next weekend unless I had no other choice."

"That's good," Jacob said, his voice soft.

"I'm not changing my mind, baby," Beau assured him. "I've missed you so much. I want to lie in bed with you and wrap myself around you and never let go. I want to walk down the street in Key West and hold your hand and not worry about what anyone thinks. Even if it's just for the weekend, I want a normal life with you."

"I believe you," Jacob said, "but it's hard sometimes, being alone."

"I know it is. Now that we don't have to worry about Melissa getting suspicious, maybe we can see each other a little more often," Beau suggested. "I could come to Elliot sometimes, too, so you wouldn't always have to make the drive."

"I'd like that," Jacob said. "My house is full of baby stuff, but you're welcome any time. I think I hear Finn crying. I should go see what he needs. I'll talk to you soon. I love you."

"I love you too, baby," Beau said, setting down the phone. Maybe he'd talk to the doctors again. Now that his mother was doing worse, familiar surroundings might not be as important as they had been when she still had frequent moments of awareness. Maybe they could find a good facility for her in Atlanta or somewhere in Florida where he and Jacob could be together. Even if they still advised against a move, it couldn't hurt to ask.

JACOB was practically vibrating as he drove toward the tiny airfield between Auburn and Opelika. It was the best place they had come up with to meet and leave Jacob's car for the weekend. He couldn't very well leave it parked in Beau's driveway, nor could Beau come to his house or to school to pick him up. The only other alternative had been to drive to Montgomery separately, but Jacob hadn't really wanted to do that.

Pulling into the parking lot, he smiled to see Beau's Prius there waiting for him. He hopped out and grabbed his suitcase, only pausing to make sure his car was locked before tossing his bag in Beau's trunk and climbing in next to him. "Hi," he said, leaning over for a quick kiss. "How was your day?"

"Way too long," Beau said with a smile. "I must have looked at the clock every two minutes all day, waiting for it to be time to leave. How was yours?"

"Long," Jacob agreed. "The kids couldn't understand why I was so distracted today. Fortunately I have them well enough trained in our routine that they could carry on without as much supervision as I usually give them. I kept counting the hours until we'd be in Key West and could make love again. It's been too long."

"It has been," Beau agreed, "but another few hours and we'll have all weekend. It'll be about a four-hour flight once we get off the ground. The faster we get to Montgomery, the faster we can get to Florida."

"What are we waiting for?" Jacob asked.

Beau laughed as he pulled the car out of the parking lot. "Sean invited us to dinner on Sunday when we get home. Assuming we get back early enough to have dinner here rather than eating before we leave."

"I knew you'd told him about us, but you didn't tell me about dinner," Jacob said, not completely comfortable with the idea of meeting Beau's friend after a weekend getaway. He'd be so blissed out from the sex that he probably wouldn't be in the mood for conversation, and he wasn't sure that was the right first impression to leave on their benefactor. "I'm not sure that's a good idea."

"Why not, baby? He just wants a chance to get to know you a little better. You're my lover, and that makes you part of his life because you're part of mine."

"Because I'm still not sure where I fit in your life," Jacob admitted. He hadn't planned to have this conversation now. He'd wanted a weekend away with no stress between them. They could deal with the rest when they got back, except that it had come up anyway. "Or where you fit in mine. Yes, the divorce is final so I'm free again from a legal standpoint, but aren't you the one always telling me we can't really live as a couple?"

"Not openly," Beau agreed, "but as Sean reminded me rather bluntly when I told him about us, he doesn't count as being open. It's like your friend in Atlanta, the one you said you told about us. If we were going to Atlanta, would you think twice about us having dinner with him?"

"No," Jacob replied slowly, "but I know Billy already. There's no awkwardness with him."

"For you," Beau said. "For me, there's none with Sean. Think about it this weekend and if you really don't feel comfortable with the idea, we'll tell him we're too tired when we get back on Sunday. Of course he'll probably make some comment about how we shouldn't have fucked that last time if it left us too tired to have dinner with a friend, but we can still decline."

Jacob flushed slightly. "Would he really say that?"

"To you, maybe not, since he doesn't know you very well yet," Beau said. "To me, definitely."

Silently, Jacob scolded himself for his reticence. He should be happy Beau's friend hadn't reacted badly to the news of their relationship. If nothing else, he could remind Beau of that reaction when they considered telling other people. "Let's see how Sunday goes," he decided. "If we're back in time for dinner, we can accept his invitation."

"IT'S even more beautiful than it looked online," Jacob said, getting out of the taxi they had taken from the Key West airstrip to the bed and breakfast. The yellow wood siding gave an air of freshness to the two-story house. A porch ran invitingly along the front of the inn, wicker chairs beckoning. "We could check in and come sit on the porch for a few minutes."

"Or we could check in and I could take you to bed," Beau murmured in his ear.

Jacob's body reacted predictably to the suggestion, but he held back. Beau had told him Key West was gay friendly, that they wouldn't have to hide here, but knowing it intellectually and feeling comfortable with it on a gut level were two different things. "I was trying to be civilized."

"Forget civilized," Beau growled. "It's been six weeks since we've made love, and that's six weeks too long."

There was that, Jacob thought, his body flushing at the tone of Beau's voice. He could feel his students' sticky hands, though, added to the inevitable feeling of grunginess that came from traveling. Before they did anything else, he needed a shower.

Dealing with the hotelier forestalled the conversation long enough for him to show them upstairs. The walls of their room matched the siding, a beautiful lemon yellow that made Jacob think of sunny days and warm sand. The blue china plates on the walls and the matching comforter and pillows completed the ambiance of French country charm. It would be a perfect hideaway for the weekend.

When they were alone again, the door safely locked behind the departing innkeeper, Jacob toed off his shoes and turned to Beau. "We should get some dinner, and I don't know about you, but I need a shower before we do anything else."

Beau hid his disappointment. They had all weekend. They didn't have to make love the minute they walked in the door. "If that's what you want, baby," he said. "Let me take a quick shower, then you can, and then we can find something to eat. Just promise me you'll let me make love to you when we get back."

"I promise," Jacob said, grateful for Beau's understanding. "It's not that I don't want to make love now, but I'm tired and grimy and hungry and—"

"And you'll be more relaxed and more in the mood later," Beau finished. "I understand completely. Get unpacked and settled in while I take a shower. That'll help too. It's been a hard few weeks for you."

Beau grabbed his toiletries bag from his suitcase and disappeared into the bathroom. A few seconds later, Jacob heard the water start. He forced himself to do as Beau suggested, opening his bag and hanging up his clothes rather than sitting on the bed and fantasizing about Beau in the shower. It *had* been a hard few weeks, with the strain of the divorce and keeping up appearances at school and not being able to see Beau except for their Autism Society planning meetings and the one truncated visit on his way home from Vicksburg. He wanted them to have a life as a couple, and the past six weeks hadn't facilitated that at all, even less than their time together before their breakup had. That could change now, at least a little. They had already started to change it some, talking on the phone every night, not just to have phone sex, although they did plenty of that, but talking about their days, their plans, all the things couples did except that couples usually had those conversations over the dinner table instead of on the phone in different towns.

Jacob hoped things would get better now that his divorce was final. He couldn't exactly move in with Beau, but they wouldn't have to worry about making Melissa suspicious. They could start meeting at Beau's house again, where they would have the privacy to hold hands, kiss, make love, or simply be together without having to worry what people would think about seeing them together.

The water turned off, drawing Jacob's thoughts back to the present and to the man currently drying off on the other side of the door. Jacob could see it as clearly as if he stood right there, the white cotton moving across winter-pale skin, lapping up the drops of water shimmering in Beau's chest hair and down his treasure trail to the slightly darker hair at the base of his cock. The door opened, and Beau walked out, towel around his waist, his short blond hair dripping water onto his shoulders, and Jacob cracked.

He pounced on Beau, tearing the towel aside and pushing him toward the bed. They could eat dinner later, or not at all, for all Jacob cared. Right now, he needed Beau and nothing else mattered.

"What about dinner?" Beau asked, though he made no move to get out from underneath Jacob.

"Later," Jacob said, diving down for a kiss. Beau subsided beneath him, returning the kiss with the same fire that licked along Jacob's skin.

The feeling of Jacob's weight pressing down on him twisted Beau's gut, sending tingles out along his nerves as he waited to see what Jacob would do next. It went against his instincts to lie back this way and leave Jacob in charge, but Jacob wasn't giving him any chance to reassert himself. Maybe, under the circumstances, it was better to let Jacob do this his way. They had all weekend. Beau would get his chance.

Jacob intensified the contact, attacking Beau's mouth in a kiss designed to steal his lover's wits and leave him breathless and open to whatever Jacob might want. Not that he intended to do anything Beau might object to. They had made love plenty of times before, but things were different this time. This time Jacob didn't have a wife to make him feel guilty or the fear of being found out to make him cautious. They didn't have all the tension between them from two years of fighting over keeping their relationship secret. They'd talked about getting married someday, about moving in together when circumstances allowed and building a family. That made tonight special. Maybe they weren't quite on their honeymoon yet, but Jacob finally felt like they might have a chance of moving in that direction.

To that end, he invaded Beau's mouth, a prelude of what he intended to do with his body. When Beau responded, burying his fingers in Jacob's hair and holding him tight, Jacob smiled into the kiss. It felt good to be irresistible.

The kiss, frantic as it was, soothed the ragged edges of Beau's mind and heart. He stood by his reasons for their separation as Jacob waited for his divorce to go through, but he had missed Jacob's touch, all the more because he no longer felt like it was a fluke to have it. The reality of their lives might still keep them apart more than together, but it was a momentary separation, to be ended as soon as the circumstances of their lives changed. He was committed to that now and believed Jacob shared that commitment. That had made the self-imposed distance between them all the harder to bear.

That was over now, though. Jacob's divorce was final, and they were somewhere safe for the weekend. They could indulge in all the intimacies their limited time together usually denied them.

Jacob released Beau's mouth, panting hard. "Don't move."

Beau watched with desire in his eyes as Jacob stood and stripped swiftly, rummaging in his toiletries bag for a sachet of lube and a strip of condoms. He could have taken advantage and taken control of their lovemaking, but he found the need to be in charge all the time had faded as he had come to believe he and Jacob would have a life together. His old defense mechanisms no longer applied.

Jacob tossed the necessities on the bed and climbed back onto the thick mattress, nudging Beau's legs apart with his knees. He lingered a moment to lick a stripe up the length of Beau's erection before covering his lover's body with his again, rubbing against Beau's chest with a happy sigh. "I could do this forever."

"You could," Beau agreed, "but I can think of other things you should do at the same time." He spread his legs wider, draping his calves over the back of Jacob's legs in silent invitation.

That was all Jacob needed. Pushing up on his knees so he could reach between Beau's thighs, he tore open the lube, laughing as it squirted all over his hands. The carefree sound brought a smile to Beau's lips. Jacob should always be this happy. "Come on, baby," he urged. "Get me ready. I want to feel you."

Jacob nodded, rubbing over Beau's perineum with one hand while he fondled the heavy sac with the other. Beau shuddered and gasped, his eyes closed, his face set in a mask of pleasure that encouraged Jacob to continue. Beau's buttocks clenched reflexively when Jacob probed between them, but he persisted, circling the tight entrance with his fingertips. Beau was always tense at first when Jacob topped, but he could usually convince his lover to relax for him. It took a few minutes, longer than it normally did, making Jacob worry he had misjudged the situation, but finally the tension eased and Jacob slid a finger inside to the first knuckle. Need pulsed in his veins and in his cock, spurring him to hurry, but he ignored it. As much as he might want it, he wouldn't rush Beau, not with this.

"Go ahead," Beau said. "I'm ready."

He didn't feel ready, but Jacob made the choice to trust him, probing deeper until he found Beau's prostate. He flicked it a couple of times, smiling as Beau thrashed on the bed. "Oh, fuck."

"We will," Jacob promised, "as soon as you're loose enough I won't worry I'm hurting you the whole time."

"Only one part of me is hurting right now," Beau replied.

Jacob glanced down at Beau's neglected cock, hard and flushed with blood. "You don't need my permission to touch yourself," he teased. The thought of watching Beau stroke himself while Jacob played with his ass added another layer of lust to the whirlwind already rushing through him.

"It's not my hand I want to feel," Beau countered. "I've had enough of that over the past six weeks to last me a while. I want to feel your hand."

"All you had to do was ask," Jacob said, moving his free hand from Beau's balls to his erection, stroking it in time with the thrust of his fingers. "Is that what you wanted?"

The strangled sound that escaped Beau's throat could have been a curse, an assent, or simply Jacob's name. It didn't matter which because Beau bucked up into Jacob's fist, making his approval obvious.

His own need growing desperate, Jacob slid his fingers free and tore open the condom with his teeth, sliding it on one-handed as he continued to work Beau's cock. He draped Beau's thighs over his own, tilting his hips up to a better angle. Beau planted his feet on the mattress and lifted up even more, offering himself to Jacob, but the moment Jacob pressed his cock against Beau's entrance, Beau tensed, making it impossible for Jacob to slide inside without more force than he was willing to use. "Relax," he urged. "I don't want to hurt you."

Beau nodded, his face set as he tried to do what Jacob requested.

"Do you need to come first?" Jacob asked, increasing the pace of his hand.

"No," Beau gasped, catching Jacob's wrist. "Just do it."

Jacob hesitated a moment longer, but Beau reached for his hip, pulling him forward. Doing his best to be careful, Jacob pressed harder against the resistant muscle, letting his weight drive him forward until the head popped inside. Beau groaned, and Jacob froze. Then, like someone had flipped a light switch, Beau let out a shuddering breath and suddenly relaxed. "Okay?" Jacob asked.

Beau smiled up at him. "Okay."

Jacob kept his first few thrusts measured, not wanting to cause a return of the dreadful tension, but whatever mental block Beau had needed to overcome, he had clearly done so because he lifted his hips to meet every thrust, their bodies slapping together wetly.

Jacob wanted to draw out the moment, but it had been too long for either of them to have that kind of patience. Within minutes, Beau's muscles seized, massaging Jacob's cock until they both climaxed hard. Jacob collapsed on top of Beau, barely retaining the presence of mind to pull out and wad the condom into a tissue before snuggling back against Beau's side and dozing in repletion.

Jacob had no idea how long they lay that way, half awake, simply basking in the freedom to enjoy the post-coital stupor. Eventually, though, his stomach's growling grew too loud and insistent to ignore.

"Where should we go for dinner?" he asked.

"Anywhere you want," Beau replied languidly, not at all interested in moving. His own stomach hadn't started rumbling yet, and he was far too comfortable with Jacob curled up naked against him to think about getting up. "Just not yet."

"Lazy bum," Jacob teased, sitting up. "I thought you brought me down here to celebrate my divorce being final."

"Isn't that what we just did?" Beau asked, running a finger down the line of Jacob's spine. He lingered on each bump, cherishing the time they had to simply be together without having to worry about appearances or rushing off.

"I want to go out," Jacob insisted. "You told me Key West was gay friendly, and I want a chance to be out with you like we were on the cruise, just a normal couple amid all the others."

Beau could hardly argue with that request when it was one of the reasons he had picked Key West in the first place. "Fine," he said, pushing up on one elbow and kissing Jacob's back, "but this time you have to take the first shower."

"No way," Jacob replied, tugging on Beau's hand. "Surely that shower is big enough for both of us."

Beau's smile grew wider. "Why didn't you say so sooner?"

Jacob laughed and stood. "Come on. The sooner we get clean, the sooner we get food. And the sooner we do that, the sooner we can go back to bed."

Beau liked the sound of that. "You're on."

They showered quickly, washing each other playfully, enough to have the arousal simmering between them again without it exploding out of control. By the time they were dry and dressed, Beau could see the tension fading from Jacob's stance. He hoped it would be gone completely by morning. "Let's find something for dinner."

They wandered along the historic streets, stopping to read menus until they found one that appealed. "Two for dinner?" the hostess asked.

"Yes," Beau said.

"I have the perfect table," she said, "out on the patio but protected from the breeze so it isn't too cool even after it gets dark. Very romantic."

Beau smiled at the casual assumption they were a couple. They could be one here without worrying what people thought or having to correct the assumption. "It sounds perfect," he said, his hand resting on the small of Jacob's back. "We've been looking forward to getting away."

"You've come to the right place," the hostess said as she led them out onto the patio. "Key West, the perfect winter getaway."

"It's been perfect so far," Jacob agreed, smiling over his shoulder at Beau, the expression so unbearably intimate that Beau was tempted to lean forward and kiss him right there. The hostess showed them their table and gave them menus. As she disappeared inside, Beau gave in to the temptation and brushed his lips over Jacob's.

Jacob smiled. "That makes it even more perfect. I like being with you and not having to hide."

Beau liked it too. Too much. It was getting harder and harder to stop from reaching for Jacob's hand in public at home. He wondered if this trip was a good idea, if going home afterward would be even more difficult because of the freedom of the weekend, but he couldn't bring himself to regret it, not looking across the table at Jacob's smile.

"Good evening, gentlemen," the waiter said, approaching the table. "I'm Kevin, and I'll be taking care of you this evening. Can I get you something to drink while you look over the menu? A pitcher of sangria to share or maybe a bottle of wine?"

"Sangria sounds good," Jacob said to Beau. "What do you think?"

"Whatever you want," Beau said.

"We'll take a pitcher of the sangria," Jacob told the waiter.

The waiter smiled and went over the specials with them before leaving them alone again. "So what are our plans for tomorrow?" Jacob asked.

"Whatever you want, baby," Beau repeated, the nickname slipping out easily now that they were alone. "We can wander the beach, visit the shops and museums, or we can stay in bed all day."

"As nice as that sounds, it seems like a waste to come all this way and not see at least some of the town," Jacob said.

"Then we'll visit the town," Beau said, "as long as you let me take you to bed too."

"Oh, definitely," Jacob said, his voice dropping as he leaned closer. "And in the shower and on the lanai and anywhere else we can get away with it."

That did nothing for Beau's composure. Fortunately the waiter returned with their drinks, breaking the tension of the moment. He took their orders and left them alone again.

"You really shouldn't say things like that when I can't do anything about them," Beau scolded gently.

"Why not?" Jacob said. "I like getting you all worked up. Anticipation makes the moment sweeter, doesn't it?"

"It can't get any sweeter than watching your ass stretch to take my dick," Beau replied, determined to give Jacob some of this own medicine.

Jacob's eyes widened, his breath catching in his throat. "Damn, Beau," he whispered. "How soon can we go back to the hotel?"

"As soon as we have our dinner," Beau said, leaning back in his chair smugly. He loved how responsive Jacob was to a word, a touch, a kiss. He intended to take full advantage of it this weekend.

"Can't we just cancel our order and pay for our drinks?" Jacob asked.

Beau laughed. "Anticipation, baby, remember?"

Jacob pouted, but Beau could see the laughter in his eyes. He leaned forward and sucked on the protruding lower lip, drawing it between his teeth and nipping it lightly. Jacob's lips parted with a soft gasp, inviting Beau's tongue to slip between them.

Desire sparked in Jacob's belly at the intimate caress, but the table between them kept it from going beyond that. Not that it could go much farther than that on a patio out in the open the way they were. It felt good, though, to not worry about who might be watching. Jacob wasn't an exhibitionist by any stretch of the imagination, but the freedom of acting like a couple with Beau was intoxicating.

They lingered over the kiss, keeping the contact light by silent agreement. Their waiter could return at any time, other customers could arrive, anyone could walk by on the beach. They had no guarantee of privacy for anything more than the soft, loving meeting of mouths, but they reveled in that, a celebration of love and freedom and openness.

"One day," Beau said, breaking the kiss and resting his forehead against Jacob's. "One day we'll live in a place where this is normal instead of special."

"One day," Jacob agreed, stealing one more quick kiss before leaning back in his chair and sipping his sangria. "How's your mom doing? Any more change?"

"No," Beau said, "nothing since the last meeting I had with her doctors. She took a decided downward turn and then plateaued again. She could stay like this indefinitely."

Jacob held out his hand, squeezing Beau's fingers when his lover reached across the table and entwined their hands. "I'm sorry. I know this is hard on you."

"If there was something we could do for her, if there was some hope of her getting better, I'd at least feel like I wasn't just sitting around waiting for her to die," Beau admitted. "I hate feeling helpless."

"We all do," Jacob said, squeezing more tightly. He so rarely saw this vulnerable side of his lover. It only endeared Beau to him more. "You're doing the right thing for her by making sure she's getting the best possible care and by staying near enough to oversee that closely. I haven't always made that easy, and for that, I'm sorry. I saw it as a question of choosing her over me, and that wasn't fair to you. We'll keep going like we have been the past couple of months as long as she's with us, and we'll deal with the rest later. I'm not going to make the same mistake again. I love you too much to do that."

Beau summoned a weak smile, trying to shake the suddenly dour mood. Jacob's promise helped because he wouldn't be facing his mother's illness and eventual death alone. He wondered if he could find an excuse to take Jacob to see her. Even if his mother never understood the true nature of their relationship, Beau would feel better for having introduced them.

The waiter returned with their dinners, giving Beau something less grim to focus on. After a few bites, he slid his foot against Jacob's beneath the table. "No more sad thoughts, okay? This weekend is for us to celebrate being together again. We'll worry about Mom when we get back to Prestonsburg."

"Okay," Jacob agreed, returning Beau's caress.

They chatted about things to see and do in Key West as they ate, deliberately putting aside thoughts of anything outside this bubble of time. When they had finished, the waiter returned to clear the table. "Can I tempt you with dessert? A crème brûlée or a slice of fresh pie?"

"We'll look at a dessert menu," Jacob said. "Something sweet sounds good."

The waiter left the menu for them. "I don't think I can eat a full dessert," Beau groaned.

"So we'll share one," Jacob said. "I just want something sweet so the meal feels finished."

"Pick one," Beau said. "I'll take a bite or two and you can have the rest."

Jacob skimmed the menu, finally deciding on the crème brûlée. When the waiter returned, Jacob placed their order to share.

"Very good," the waiter said. "One spoon or two?"

"Oh, I think we can share a spoon," Jacob said with a grin for Beau.

The waiter smiled and went to get their desert.

"So you're going to feed me dessert?" Beau teased.

"I thought I might," Jacob replied, feeling suddenly defensive. "Unless you'd rather I didn't?"

"Not at all," Beau replied quickly, squeezing Jacob's hand for reassurance.

Jacob relaxed, turning to stare out at the water. "It's a beautiful night. We should walk along the beach to work off dinner before we go back to the hotel."

"Sounds like a plan," Beau said.

Kevin brought their dessert and the single spoon, checking to see if they needed anything else before returning inside. Jacob dipped the spoon in the creamy concoction and held it out for Beau to taste, shivering as his lover opened his mouth, his tongue darting out to catch a bit of caramel before it dropped off the side.

"How is it?" Jacob asked, his voice hoarse as desire swamped him again.

"Delicious," Beau replied, taking the spoon from Jacob's lax grip and scooping up some more. "Try it."

The dessert was indeed delicious, but it was the look on Beau's face as Jacob sucked it off the spoon that was nearly Jacob's undoing. "Maybe we should go straight back to the hotel."

Beau shook his head, offering Jacob another bite. "Walk with me in the moonlight."

Jacob nodded, swallowing again.

They finished the meal, Beau picked up the check, and they stepped from the patio into the shadows of the beach. They had only gone a few yards when Beau pressed Jacob against the pillar supporting the next building and kissed him thoroughly. Jacob wrapped his arms around Beau's shoulders, holding tight and keeping him close as he rubbed against the firm body, reveling in the erection that matched his own. "You're too beautiful for your own damn good," Beau growled, pulling Jacob's hair free from the tie that held it back and burrowing his fingers into the messy curls.

Determined to give as good as he got, Jacob ran his fingers through Beau's short blond hair. It wouldn't show his attention the way his own hair would show Beau's, but that didn't make it less arousing. He attacked Beau's mouth, nipping and biting, the tender kisses at the restaurant having whetted his need for more. He wondered wildly if anyone would see them if Beau spun him around and fucked him right there against the post, but Beau pulled back before Jacob could suggest it. "We can't do this here. If we get arrested for public indecency, we'll never manage to keep it quiet at home."

"Then take me somewhere we can do it," Jacob demanded, grabbing Beau's hand and pulling him down the beach in the general direction of their hotel.

By the time they reached the bed and breakfast, they were all but running, barging through the door and up the stairs to their room with no thought for the assumptions anyone would make at seeing them that way.

Jacob tore at Beau's clothes, uncaring of buttons flying or seams ripping. He needed skin and nothing else would do. When their mutual attempts at undressing only resulted in frustration, Jacob pulled back.

"Get naked," he snapped, jerking his own shirt over his head and tearing off his jeans. Beau did the same, stripping quickly and opening his arms in invitation. Jacob pounced, knocking Beau back onto the bed and following him down, straddling his lover's hips so he could run his fingers through the hair on Beau's chest. "I love this," he said, tugging on the short curls lightly.

"I love this," Beau countered, sliding his hands over the curve of Jacob's ass. "Perfect, perky, and all mine."

"All yours," Jacob agreed, leaning down for a kiss as he played with Beau's nipples. He gasped when he felt cool, wet fingers probing his entrance, but he wasn't about to complain when they slid inside and rubbed over his prostate. "Oh, fuck."

"We will, baby," Beau promised. "I want to see your ass stretched around me just like I said at the restaurant."

"Then we're in the wrong position," Jacob said, moving to the side and bracing his elbows on the bed so his back arched and his buttocks lifted in invitation. "You need to be behind me for that."

Beau moved swiftly into place behind Jacob, rolling a condom on as he scissored his fingers roughly. His patience had reached an end, but even so, he didn't want to hurt Jacob. Fortunately, Jacob seemed to share his urgency, rocking back against his fingers demandingly.

"Now," Jacob begged as Beau pulled his fingers free and replaced them with his cock.

"Now," Beau agreed, thrusting home, his eyes fixed on the spot where they joined, the rippled skin stretched smooth around his erection, a slightly darker shade than the faint olive cast of the rest of Jacob's skin. "Look at the way you take me in," he groaned. "You need this, don't you?"

Jacob had no idea where Beau's sudden need for reassurance came from, but he didn't hesitate to provide it. "Yes," he gasped. "I'm only half alive without you. Harder, Beau. Fuck me harder."

Beau obliged, pummeling the clinging passage, giving Jacob all his strength, all his devotion in the joining of their bodies.

It couldn't last long at that pace, the entire evening one long foreplay session, but Jacob was as eager as Beau, his cock jerking untouched beneath him as Beau hit his prostate with every pass, forcing burst after burst of fluid from his balls until he finally shot all over the sheets.

The contractions of Jacob's inner muscles massaged Beau's shaft, teasing him with Jacob's release until he, too, succumbed to the lust driving him and spilled into the condom.

"Wet spot," Jacob grimaced as Beau's weight bore him down onto the bed.

"And whose fault is that?" Beau teased, withdrawing and tossing the condom in the nearby waste bin.

"Yours," Jacob said. "Definitely yours."

"And how do you figure that?" Beau asked, getting a wet cloth from the bathroom to clean them up and a dry towel to cover the mess they'd made on the bed. "I was wearing a condom."

"I wouldn't have come if you hadn't fucked me so well," Jacob retorted, smiling sleepily up at Beau as his lover wiped him clean. "Get rid of that and come to bed. I want to sleep in your arms."

It had been too long since they'd done that. They'd made love, but sharing a bed through the night was an intimacy they hadn't shared since they returned from their cruise two years before. "That sounds like heaven."

When Beau came to bed, having hung up the washcloth, and Jacob wrapped around him, it felt like heaven too.

THEY spent the next day wandering the island, visiting the Key West Audubon House and then taking a dolphin watching tour. To their delight, they saw dozens of dolphins playing in the boat's wake and even racing along beside it. By the time they returned to the hotel to change for dinner, they were smiling and sunburned despite the mild temperatures and the sunscreen they'd slathered on each other that morning.

"Let's go dancing tonight," Jacob suggested as he brushed his hair after his shower. He had worn it loose all day at Beau's request, and he was paying for it now with all the tangles. "There's nowhere in Prestonsburg or Elliot where we can dance with each other. We had such fun on the cruise, and I'd like to do it again."

"I'm sure we can find somewhere," Beau agreed, pulling on a casual pair of khakis and a polo shirt. "We can ask the innkeepers."

The owners of the bed and breakfast recommended several clubs on the island where they would be welcome, including one where they could have dinner first, so Beau and Jacob decided on that one. The food wasn't quite as good as at the restaurant the night before, but the ambiance made up for it. All the employees in the restaurant wore costumes, some of pirates, others of British or American military, and every hour, they performed a battle between the pirates and the military forces. Jacob had to smile at the inaccuracies, but for pure entertainment during their meal, it was perfect.

Between shows, the dance floor was packed with couples of all varieties, so when Jacob and Beau finished eating, Jacob grabbed Beau's hand and pulled him out into the crowd.

Beau went along willingly enough, the smile on Jacob's face more than sufficient reason to give in to his lover's request. The music was perfect for dancing, with a variety of big band selections from the forties and fifties. "You lead," Jacob said as he turned into Beau's arms. "You're a much better dancer than I am."

Beau smiled and drew Jacob closer, leading him through some simple steps to make sure Jacob could still follow before undertaking any more complicated moves. They played around with steps and twirls for the first few minutes, but eventually the desire to be together won out and they abandoned fancy footwork for simple steps and the illusion of being the only two people in the room.

When they finally returned to their room that night, the same slow, sweet mood carried through their lovemaking and into their dreams.

[7]

"ARE you sure we have to have dinner with your friend?" Jacob asked as they left the airstrip on their way home from Key West.

"If you really don't want to go, I'll call and cancel," Beau said, although he couldn't keep the disappointment out of his voice, "but I would like to see him, and he did let us borrow his plane. It won't be that bad, baby. He said Marlene and the kids are visiting her mother, so it'll just be the three of us. A group of guys hanging out and drinking beer."

Except that Beau and Sean were already friends and Jacob would be the outsider.

"Okay, let's go," Jacob said. It had been a good weekend. He didn't want it to end with tension between them because he was afraid to meet Beau's best friend. "Just remember that I have to be at work early tomorrow so we can't stay too late."

"I already told Sean that," Beau promised. "He said he'd send us on our way no later than eight. You don't have to pick Finn up tonight, right?"

"Right," Jacob said. "Melissa will take him to daycare in the morning, and I'll pick him up after school. Don't take this the wrong way, because I had a wonderful weekend, but I miss him."

"Of course you do," Beau said. "He's your son and you love him. Part of being a parent is juggling his needs and your needs. I only had two years with Harrison before Christine moved away, but I remember that part clearly. I also remember figuring out that I couldn't take care of Harrison if I didn't take care of myself sometimes."

"I'm learning that," Jacob assured him. "That's why I went ahead and divorced Melissa. Even if things don't work out between us, being with her was never going to be good for me."

"Things will work out," Beau insisted. "We'll make sure of it."

If their lives could be like they had been this weekend, Jacob wouldn't have any doubts about that. He didn't question what was in their hearts, just the effect secrecy would have on their ability to live by what they felt.

"Enough dour thoughts," Beau scolded, making Jacob realize his distraction must have shown on his face. "We'll be at Sean's house in a couple of minutes. If you're frowning, he'll think I didn't take good care of you this weekend."

"Since when do you have to take care of me?" Jacob asked, keeping his voice deliberately light despite the urge to get defensive.

"Your divorce went through a week ago," Beau said. "If anyone deserves at little TLC, it's you. I'm sure a time will come when you'll have to take care of me too. It's what couples do."

"Sorry," Jacob said. "I didn't mean to overreact. I'm still feeling my way, trying to balance being a couple with being in the closet."

Beau reached across the gearshift to squeeze Jacob's hand. "We both are, baby. We'll figure it out together."

After this weekend, Jacob could almost believe it.

They pulled up in front of a huge house behind an imposing wrought iron gate. Beau pressed the buzzer and waited for the intercom to crackle to life. A moment later, the gate swung open, letting them inside. Jacob swallowed nervously and looked down at the jeans and light sweatshirt he was wearing. "I'm not dressed for this."

"Marlene isn't here," Beau reminded him. "Sean will have given the staff the night off, and it'll be steaks on the grill and beer in a bottle. If you come back when his wife is here, that might be different, but tonight it's just us guys."

Jacob fidgeted on the seat, not completely reassured by Beau's words. Beau didn't share his nervousness, though, and that helped calm Jacob as well. He might not come from the kind of wealth obvious in the house and grounds in front of him, but his mother had insisted all her children learn enough etiquette to behave appropriately in society.

Beau followed the driveway around to the side of the house, parking next to a garage that was nearly as large as Jacob's whole house. Before Jacob could voice his concerns again, a blond man similar to Beau in age and build came around from the back of the house, wearing jeans and an Auburn sweatshirt and carrying a pair of tongs from the grill. Jacob relaxed a little. At least his attire wouldn't be out of place.

Beau bounded from the car, hugging Sean swiftly, the kind of masculine one-armed embrace that separated friends from lovers. Jacob got out of the car more slowly, giving the men a chance to finish their greetings.

"Jacob, come meet Sean."

Jacob crossed to Beau's side, offering his hand to Beau's friend. He was so focused on the other man that Beau's arm going around his waist caught him off guard. He swore he jumped a foot at the unusual gesture, but neither man seemed to notice his reaction, although Jacob saw Sean's gaze linger on Beau's hand against Jacob's side before he looked up and shook Jacob's hand. "Sean McAlvoy. Nice to meet you. Any friend of Beau's, and all that."

"Jacob Peters," Jacob replied, reassured by the casual greeting and firm handshake. "It's nice to meet you as well. Thank you for letting us borrow your plane this weekend."

"Beau's the closest thing I have to a brother," Sean said honestly. "There's not a lot I wouldn't do to help him out if it was in my power to do it. Letting him use the plane was easy."

"That doesn't make us appreciate it less," Beau said. "So what's for dinner?"

"I just tossed some steaks on while I was waiting for you to get up to the house," Sean said. "There's baked potatoes that just need to be heated back up and some leftover green bean casserole. Or there might be stuff for a salad if you don't want the beans."

"I love green bean casserole," Jacob said. "What can we do to help?"

"Not a thing," Sean said. "It's all ready except the steaks. I've got cold beer in the fridge. You can tell me all about Key West—not the X-rated stuff, I don't need those details—while the steaks cook. How do you like your meat?"

Jacob glanced at Beau, seriously tempted to make an off-color comment, but he held back, not sure it would be appropriate. Beau had no such hesitation.

"About eight and a half inches and—" He broke off when Sean smacked him on the shoulder with the tongs, eliciting a sharp yelp.

"I told you I didn't want details. There are things about Jacob I just don't need to know."

"I was talking about myself," Beau muttered.

"Still things I don't need to know," Sean retorted.

Jacob couldn't hold back his laughter, the exchange enough to break any lingering tension. "On the red side of medium rare," he said, answering Sean's original question.

"Someone who appreciates a good piece of meat," Sean said, winking at Jacob as he said it. "I knew there had to be someone out there who could appreciate Beau."

Jacob snorted, his smile widening. "He has his uses."

"Hey, I'm standing right here," Beau said, although he'd let Sean and Jacob take potshots at him all night if it kept the smile on Jacob's face. Jacob might not realize it, but to Beau, the teasing was a sign that Sean had accepted Jacob.

"And you look so pretty doing it," Sean said. "Be useful and get Jacob a beer. He and I need to get better acquainted."

Beau huffed in mock indignation and walked over to the portable refrigerator Sean had installed on his deck, pulling out beers for Jacob and himself. "Do you need a refill, Sean?"

"No, I'm good."

Beau carried the drinks back to where Jacob now sat in one of the gliders as Sean checked on the steaks. "These need a few more minutes," Sean said. "I'm going to heat up the potatoes and casserole. No funny business while I'm gone."

Jacob laughed as Sean went inside. "I like him."

"He likes you too," Beau said. "Maybe this isn't a fair comparison, but he never relaxed with Christine the way he has with you. He always wore his formal façade with her, the one he uses when company comes over. I probably should have known then that it wouldn't work out, but I figured it was because his mother had very strict ideas about how to treat a woman, and it didn't include the kind of banter he likes when we're alone."

Jacob took a sip of his beer. "I wouldn't have said the things I did if his wife were here, so I'm sure that was part of it."

"I'm sure it was," Beau agreed, "but he doesn't always relax that way when it's just men either. It's a side of him only close friends see. He chose to let you see it, and that says a lot about his willingness to accept you and us as a couple." Beau leaned over and kissed Jacob lightly. "Thank you for coming with me."

"Hey, I said no funny business," Sean shouted from the kitchen door. "I go inside to make sure you have food to eat and this is the thanks I get?"

Beau looked over his shoulder at Sean, kissed Jacob again, more firmly, and then got up to help Sean carry things outside.

"I'll kiss my boyfriend when I feel like it," Beau insisted.

The words struck Jacob hard. It was the first time Beau had referred to him as his boyfriend, which felt like a huge step forward, but it was also a stark contrast to the separation they were about to go back to. If Beau had really meant those words, if he was ready to forget about hiding and come out, Jacob would have been totally thrilled to hear it, but Jacob knew better than to expect that.

"Really?" Sean challenged. "If we were sitting on your front porch instead of my deck, you'd be as bold?"

Sean's defense surprised Jacob nearly as much as Beau's comment did. He sank into the glider, not wanting to draw attention to himself. Maybe Sean could achieve what all of Jacob's arguments had not.

"No," Beau admitted softly. "You know what Prestonsburg is like, Sean. Can you really see that going over there?"

"That doesn't make it any better," Sean said. "I've known you a long time, Beau. I look at you, I see you look at Jacob, and I can tell you're happy right now, probably the happiest I've seen you in years. That's wonderful. But how long are you going to be able to live the way you say you have to without resentment destroying that? How long before one of you screws up the lies you have to tell to protect your secret? And then, instead of being able to control the situation, you're stuck trying to mop up afterward? Take a look at national politics and learn from their mistakes."

"It's still a clusterfuck, even when they come out rather than being found out," Beau said.

"That doesn't answer the rest of my question," Sean insisted. "How long are you going to be able to hide before you start resenting each other?"

Jacob bit his tongue to stop from reminding Beau that they'd been down that road once before and that it had ended in a breakup and in Jacob sleeping with Melissa. He didn't want to bring that up in front of

Sean, though, since he didn't know how much Beau had told the other man of their history. It wasn't a pretty story, and while Jacob had told Billy, that didn't mean Beau had been comfortable telling his friend.

"It won't be like that this time," Beau said.

"This time?" Sean asked, jumping on Beau's slip of the tongue.

"We, um...."

"We had a fight over a year ago," Jacob said, rising from his chair and coming to Beau's side. "We didn't talk for almost a year because of it, but I think we both learned something from that time."

"Learned what?" Sean asked. "It seems to me you're making the same mistakes all over again."

"We learned we wanted to be together even if it meant making some sacrifices," Jacob explained. "Maybe we aren't making the right sacrifices. Maybe you're right and we should be going about it differently, but at least this time we're going about it consciously."

"In what sense?"

"We know where things went wrong last time," Beau said, giving Jacob a grateful smile for his support. He had told Sean some of what had happened between them, but having Jacob at his side, defending their current decisions, made Beau feel better about their future. "We're watching for that resentment, trying to head it off, actually talking instead of assuming we know what the other person is feeling. We're trying to act like a couple, within the limits of acceptability, instead of just having an affair like we did before."

"Fuck acceptability," Sean said. "You shouldn't ever have to act any different than you do right here on my deck. It shouldn't matter where you are or who's around. If you want to kiss your boyfriend, you should."

"It shouldn't matter," Beau agreed, "but unfortunately, it still does."

Sean looked like he wanted to argue more, but the steaks were ready, so he let it go. They talked of inconsequential things over dinner, and Sean made them promise to come back for a visit soon as they were leaving.

"You think Sean's right, don't you?" Beau asked Jacob as they drove back toward Prestonsburg.

"Yes and no," Jacob replied. "If I come out, I run the risk of losing my job, so I'd want to plan things out, find another job first in a school that wouldn't fire me the moment I admitted to my sexuality. Whether that's in Elliot, in Prestonsburg, or in Auburn or farther afield. I'd want you to have a backup plan in place in case you lost the next election or in case people tried to remove you from your position now, if that's even possible. I'd want to know we'd done everything we could to minimize the disruption for Finn and for your mother, so no, I don't think we should go home tonight and kiss on the front porch of either of our houses. On the other hand, even now, with all the effort we're making to do this right, I catch myself wanting more and getting angry that we can't have it. I hate leaving to drive back to Elliot on the nights we're together. I hate being alone in my bed on the nights we can't be together. Being with you in Key West, holding hands as we walked along the beach, being a couple at the restaurant instead of having to pretend to just be friends, going dancing together.... I want those things all the time. I want that life. I'm willing to wait to have it, but Sean's right. It would be easy to let resentment drive us apart again. "

He reached for Beau's hand. "I also worry what will happen between us if we're found out and all the worst-case scenarios come to pass. If I mess up our stories or you do, are we going to end up blaming each other for it? I don't want to even think about that."

"If it happens, we'll deal with it," Beau promised. "We're in this together. Isn't that what we said?"

It was what Jacob wanted, but a part of him had held back still, not fully able to commit to something when he didn't feel like Beau was equally committed. This weekend had gone a long way toward easing those fears, as had Beau's behavior at Sean's house. He wouldn't have taken Jacob to meet his friend, wouldn't have been so open about their relationship, if he wasn't committed to it. "Yes," he said, squeezing Beau's fingers. "That's what we said."

Now he just had to figure out how to keep that promise.

BEAU looked up when his cell phone rang. He usually kept it off at the courthouse, but he had finished his cases for the day and was just dealing with some paperwork before going home, so he had switched it back on in case Jacob called. They had their weekly "committee meeting" tonight, but Finn had been feeling poorly yesterday, and Jacob hadn't been sure he would be able to come. "Hello?"

"Hi, Beau. I hate to do this, but Finn is running a fever now. I have to take him to the doctor," Jacob said. "I don't know how long that will take, but even if we get done in time, I don't know if it's a good idea for me to take him out. It's getting cold at night, and if he's already sick, it's even more important to keep him warm."

"I'm sorry he's sick," Beau said. "Why don't I come to your place tonight? I can pick up a frozen lasagna or something, we can work while it cooks, and then I can help you with Finn."

"Are you sure?" Jacob asked. "My neighbors aren't used to seeing you around. I don't want to cause problems."

"I'm a friend dropping by to help you out with dinner because your son's sick," Beau reminded him. "The fact that I'm hoping he'll fall asleep so we can have a little time together isn't something they need to know."

"If you're sure," Jacob said. "I swear, the weeks get longer and longer."

"I know," Beau agreed. "If the doc says he's really too sick for company, I won't come, but if it's just an ear infection or something like that, there's no reason I can't come see you. I've missed you."

A knock on his door interrupted them. "Hold on a minute. Someone's at the door." Holding the phone away from his ear, he called for his secretary to enter.

"I'm sorry to disturb you, sir, but Mr. Nicholson is here to see you."

"Give me one minute to finish this call," Beau said, gesturing to his cell phone.

His secretary nodded and closed the door.

"I've got to go," he told Jacob. "I'll call you when I leave the courthouse to see what the doctor said and to let you know what time to expect me."

"See you tonight," Jacob said. "I love you."

Beau got ready to reply, but the door opened and Parker Nicholson barged in. "See you tonight," Beau said simply, disconnecting the phone.

"Got a hot date?" Parker asked.

Beau stifled a sigh. "No, I was supposed to meet with Jacob Peters to work on our Autism Society planning tonight, but his son is sick. I offered to take dinner over to him. He can't be expected to cook with a sick baby."

"Where's his wife?"

"He's divorced," Beau said. "He got full custody."

"That's not something you see often around here," Parker commented.

Beau shrugged. "He's a good father, and from what I heard, his ex didn't have much idea what to do with a baby. It's better for everyone this way. You didn't come to talk about my plans for the evening. What can I do for you?"

"I wanted to talk to you about this case I'm working on," Parker said. "It's on the docket for next week, and I was hoping—"

"On my docket?" Beau interrupted.

"Well, yes," Parker said.

Beau shook his head. "Then save it for the courtroom, Parker. We may be friends," he said, although that was a generous description of their relationship, "but that doesn't change anything where my cases are concerned."

"I just had a technical question," Parker said.

Beau shook his head again. "Ask a different judge or else get the case transferred to a different judge and then ask me, but as long as it's my case, we can't talk about it outside of court. You know that."

Parker huffed. "I tell you, what's the point in knowing people if they can't do you a favor now and then?"

"I'll be happy to do you a personal favor," Beau said, "but I don't do favors in the courtroom."

"I know," Parker said, "but there's no harm in asking occasionally, is there?"

Beau didn't agree, but he kept his opinion to himself. "If there's nothing else, I really need to get this done so I can get to the store. I have to drive all the way to Elliot and back tonight. *Those* are the kind of favors I do for my friends."

"Yeah, yeah," Parker said, leaving the office. Beau rolled his eyes and got back to work.

TWO hours later, Beau pulled into Jacob's driveway, a frozen lasagna and a loaf of garlic bread on the seat next to him. The lasagna would take an hour to cook, giving them a chance to discuss the curriculum for the summer program. They had gotten approval at the last monthly meeting for the weekly themes they'd proposed and so had moved on to the day-to-day activities around each theme, all structured with the needs of autistic kids in mind. And if they didn't get to that tonight, they could wait until next week. With all the holidays, they wouldn't have another monthly meeting until January.

Beau knocked on Jacob's door and waited for his lover to answer. The sound of a car driving down the street made him flinch, but he forced himself not to act like he had anything to be ashamed of. Jacob's neighbors might not know him, but that didn't mean they'd immediately assume anything illicit. Jacob answered the door before Beau's nerves got the better of him.

"How do you do it?" Beau asked when they were inside. "How do you walk up to my house every week, knowing the neighbors could be watching and thinking all manner of things?"

"I remind myself that we have a perfectly valid excuse to give them if anyone says anything," Jacob said, "and then I remind myself it's none of their business anyway. Mostly, though, I just grit my teeth and do it because you're waiting for me inside, and that makes it worth it."

Beau kissed Jacob lightly, offering him the bag of food. "Dinner," he said, "although it'll have to cook first."

"Let's get it in the oven," Jacob replied, "and then we can talk."

"How's Finn?" Beau asked, following Jacob into the kitchen and watching as his lover stuck the pan in the oven to bake.

"He's asleep right now," Jacob replied. "Fortunately it's just an ear infection, and only in one ear. He's on antibiotics and ibuprofen for the pain. The doctor said he'd probably still be fussy for forty-eight hours as the painkillers wore off, but that he wasn't contagious and could still go to daycare tomorrow, so I won't have to miss work."

"That's good," Beau said. "Do we want to get some work done while he's asleep?"

"Sure," Jacob said, pulling out the binder they used to keep their notes organized.

They spent fifteen minutes discussing how to organize the kids into groups to best accommodate their individual needs before Finn's cries interrupted them. "I'll get him," Beau said when Jacob started to get up. "You'll have to deal with him during the night. Let me take care of him for you now."

"Thanks," Jacob said. He hadn't been looking forward to Finn's fussing. Not that he blamed the baby. Ear infections hurt, and Finn was too young to understand his daddy's reassurances that the pain would go away and that he'd get better soon. "His bedroom is the last door on the right."

Beau went down the long hallway, resisting the urge to peek in the other doors to see what the different rooms looked like. He found Finn's nursery and walked in, smiling as he bent down to pick up the fussy baby. "How are you, little man?" he asked, leaning Finn against his shoulder as he fumbled with the blanket. "I'm not as good at this as your daddy, but he needs a bit of a break so I'm going to hold you for a bit if that's okay with you."

Finn's cries calmed now that he was no longer alone in his crib. Beau smiled and kissed the soft dusting of hair on the crown of his head. "You were just lonely, weren't you?" he asked. "Let's go back to the kitchen and you can sit on my lap while your daddy and I work. How does that sound?"

Finn didn't answer, of course, but he seemed perfectly happy in Beau's arms, so Beau took that for assent, returning to the kitchen and Jacob.

"He just wanted some company," Beau said, taking his seat again and juggling Finn so the baby faced Jacob. "He can sit right here with us while we talk. You never know. He might have a good idea or two."

Jacob smiled, charmed by the image of Beau and Finn. "I love you."

"I love you too," Beau said. "I'm sorry I didn't say it earlier, but Parker Nicholson walked in before I could, and he asked enough questions just hearing me say I'd see you tonight."

"I figured something like that had happened," Jacob said. Seeing Beau holding Finn made Jacob think about Beau's son. "Are you going to get to see your son at Christmas this year?"

"The week between Christmas and New Year's," Beau said. "I'll fly to New York on the twenty-sixth and come home on January first. Do you have plans for your vacation?"

"I'll go to Vicksburg like I always do," Jacob replied. "Maybe not for the whole two weeks, but Mama won't forgive me if she misses Finn's first Christmas. I thought about suggesting they come here, but I don't have much in the way of decorations and stuff. He'll have a much better celebration at their house."

"Speaking of celebrations, we should find a time to have one for ourselves," Beau said. "I have something for you and Finn, but it's at my house, and I didn't go home tonight before coming here."

"I noticed," Jacob said with a pointed look at the dress shirt Beau still wore, his tie loosened around his neck and the top button undone. "I'm enjoying the view."

Beau grinned. "I didn't know you had a suit fetish."

"Only if you're the one wearing the suit," Jacob replied. "Or not wearing it, in this case. I'm hoping Finn will go to sleep early tonight. I'm getting ideas just looking at you."

"I always get ideas looking at you." Beau winked at Jacob over Finn's head. "First, though, we should eat and get this one settled again."

Jacob glanced at the clock. "It's time for him to eat. Do you want me to feed him so he doesn't spit up all over your suit?"

"What's he eating these days?" Beau asked as Jacob opened the pantry and pulled out a couple of jars of baby food.

"Green beans and peaches tonight," Jacob said, "but his favorite is sweet potatoes."

"Maybe I will let you feed him," Beau said, looking down at his white shirt. "Somehow I think I'd have a hard time explaining green and orange splotches on my shirt."

"You could take it off," Jacob teased. "I wouldn't complain."

"That doesn't protect my pants," Beau replied with a grin.

"You could take those off too," Jacob answered. "We'd be taking them off after dinner anyway."

"You think I'm that easy?" Beau joked.

Jacob set the baby food on the table, lifted Finn out of Beau's lap, and straddled his lover's knees, grinding their bodies together. "I know you're that easy."

Beau's hands went automatically to Jacob's ass, steadying him. "You're right."

Jacob leaned forward around Finn's bulk in his arms and kissed Beau hungrily. "After Finn goes to bed."

The promise in Jacob's voice sent a shiver down Beau's spine. "I'll hold you to that."

The buzzer on the oven sounded. "I'll get that," Beau said. "You feed Finn."

Jacob nodded and put Finn in his high chair, enjoying the quiet domesticity of Beau working on dinner while Jacob took care of Finn. It wasn't the heady freedom of being completely open as they had done in Key West, but it was a different kind of contentment, the quiet moments of being a family. Beau would have to leave eventually, but for a few precious hours, Jacob could imagine what it might be like at some future point when they didn't have to hide anymore, when Beau wouldn't have to walk out the door at an "acceptable" time.

"It needs about twenty more minutes to cook," Beau said, joining Jacob beside the high chair. "Is there anything I can do to help?"

"You can get a washcloth for me," Jacob said. "He's spitting it out more than usual, probably because he doesn't feel good."

"Sure," Beau said, going over to the sink and wetting a washcloth. He handed it back to Jacob, rubbing his lover's back gently. "I could get used to this."

"To what?" Jacob asked, although he hoped he knew.

"To sharing moments like this with you. To sharing everything with you."

"Say the word and I'll start looking for another job," Jacob offered immediately. "It would be for next year, obviously, but that would take the pressure off me to stay in the closet."

"Let me tell Harrison first," Beau requested. "I know he's not around like Finn is, but he's still a part of my life, and he deserves to know about us before we make any decisions. I'll tell him when I'm in New York at Christmastime, and we can start thinking about plans when I get back. In the meantime, when are we going to celebrate Christmas?"

Jacob checked his calendar. "I'm free this weekend, if you think we can justify a second meeting this week, or if not, we could celebrate next week during our usual time."

"You didn't come to my house tonight," Beau pointed out. "If you come on Saturday, they'll just figure we had to change our usual meeting time. What time would suit?"

"Finn usually takes a nap in the afternoon around one," Jacob said, "so either we have to be there before that or wait until he wakes up."

"Why don't you come for lunch?" Beau suggested. "That way I can give Finn his present before he takes his nap and then we'll have the rest of the afternoon to ourselves while he sleeps."

"How did you explain buying a baby present?" Jacob asked curiously.

"I always give a big donation to Toys for Tots," Beau explained. "I simply bought a couple of extra things this year and kept them aside when I made the delivery."

"You're good," Jacob said. "I wouldn't have thought of that."

"I might not have thought of it either if I weren't already doing it," Beau admitted, "but I've been doing it for years, so it was logical to buy everything at once, even if I hadn't been trying to be discreet."

Jacob finished feeding Finn and cleaned him up. "That makes sense. So we'll come around eleven thirty on Saturday?"

"That would be perfect."

THE weather on Saturday was absolutely miserable, the heavy clouds spitting a dangerous combination of rain and ice. Jacob considered canceling, but he wanted to see Beau. Deciding to err on the side of caution, he packed enough food and diapers for Finn to hold them through a couple of days, just in case the weather worsened. He doubted it would come to that. It was only December, and the bad storms, if they got them, didn't usually hit until January, but better safe than sorry. He bundled Finn up against the cold, making sure to pack the antibiotics as well. The pain had gone, but the doctor had been very clear that it would take the full ten days for the infection to go away entirely, going on to elaborate on the dangers associated with repeated infections and drug-resistant strains. It had been enough to make Jacob blanch.

The drive to Beau's house was harrowing. Jacob almost turned around several times, except that the roads behind him were as bad as the roads ahead of him, and Prestonsburg was the county seat. If the power went out, the utility company would restore power there before working their way to the outlying towns. Furthermore, Beau had a fireplace and a stack of wood, and Jacob's house did not. Not that Jacob expected it to come to that, but the storm was already worse than the weatherman had predicted.

By the time he reached Beau's house, his hands were shaking from the adrenaline rush and tension of driving on the icy roads with Finn in the backseat. He had to sit for several seconds after he pulled into Beau's driveway before he could make his hands unclench from the steering wheel.

Beau came rushing out to the car while he sat there. "Are you all right? Your phone was off, and I couldn't reach you. I was going to tell you not to come."

"I turned it off so it wouldn't ring and distract me while I was driving," Jacob said, the sight of Beau's concerned face enough to finally relax his tense muscles. "I probably should have stayed home, except that I wanted to see you."

Beau looked at him like he'd lost his mind, which, Jacob admitted, he probably had for driving in the now steady sleet.

"I'm here now," he continued, "and Finn and I are both fine. Let's go inside. You can yell at me there, where it's warm."

Beau's expression suggested that was exactly what he intended to do, but he got Finn out of the backseat without further comment. Jacob grabbed the diaper bag with all of Finn's necessities and followed Beau inside.

"You can put Finn's bag in the spare bedroom," Beau said. "I hope you brought plenty, because if not, you'll be walking to the grocery. There's no way you're driving home in this mess."

"I brought plenty," Jacob said. "I didn't expect to have to stay, but I figured better safe than sorry when I saw the weather."

"Idiot," Beau muttered. "Why didn't you just stay home? It would have killed me if anything happened to you and Finn."

"Nothing happened," Jacob said. "And I didn't stay home because I didn't want to miss Christmas with you."

"We could have rescheduled."

"We could have," Jacob said, "but if we had to be iced in somewhere with maybe no power, it was better to do that here than at home where I don't have a fireplace. It's done now, so there's no use fussing at me over it."

"I'm sorry, baby," Beau said, hearing the annoyance in Jacob's voice, "but the idea of something happening to you scared the shit out of me. I'll try to keep it under control."

"I was scared too," Jacob admitted, "but what's done is done. I'll stay here until it's safe to drive home, and the neighbors can just deal with it."

Beau was not quite as sanguine about the neighbors' reactions, but he was not about to send Jacob back out in this weather. They'd just have to deal with it if anyone said anything.

"I started lunch," Beau said instead. "Tomato soup. And I thought I'd make grilled cheese to go with it. A nice, hearty winter lunch. Maybe not very Christmasy, but good for warming cold bones."

"It is cold," Jacob agreed. "I'll help you with the sandwiches. Finn can play on his blanket while we do. He's starting to roll over now, which is a little scary, but very exciting."

They fixed lunch and ate quickly. "Shall we give Finn his presents?" Beau asked when they were done. "And then he can take his nap and I can give you your present."

"Just being here is already a gift," Jacob said.

Beau smiled. "Maybe so, but I bought something for you anyway."

They moved into the living room. Beau tossed another log on the fire in the fireplace, the crackling flames adding to the feeling of the holidays. Jacob noticed Beau had put up his Christmas tree in the corner but not decorated it yet. "Maybe while Finn's asleep, we can decorate your tree," Jacob suggested.

"That was my plan," Beau said. "I know we can't spend Christmas day together, but I wanted us to have as much of a real holiday as we could."

Jacob did not repeat his offer from earlier in the week to start looking for another job. Beau had asked him to wait until after Christmas, and Jacob would honor that request. He only hoped Beau's ex-wife was raising an open-minded child, because Jacob didn't want to end up in a tug-of-war with Beau's son. As much as he loved Beau, if it ever came to a choice between Beau and Finn, he would have a hard time choosing Beau.

"Stay here," Beau said, disappearing into the closet under the stairs.

Jacob waited patiently while Beau dug through the closet. A few moments later, he returned with two brightly wrapped packages. "Merry Christmas, Finn," he said, placing the boxes on the blanket next to the baby.

Jacob chuckled and knelt beside his son. "We might have to help him open them," he said.

Beau picked Finn up and settled him on his lap. "He can do it himself," Beau said. "We just have to show him how." He guided Finn's fingers to the loose seam in the wrapping paper. "Now pull," he said.

Finn gurgled happily, ripping the paper by an inch.

"He'll be here all afternoon at that rate," Jacob said.

"We'll help him a little," Beau compromised, guiding Finn's hand back to the torn paper and helping him tear the package open. Inside was a big blue pig with wheels instead of feet. "Look at that," Beau said. "You pull it back and it goes rolling across the room."

"Just what I need," Jacob said with a laugh.

"Harrison loved his pig," Beau explained. "He learned to crawl so he could chase it across the room. I know Finn isn't quite to that point yet, but it won't be long. And in the meantime, it rattles too."

Jacob nodded.

"Are you ready to open your other one?" Beau asked Finn. Finn batted his hands up and down, bringing a smile to both men's faces. "You want to help him with this one?"

Jacob shook his head. "I'll have plenty of chances at Mama's house. You go ahead since you gave it to him."

Finn seemed to have figured out the unwrapping, because as soon as Beau put the box within his reach, he clawed at the paper. Beau had to help him find the seam again, but Finn did a much better job of tearing by himself. When they got all the paper pulled off, Beau opened the box and pulled out an engine and six train cars. "These were Harrison's," he admitted. "The engine sings and counts depending on which cars you attach to it. I couldn't ever bring myself to get rid of it after he moved to New York."

"Are you sure you want to give it to Finn?" Jacob asked.

"I'm sure," Beau said. "It was meant to be played with, and I'm sure Finn will love it as much as Harrison did. If he doesn't, that's okay too. I'll have given it to another special little boy."

"If it sings, he'll love it," Jacob said. "He loves anything with lights or music. I swear, he could watch his aquarium for hours."

They put the train in front of Finn, and Beau showed him how to push down on the engineer so it played music. Finn clapped delightedly and pushed down on the figure repeatedly. "We'll let him play for a bit before I put him to bed," Jacob said. "Do you want your present now or later?"

"Is it kid safe?" Beau teased.

"Yes," Jacob replied. "I figured I'd save the adult toys for our anniversary."

Beau grinned. "Then I can open it now. Let me get yours too. Then we can do the tree while Finn sleeps."

Jacob fished the present he'd bought out of Finn's diaper bag and waited for Beau to return. He was a little nervous about Beau's reaction. This was the first time they'd exchanged presents for any occasion, and he wanted it to be perfect.

"Merry Christmas," he said, offering the package to Beau when his lover came back into the living room.

"Merry Christmas," Beau echoed, taking the gift from Jacob and handing him one in return. "Go ahead and open it."

Jacob took his time with the wrapping paper, a habit left over from his grandmother's insistence that it could be reused rather than wasted, setting it aside carefully before opening the white gift box. A silver picture frame rested amid the wealth of tissue paper. "If you turn it on," Beau said, "it's loaded with our pictures from Key West. It's a digital frame, so you can put different pictures on it and have it do a slideshow or set it to show just one, whichever you prefer."

"Thank you," Jacob said. "I can't wait to look through the pictures. Now open yours."

Beau unwrapped the small box with far less care than Jacob had shown, opening the box to find a pair of gold cuff links. "I know you already have other sets," Jacob said quickly, "but I thought you could wear them without anyone noticing they were different, and that way you could discreetly wear something I gave you."

"I'll wear them every day," Beau promised. "That way I'll always have a piece of you with me, even when we're apart."

"Not all your shirts require cuff links," Jacob replied automatically, remembering more than one occasion when he had unbuttoned the cuffs on Beau's shirts.

"No, but I have enough that do to go at least two weeks without repeating, and after that, no one remembers anyway," Beau said, "so I'll wear those shirts unless it's a day we're going to be together. Thank you."

"Do you really like them?" Jacob asked. "I wasn't sure about the style, and I had to order them online so no one would wonder why I was buying them."

"They're wonderful," Beau said, kissing away Jacob's insecurities. "Now, is it nap time for Finn yet? We have a tree in need of decoration."

Jacob looked over to where Finn lay on the blanket, beginning to yawn slightly. "Yes, I think so. I'll get him settled and be back."

He took Finn into the guest room, where a port-a-crib had appeared several weeks earlier. He had tried thanking Beau, but his lover had brushed it off, saying he'd found it in the attic mixed in with a bunch of other stuff he'd thought he'd gotten rid of. Jacob wasn't entirely sure how true that was, but he had decided not to argue. Finn dozed off in a matter of minutes, leaving Jacob free to return to the living room and Beau.

"Is he asleep?"

"Out like a light," Jacob said.

"Good," Beau replied, pulling Jacob in for a kiss. "I wanted to thank you properly for my present."

Jacob relaxed into the kiss, the crackling fire, the smell of pine, and the scrape of Beau's stubble combining into the perfect mix. When they finally parted, Jacob smiled at Beau. "Let's decorate the tree."

[8]

BEAU exited the plane, tugging his coat around him more tightly. He really should have pulled out his ski jacket to visit Harrison at Christmas, but it was so casual, and it seemed like a waste of money to buy a more formal topcoat for no more than a week each year, and sometimes not even a full week. He'd just put on extra layers and think of Jacob.

Picking up his bag, he caught a taxi to the hotel and checked in. He wished he had a better place to spend time with his son than a hotel room, but it would have to do. He hated the idea that Harrison was used to it, but while Beau took him out places, the hotel was it for sitting and talking together. They needed to talk too. If Beau wanted to have a life with Jacob, however hidden, Harrison needed to know about it.

The thought was just this side of terrifying. If Harrison rejected him, Beau didn't know what he would do. He couldn't keep it a secret, though, not from his son. Not when he'd already told Sean. Not when he had started looking into options for moving his mother to Atlanta, where the anonymity of the big city would provide a measure of protection for them. He hadn't made any decisions yet, but Harrison needed to know these potential changes were in the works.

Taking a deep breath, he dialed his son's phone and waited.

"Hi, Dad! Are you in Buffalo already?"

"I am," Beau replied, "and I can't wait to see you. What did your mom say about when we could get together?"

"She said I could go with you whenever you came to pick me up," Harrison replied, his voice high and fast with excitement. "She said I could stay overnight at the hotel with you if that was all right with you. Is it all right, Dad? Please?"

"Of course it's all right," Beau exclaimed. "I never get enough time with you, so this will give us a few extra hours. I'll be there to pick you up as soon as I can."

Wishing he'd rented a car, Beau returned to the lobby of the hotel and waited while the bellhop hailed a cab for him. He gave the driver Christine's address and explained about picking up his son. The cabbie smiled at him sympathetically as he whisked Beau across town. The moment the cab pulled up, Harrison came flying out of the house into Beau's arms. "My suitcase is just inside," he said, his voice muffled against Beau's shoulder.

"Get in the cab," Beau said. "I'll get your suitcase. Did you tell your mother you were leaving?"

"She was waiting inside with me," Harrison replied, pulling away so he could get in the cab. "She won't come out, but she knows you're here."

Beau nodded and walked up the sidewalk to get Harrison's suitcase. "Christine," he acknowledged when he saw her on the other side of the door. "When do you want me to bring Harrison home?"

"Before your flight leaves," Christine replied. "John has convinced me to let you have the whole week with him. If that goes well, maybe he could come see you in Prestonsburg next summer."

"I'd like that," Beau said, hoping Harrison would still want to come after everything Beau had to tell him. "Thank you, and I'll see you on Thursday morning. My flight is at two, so I'll bring Harrison home around eleven."

Christine nodded, gesturing to the suitcase next to the door. "He should have everything he needs."

"If he doesn't, I'll call or replace it," Beau said. "Have a good week."

Beau returned to the cab, directing the driver to take them back to the hotel. "So what do you want to do this week?" he asked his son.

"Eat lots of junk food and swim in the hotel pool," Harrison said immediately.

"We'll see about the junk food," Beau cautioned, "but we can definitely go swimming. Did you have a good Christmas? Was Santa good to you?"

Beau let Harrison's excited chatter fill the drive back to the hotel. Half of what the boy said went right over his head as he talked about Wii and PS3s and all kinds of other things Beau knew nothing about, but that didn't matter. He was simply happy to be with his son and to have six days together without interruption. Now he had to find the right time to tell Harrison about Jacob.

Two hours later, having finished dinner in the hotel restaurant—a huge hamburger for Harrison and filet mignon for Beau—they changed into their swim trunks and headed for the pool. "How's school?" Beau asked.

"It's okay," Harrison said with a typical twelve-year-old's shrug. "My teacher is pretty cool."

"Really?" Beau asked. "What's her name?"

"His name, Dad," Harrison said, rolling his eyes. "Why does everyone assume teachers are female?"

It was a good question, particularly since Jacob was a teacher too. "I'm sorry," Beau apologized. "What's his name?"

"Mr. Enoch," Harrison said. "He's great. We had a Christmas dance, and he was there with his partner."

"His partner?" Beau asked, surprise growing.

"Come on, Dad," Harrison groaned. "How out of it are you? Mr. Enoch and Mr. Lee are engaged, but they haven't gotten an appointment yet to get married. Mom said I shouldn't tell you. She said you wouldn't be able to handle it. You aren't going to get all weird because my teacher's gay, are you? I'm learning so much from him this year. I don't want you to freak out over this."

"I'm not going to freak out," Beau promised, his voice soft as the full import of Harrison's words sank in. "It doesn't bother you that he's gay?"

"Why would it?" Harrison asked. "If they love each other, that's their business. It doesn't change what kind of teacher he is."

"That's a very adult opinion," Beau said, "and I'm glad you feel that way. Let's swim. When we're done, I have something I want to tell you."

They played in the pool for nearly an hour before Harrison was ready to get out. Beau insisted his son rinse off and put on clean clothes before they talked.

"So what did you want to talk about?" Harrison asked when they were both clean and dry and snuggled under the blankets.

"I've met someone special," Beau began. "I thought it was only fair to tell you."

"So you're getting married again?" Harrison asked, his face pensive.

"Well, not right away," Beau replied. "Your grandmother is too ill for me to move her, and not everywhere is as liberal as New York."

Harrison had already started nodding his head, having heard the bit about his grandmother more than once, when the second half of Beau's statement sank in. "Wait, what?"

"His name is Jacob," Beau said, "and I love him very much."

"Oh."

"Oh?" Beau repeated. "Is that all you have to say?"

"I'm sure I'll think of something else," Harrison said. "In a minute, after I have a chance to think of it."

Beau couldn't help it. He laughed at the perplexed look on Harrison's face.

"So what about me?" Harrison said after a moment.

"What about you?" Beau asked. "You're my son, just like you've always been. Loving Jacob doesn't change that."

"But what if he doesn't want me around?" Harrison asked. "I won't be able to come see you next summer if—"

"Stop," Beau ordered. "First of all, you can always come see me, no matter what. More importantly, though, Jacob wants to meet you. He knows I have a son, and he's fine with that. He has a baby too. Finn is about six months old."

"How does he have a baby if he's gay?" Harrison asked.

"He was married just like I was," Beau said, glossing over the circumstances of Jacob and Melissa's relationship, "but he got divorced too."

"So do you live together?"

"No," Beau said. "Like I said, Prestonsburg isn't as liberal as New York. Jacob lives in Elliot, about half an hour away. He teaches elementary school, a lot like your Mr. Enoch, I bet. The kids love him, and he's really good at his job. I don't want to do anything that would make him lose his job, so we haven't told anyone about us."

"Can they do that?" Harrison asked.

"Unfortunately they can," Beau said. "He works in a private school, and they have very strict rules about what people can and can't do if they want to work there. Jacob signed the contract, so now he has to abide by those rules."

"So what are you going to do?" Harrison asked. "Don't you want to marry him?"

"I do," Beau said, "but right now that isn't a choice for us."

"You could move up here," Harrison suggested. "I could see you more often, and you could get married. Mr. Enoch is always talking about how hard it is to find good teachers, and you could be a lawyer here, even if you weren't a judge."

"We might do that someday," Beau said, "but right now we have to stay in Prestonsburg with your grandmother."

"It's not fair," Harrison said.

"What isn't?"

"You shouldn't have to put one part of your life on hold because of another part. Grandmother wouldn't want you to do that."

"No, I know she wouldn't," Beau said, "but right now I don't see any other choice. Maybe someday Alabama will be ready to accept gay couples, but that's still a while off. In the meantime, we'll be together quietly like we're already doing."

"Will you bring Jacob with you the next time you come to visit?" Harrison asked.

"If he's free," Beau promised. "He had to go to Vicksburg to visit his parents this week, but maybe the next time I come, he can come with me."

"So do you have a picture of him or something?" Harrison asked. "Is he cute?"

Beau laughed, relieved, and pulled out his phone to show Harrison the pictures he'd taken on the trip to Key West.

JACOB hadn't expected Christmas to be any better than Thanksgiving where his parents were concerned, so he was surprised when his mother didn't bring up Melissa and their divorce as soon as he walked in the door. Instead, she cooed over Finn and treated Jacob as if the snide comments at Thanksgiving had never been spoken.

After Christmas dinner, with Jacob's father snoring in his chair, Jacob's mother joined him on the couch. "Are you seeing anyone?" she asked.

"I am, actually," Jacob replied, snuggling Finn a little closer as if having his son in his arms could protect him from his mother's reaction. "Beau and I met a couple of years ago and ran back into each other recently."

His mother pursed her lips slightly, as if she'd eaten something sour, but Jacob had come out in college, even if his life in Elliot had forced him back into the closet somewhat. His mother had to have known there was a fifty-fifty chance of anyone he was seeing being male. "Are you sure that isn't too fast?"

"It's not," Jacob assured her. "We dated a bit before I met Melissa. I'd decided he wasn't interested in anything serious, but it turns out I was wrong."

"If you were seeing him, how did you end up with Melissa?" his mother asked.

Jacob sighed. He really didn't want to get into this, but his mother wouldn't be denied. "Like I said, I'd decided he wasn't ready to be serious about us, so I broke things off. I met Melissa the next night, and you know the rest."

"I suspect there's far more you aren't telling me," Mrs. Peters said, "but I won't press you for details. Are things really different this time?"

"Yes, Mama," Jacob said, thinking of Beau with Finn, of their trip to Key West, of Beau coming out to his friend. "I'm not saying everything's perfect, but things are better this time. He's decided I'm what he really wants, Finn and all, and he's been all I wanted since I first met him. We have to be discreet because of school policies and because he's a county judge, but I really think we'll make it work this time."

"Well, in that case, I'm happy for you," his mother said, hugging him gently. "Bring him with you next time you come to visit."

"Yes, Mama," Jacob said, smiling at her. "I love you."

"I love you too, Jacob. Now put that baby to bed and come help me with the dishes."

Jacob laughed. Some things never changed.

JACOB put away the last of the papers he had been checking and pulled his coat out of the cupboard where he kept it during the day. He glanced around the room one more time to make sure everything was ready for the next day's classes, flipped the light switch off, and locked the door. It had been a good day, but he was ready to go home. He smiled as he thought about the evening to come. Melissa had Finn tonight, so Jacob and Beau had dinner plans. Jacob hoped that would segue into after-dinner plans as well.

"Before you leave, Mr. Peters, I need a word with you."

Jacob looked up to see the school's principal, William Varner, standing at the door of his office, a frown on his face. That didn't bode well, but Jacob reminded himself that the expression could have many causes, not just him. "Of course, Mr. Varner."

He went into the office and took a seat, setting his coat and bag on the chair next to him. "What can I do for you, sir?"

"I received a most distressing phone call today," Mr. Varner said, his face pinched. "It would seem you haven't been honest with us."

"Honest about what?" Jacob asked, stomach churning.

"You've been seen frequently in the company of Judge Braedon in Prestonsburg," Mr. Varner replied.

"We're working together on a summer project for the Autism Society," Jacob said defensively. "I don't see how that poses a problem."

"Volunteer work doesn't pose a problem," Mr. Varner said. "Homosexuality does."

"How does my volunteer work with Judge Braedon equate to homosexuality?" Jacob protested, feeling the life he loved slipping through his fingers. *They don't have proof. They can't have proof.*

"As I said, your volunteer work is not the problem, but you've been seen with him in other situations as well. Situations not explained by your summer project. Unless perhaps he is your summer project?"

Jacob took a deep breath. "I think we shouldn't continue this conversation without representation."

"As you wish," Mr. Varner replied. "You're suspended pending a hearing in front of the board of directors. I will inform you when it's been scheduled. You may leave your key with my secretary on your way out."

Jacob rose, hands shaking as he reached for his belongings. "Is what I do or don't do in my private life really worth this?" he asked.

"Our teachers are role models of a Christian life," Mr. Varner replied piously. "We expect them to be above reproach at all times. You knew this when you signed your contract."

I wasn't in love with Beau when I signed the contract, Jacob thought bitterly. "Expect a phone call from my lawyer," he said instead. "I won't simply let you fire me."

He didn't wait for a reply, tossing his school keys on the secretary's desk as he walked by. When he got to the car, he climbed in, shaking with anger and not a little fear. He had no idea what "proof" his accusers had, but even if he managed to defend himself, he already knew what would happen. His contract wouldn't be renewed at the end of the year because of the scandal he'd caused, even if he was vindicated. Except that how could he be vindicated when the accusations were true? He was gay, and he was involved with Beau.

He needed to talk to his lover.

"Hello?"

"We have a problem," Jacob said without preamble. "Varner called me into his office just now to tell me I've been accused of homosexuality. I'm suspended until they can organize a hearing. I don't know what proof he has, or thinks he has, but he specifically mentioned you."

"Take a deep breath," Beau said. "Are you okay to drive?"

"Mad as hell, but I'm okay," Jacob said, realizing it was true. Just talking to Beau had steadied him enough that his hands no longer shook.

"Then go home. Find your contract if you can and call me back. We probably shouldn't meet in case they're watching you, but we can talk it out. You can fax me anything I need to see. Don't worry, baby. We'll beat this. I promise."

Jacob didn't see how that was even remotely possible, but he decided to trust Beau. He was the lawyer, after all.

He drove home and dug through his file cabinet until he found the contract. "Okay, I have it," he said when Beau answered the phone again.

"Skim through it to the morals clause," Beau directed, "and tell me exactly what it says."

"The Board may terminate an Employee in the following circumstances: Any serious act of misconduct by Employee, including (but not limited to) an act of dishonesty, theft or misappropriation of Academy property, moral turpitude, insubordination, or any act injuring, abusing, or endangering others," Jacob read.

"They're going to use moral turpitude," Beau said. "Keep reading. Does it mention homosexuality specifically anywhere in the contract?"

Jacob's hopes lifted as he continued to read and saw no specific definition of moral turpitude. "I don't see it," he said, "although Varner did say it was in there."

"He can say all he wants," Beau replied. "If it isn't on paper, we have room to argue it. Can you scan a copy of the contract and e-mail it to me? I want to look over it. If we're going to fight this, I'll need to be prepared."

"You realize that if you help me fight it, there will be no denying our affair," Jacob said. "Not really."

"I wasn't planning on denying it," Beau replied. "I was planning on forcing them to face the fact that their definition of morality doesn't match twenty-first century law."

"What about your job?" Jacob asked, feeling sideswiped by Beau's comment. "What about the next election?"

"If rumors have started about us, they're not going to stop," Beau explained. "It's like Sean said when we had dinner with him. Even if we managed to spin everything they say against us into something perfectly harmless, people will keep looking for more because their suspicions are raised. The way I see it, we have two choices. We can deny it, break off our relationship, and never see each other again, and hope that's enough to stop the rumors, or we can come out and deal with the consequences. I've done a lot of thinking since you left me and even more since you took me back. I don't like hiding. I think it's time to come out and deal with it."

Jacob nodded, knowing Beau couldn't see him. He could wish Beau had felt this way two years ago, before they landed themselves in this mess, even if coming out two years ago would have resulted in this same suspension and hearing, but as his mother was fond of saying, there was no use crying over spilt milk. "So what do we do?"

"Did the principal tell you when the hearing was?" Beau asked.

"No, he said he'd inform me once it was scheduled," Jacob replied. "Maybe he thought I'd deny it or something and it wouldn't be necessary. I didn't admit to anything, but it caught me so off guard, and a part of me couldn't stand to lie."

"That's one of the reasons I love you," Beau said. "So here's what we do. E-mail me a copy of your contract so I can look at it while you drive into town. I'll order pizza so we can talk without being interrupted, and we'll make a plan over dinner."

"Really?" Jacob asked, miserably grateful to hear that Beau still wanted him to come over. "I was afraid…."

"I'm not going to run away this time," Beau promised. "I know I screwed up before, but things are different this time around. Whatever happens, we'll face it together."

TWO weeks later, Jacob walked into the auditorium of the school where he had expected to spend his career, fully aware he would probably walk out without a job. He and Beau had gone over his contract and his options repeatedly. In a public school, where they were governed by state and federal law, the *Lawrence v. Texas* decision would have protected Jacob when it struck down all state sodomy laws, but Jacob worked in a Christian school. They could impose their definition of Christian morality through the moral turpitude clause even though Jacob had done nothing illegal. He could threaten to sue for discrimination, but Jacob was not sure he could make good on that threat. Not when doing so would drag him and Beau into a spotlight that could last for years and still might not result in a victory.

Every head in the room turned as he and Beau walked down the aisle to the table set up at the front of the room. Jacob's stomach clenched when he saw not a single empty seat and a fair number of people standing along the walls. This was not going to be pretty.

He took his seat, resisting the urge to turn to Beau for comfort. It would certainly not help his case if he did.

"This meeting is called to order," Mr. Varner said. "We are here to discuss the allegations of misconduct on the part of Jacob Peters, a teacher in the fourth grade. We have received reports of homosexual conduct, an act expressly forbidden in our contract."

"Actually," Beau said, rising to his feet, "there is no mention of homosexuality anywhere in your contract."

"Homosexuality is a sin," Mr. Varner declared. "It says so in the Bible. 'If a man lies with a male as those who lie with a woman, both of them have committed an abomination and they shall surely be put to death.'"

"Leviticus?" Beau verified. "I believe it also says you shouldn't eat oysters, shrimp, lobsters, crabs, and clams, and yet I'm quite sure I saw several of the board members at Third Street Bistro enjoying Mark's gumbo last week. Unless I'm mistaken, his gumbo has both shrimp and crawfish in it. Now I'll admit they didn't mention crawfish as unclean in Leviticus, but I'm pretty sure that's because they didn't know about crawfish in ancient Israel."

"We aren't here to debate Bible verses," Cecil Knightley, president of the board, interrupted. "We will not have this hearing turned into a circus."

"I was simply pointing out the flaws in Mr. Varner's argument," Beau replied with a shrug. "I can cite state law if you would prefer. As of 2003, homosexuality is not illegal in the state of Alabama and therefore not a cause for dismissal."

"As a Christian institution, we expect more of our employees than the letter of the law," Mr. Knightley declared. "They are expected to be models of Christian virtue for their students, and you cannot expect me to accept homosexuality as a Christian value."

"You cannot expect *me* to accept that Mr. Peters has said or done anything in front of his students to compromise their Christian values," Beau retorted.

"He's a known homosexual in a relationship with another man," Mr. Knightley said. "That knowledge alone compromises their Christian values."

The impulse to deny it, to demand to know what proof they had, was strong, but Beau had made his decision when he offered to help defend Jacob at the hearing. "So you're saying," he said slowly, enunciating every word for maximum effect, "that if Jacob and I weren't together, you wouldn't fire him? That the problem isn't that he's gay but that he has chosen to find someone to spend his life with?"

The auditorium erupted in shouts and jeers at Beau's admission, but he had not really expected anything else given the hostility of the board of directors. He still hoped to show up their hypocrisy, if nothing else, but it was far more important for Jacob to hear him affirm their relationship and stand by it.

Beau could practically see Jacob folding in on himself as the angry shouting continued. He wanted to offer his support, but any gesture he made would surely only add to the crowd's disapproval. Mr. Knightley called for order several times before the spectators finally settled down enough for him to be heard.

"The problem is that if the students are aware of Mr. Peters's leanings and see him continue to teach here, they will assume such behavior is acceptable," Mr. Knightley said coldly. "Since you have just confirmed both his leanings and the accusations of your 'relationship', I have no choice but to terminate Mr. Peters's employment with Elliot Christian Academy effective immediately."

Beau had other arguments he could make, but Jacob's hunched shoulders dissuaded him. "You think you're so high and mighty, all of you sitting in judgment on us." He turned so he could see the crowd behind them as well. "You wave the Bible around and cite the verses that support the positions you want to take. Let me remind you of another one. 'Judge not, lest ye be judged.'"

He closed his briefcase and touched Jacob's shoulder lightly. "Let's go home."

Jacob rose silently and followed him out of the auditorium, ignoring the insults hurled at them as they passed through the crowd.

When they were alone in Beau's car, Jacob turned to Beau with haunted eyes. "I taught there for four years," he said, his voice breaking. "Not a single parent of my students stood up and said my record was more important than my sexuality. All the volunteer work I've done at the school and elsewhere, the time and money I spent making sure I gave my students the best possible education. They just ignored all of that, like I was some... some...." Words failed him.

"In your colleagues' defense," Beau said softly, "the board had already made up their mind. Defending you would only have landed them in hot water as well, and nobody wants to lose their jobs."

"Me included," Jacob replied.

"I know you loved teaching there, baby," Beau said, "but we'll find a way to deal with this. Let's pick Finn up from Melissa's parents and go home."

"I can't make my mortgage payments if I don't have a job," Jacob said forlornly. "I won't be able to keep Finn."

"Stop that," Beau said. "You're too upset to make decisions right now. Come home with me tonight and we'll deal with the rest tomorrow."

Jacob subsided, resting his head against the back of the seat and staring blindly into the night. He had known this would be the outcome despite Beau's assurance they could fight the decision, but then it had been a future fear, and there had been the hope that Beau was right. Now it was his reality. Unemployed, and not just unemployed but terminated, outed, and humiliated. Getting another job in education would be incredibly difficult, at least here in Alabama. If it were just him or just him and Finn, he would move, go somewhere more liberal where his preferences wouldn't be an automatic mark against him, but he wouldn't ask Beau to leave his mother, and Jacob wasn't willing to leave Beau. Not after tonight.

"Thank you for trying to help me," he said into the darkness between them. "You didn't have to do that."

"Maybe not," Beau agreed, "but I wasn't about to let you face that alone. That's not what partners do. Now that everybody knows about us, I can give you the title you deserve, at least while we live here, where there's no chance for a legal title."

They arrived at Melissa's parents' house. "Stay in the car," Beau said. "I'll go get Finn."

"Thank you," Jacob said. "I'm sure they'll have a few choice words to say about my choices."

"You won't be able to avoid them forever, since they are Finn's grandparents, but I can help you put that off a little longer."

Beau got out of the car and walked up to the front porch. Jacob watched him listlessly, too numb to do anything else. He could tell from the way Mr. Winters gesticulated that he was berating Beau, for the situation, for Jacob divorcing Melissa, for who knew what, but Beau kept his calm, gathering Finn and his belongings and leaving Mr. Winters to shout after him. Beau ignored him and kept walking back to the car. He settled Finn in the backseat and climbed back in next to Jacob. "That's going to be interesting for the next few months."

"I'm sure he had plenty of unkind things to say," Jacob agreed.

"His primary concern seems to be that you left Melissa for me. I suggested he ask her what really happened the night you and she met. He didn't seem impressed."

Jacob flinched. "You know that story makes all three of us look bad."

Beau shrugged and squeezed Jacob's hand. "Maybe, but at least it doesn't turn you into the villain of the story, leaving your sweet, young, innocent wife to go live in homosexual sin with another man."

"God, it sounds tawdry when you put it that way."

"It's not tawdry," Beau said immediately, reaching for Jacob's hand as he drove them back toward Prestonsburg. "Nothing about us being in love is dirty or tawdry or sinful. We made some mistakes, but people do that. Part of being in love is fixing the mistakes so you can keep moving forward as a couple."

Jacob squeezed Beau's hand and lapsed into silence the rest of the way to Beau's house. Finn had fallen asleep in his car seat by the time they arrived, so Beau simply carried the entire contraption inside, depositing it in the spare bedroom he had begun to think of as Finn's room. Jacob had wandered as far as the kitchen when Beau came back downstairs. Beau pulled Jacob into his arms and simply held him, arms wrapped tightly around Jacob's waist, letting Jacob lean on him for support, comfort, or whatever else he needed.

"What am I going to do?" Jacob asked.

"Tonight you're going to come upstairs and sleep in my bed," Beau said. "You're going to let me hold you and take care of you. Tomorrow we'll worry about the rest."

Jacob followed Beau docilely up the stairs, but when they reached Beau's bedroom, Jacob pulled away, making a beeline for the bathroom. The sound of retching followed swiftly. Beau waited a moment, torn between helping Jacob and giving him his privacy, before he heard the toilet flush and water running in the sink. Jacob came back out, his face wan and his arms wrapped around his waist.

"Come here, baby," Beau said, patting the edge of the bed. "You're wound so tight you're about to snap."

Jacob crossed the room and sat on the bed next to Beau, making no effort to touch his lover. Beau urged him to lie down, stretching out next to him and pulling him close. He didn't speak, leaving it up to Jacob to talk or be silent.

"Did you hear what they shouted at us as we were leaving tonight?" Jacob said finally. "People think we're sick because we love each other."

"I know this isn't the first time you've encountered homophobia," Beau said.

"It's the first time it's ever been that in my face," Jacob replied. "My parents weren't happy when I came out, but they didn't hurl insults at me. I went to Austin for college, and they're a pretty liberal campus in a pretty liberal city. Sure, I heard the occasional comment, but it was easy to brush off. The things they said tonight... I can't brush those off."

"Not yet," Beau agreed. "Try not to think about it. Try to concentrate on the fact that I love you and that I'm going to stand with you, no matter what happens. Everything else will work out, one way or another."

"MRS. PETERS?"

"Yes, this is she."

"My name's Beau Braedon. I'm a friend of Jacob's," Beau began, not entirely sure how much Jacob had told his parents about them.

"I suppose that's one way of putting it," Mrs. Peters replied caustically.

Beau took a deep breath. "Have you talked to Jacob in the past few days?"

"Not since he called to tell me he was probably going to lose his job because of his relationship with you," Mrs. Peters replied.

"I tried to help him fight it," Beau assured her, "but whatever I might think of the terms of the contract, it was very clear. Jacob was fired yesterday."

Mrs. Peters sighed. "I feared this would happen when he told me about you at Christmas, but he assured me you were being discreet."

"We thought we were," Beau replied, "but apparently not as discreet as we intended to be. Look, I know you have no reason to help me, but Jacob needs to get away from all of this for a few days. I know a place I can take him, but we can't take Finn with us. I was hoping you'd be willing to come watch him while we're gone."

"So you aren't going to disappear on him like you did last time things got complicated?" Mrs. Peters demanded.

"No," Beau promised. "I'm going to stand beside him like I should have done from the beginning, and I'm going to do everything I can to make him happy, starting with this trip, if you'll help us out."

"When do you need me?"

Relief flooded Beau as he gave Jacob's mother the dates he had been able to reserve at the Domain of Killien after a cancellation left the estate with an empty cabin.

"I'll have to speak with my husband," Mrs. Peters said, "but I don't have anything on my calendar for those days. Give me your number and I'll call you back in a few minutes."

Beau gave her the number and hung up, waiting impatiently for her to call back. He felt like he'd surmounted a huge hurdle, getting Jacob's mother to agree. She could have blamed him for the entire mess and refused to do anything to help. Granted, that would have made things as hard for Jacob as it would have for Beau, but after Jacob's account of his parents' reaction to his divorce, Beau hadn't been sure Jacob would tell them the rest.

A few minutes later, the phone rang again.

"We'll come spend the week at Jacob's house," Mrs. Peters said without preamble. "That way you can leave and return when you're ready and I can spend a few days with my son as well."

"Thank you," Beau said, breathing a sigh of relief. "I was afraid you wouldn't even hear me out."

"I'm withholding judgment on you," Mrs. Peters warned. "I'm coming to help my son."

"I understand, ma'am," Beau said. "I appreciate it all the same."

After saying goodbye, Beau went in search of Jacob, finding his lover on the back porch, rocking Finn in morose silence. "We need to go back to your place and find all your warmest clothes."

Jacob looked up at him listlessly, not even bothering to ask the question Beau could see on his face.

"Your mother is coming next week to watch Finn, and we're going away for a few days," Beau explained as if Jacob had asked. "I reserved a cabin for us at a place north of Toronto. We can build a fire in the fireplace and not come out the entire time we're there. No one to see, no one to care, just the two of us holed up in a little cabin in the woods and a five-star chef to make breakfast and dinner for us."

"Oh," Jacob said, turning his attention back to Finn.

Beau wanted to shake him out of his apathy, but he settled for joining Jacob on the swing and pulling his lover into his arms. "Please say you'll come with me," he said. "I want to do something special for you."

"Why?" Jacob asked. "All I've done is bring trouble down on your head."

"Shit happens," Beau said with a shrug. "We knew this could happen. I hoped it wouldn't, but it was the risk we took. Now we have to decide how we're going to live with it."

"What choice do we have?" Jacob asked, his voice cracking. "I've lost my job, and I'm not going to find another one in Elliot or Prestonsburg or probably even in Auburn. I'll have to go to Atlanta or farther away, and that will be that. You'll come see me or I'll come see you for a while, but eventually the distance will get to be too much and—"

"Stop," Beau ordered. "You don't know any of that. You're feeling sorry for yourself, understandably, but that isn't going to help. The only decision you need to make right now is whether you'll come to Canada with me next week."

"I don't have much in the way of real winter clothes."

"You can borrow some of mine," Beau declared, choosing to take Jacob's protest as a statement of need rather than a refusal to go. "And if we have to, we can buy boots once we get there. They have ski gear at the lodge, but I don't think they have regular boots, and we don't have time to order anything online."

"Do you have winter boots?" Jacob asked, his voice betraying the first sign of interest Beau had heard in days.

"Yes," Beau said. "I used to go to this place every winter to go skiing. It's been a few years, but I still have most of the gear I bought for my trips."

"I didn't know you skied."

"It's been a couple of years since I've gone," Beau said. "I hurt my knee three years ago in Vail and haven't gone since then. I could probably do it again now, cross-country, anyway, which is what they have at the Domain of Killien. I just haven't tried. If you want to go skiing, we should go a day early and go shopping in Toronto. You don't need skis, but you'll freeze in jeans and sweatshirts."

Jacob shook his head. "Not this time. Maybe next year we can plan a trip. If we're still together and all."

There it was again, that defeatist attitude that drove Beau crazy. He could fight the bigots; he didn't know how to fight Jacob's apathy. He would have to love Jacob so thoroughly and so often this weekend that he would stop doubting the depth of Beau's commitment. "We'll make reservations while we're there, then," he declared. "We get a discount if we do."

"You're so sure."

"I am," Beau agreed. "I know what I want. I didn't want to get it at the expense of your career, but I don't regret being free to love you. I can't regret it because the other option is living without you. I tried that. I didn't like it."

"I didn't either," Jacob said, the sentiment surprising a smile out of him. "What are we going to do?"

"We're going to take a vacation to Canada and forget about everything for a few days. We'll worry about the rest when we get back."

Jacob doubted it would be that easy, but he did his best to push aside his depression. "I guess we'd better go see what I have in the way of sweaters."

[9]

THEY borrowed Sean's plane again so they could fly directly into the Stanhope Airport instead of having to rent a car and drive the four hours from Toronto. In the summer, Beau wouldn't have minded the drive, but he wasn't comfortable driving in the snow. Lynn and Régine, the manager and assistant manager at the Domain of Killien, arranged for transportation from the airstrip to the estate, and Jacob got his first glimpse of the winter wonderland. The roads were clear, but the rest of the world was covered in white. "I've never seen so much snow!"

"This has actually been a fairly mild winter," the driver told them. "We usually have at least another foot of snow at this point in the year."

"I can't even imagine," Jacob marveled as they drove past mile after mile of frozen lakes and snow-covered pines. "But I guess it's like anything else. You learn to live with it."

"Exactly," the driver said. "Lynn said you're from Alabama. It must get hot in the summer, eh? When it's cold, you put on another pair of socks. There's only so much you can take off when it gets hot."

"That's true," Jacob said, "but I grew up in Mississippi, so I've never known anything else."

"Well, you'll get a taste of snow, and if you like it, you can always come back again." They pulled off the main road onto a gravel driveway that took them onto the Domain of Killien property. The driver pulled all the way up to the main lodge and helped them carry their bags inside the rustic building. Inside, a fire crackled merrily in the huge fireplace.

"Welcome to Domain of Killien. Mr. Braedon, welcome back. It's been too long since you've come to see us."

"Thank you. Lynn, this is my partner, Jacob Peters."

"Nice to meet you, Mr. Peters," Lynn said, offering her hand. "Are congratulations in order?" she asked, looking back at Beau.

Jacob blanched, her question overriding the thrill of hearing Beau introduce him as his partner, but Beau put a reassuring arm around his waist, steadying him and bringing back the quiet glow of not having to hide. "Maybe not quite yet," Beau said, "but soon, I hope. We've had a rough few weeks and decided we needed a break."

"We'll do our best to provide one," Lynn promised. "We have a full house, so Scott and Emily have their usual variety of delights available from the kitchen. Your cabin is stocked with wood if you want to build a fire, and I went in earlier to make sure the heat was on. Will you need skis and poles while you're here?"

"I don't think so," Beau said. "The thought of relaxing in front of a fire, playing a few games of chess, and eating all the wonderful food Emily and Scott can provide is pretty much perfect at the moment."

"Let me know if you change your mind, eh," Lynn said, retrieving a key from behind the old-fashioned wooden reception desk. "I've put you in Aurelie. It's probably too cold to enjoy the front porch, but you'll still have a lovely view of the lake from your sitting room, and of course you're welcome to enjoy the lodge as well if you want a change of scenery. What time would you like to be seated for dinner in the evenings?"

"Would seven suit?" Beau asked Jacob.

"That would be fine," Jacob replied.

"We'll see you at seven, then," Lynn said, making a note in her planner. "You should have everything you need in your cabin, but let us know if there's anything we can do to make your stay more enjoyable."

"Thank you," they both said. Beau took the key and hoisted one of their bags on his shoulder. Jacob grabbed the other and followed Beau back into the cold air.

"I can hardly catch my breath," Jacob said as they crossed the snowy lakefront to their cabin.

"Pull your scarf up over your face," Beau advised. "It'll help warm the air so it doesn't burn your lungs."

Jacob fumbled with his scarf, his fingers clumsy through the thick gloves, but he finally got it pulled up over his mouth and nose. He shivered when a gust of wind eddied around his ankles. He hoped Lynn was right about the heat being on in the cabin.

They kicked the snow off their boots when they reached the porch. Jacob took one step inside and breathed a sigh of relief at the warmth. "Do we really have to go back outside?"

Beau laughed. "Take off your boots and let's get a fire going," he suggested. "We'll cuddle on the couch for a few hours until you're nice and toasty, and then we'll dash over to the lodge for dinner. I promise it'll be worth it."

Jacob tugged his boots off, padded across the floor in his socks, and sat down on the couch, pulling a thick blanket over his legs. He'd take his coat off eventually. Maybe.

Beau shucked his coat immediately along with his boots, leaving Jacob to admire his lover's ass as he bent to stack wood in the fireplace and set a match to the tinder. Before long, a merry blaze crackled on the hearth. "Is there room for me under that blanket?"

Jacob lifted the covers in silent invitation.

"Why don't you take off your coat first?" Beau teased. "I know you're still cold, but you'll actually warm up faster without it on." Jacob looked skeptical. "Come on, baby. Let me keep you warm."

Jacob smiled and shook his head at Beau's antics, but he did as Beau asked, pulling off his coat and tossing it aside. He shivered again, but he could feel the heat from the fire spilling into the room, and then Beau slid under the blanket with him and wrapped Jacob in his arms.

Jacob leaned into the comforting embrace and sighed deeply. "This isn't going to solve anything, but I'm glad we're doing this. At home, I kept feeling like everyone was staring at us, even when we were alone. We aren't even a novelty here."

"No, we're just another couple here on vacation," Beau agreed, kissing Jacob's neck lightly. "Think anyone would notice if you came to dinner with a love bite?"

"Beau!" Jacob protested. "I thought we were trying to be unremarkable."

"You'll never be unremarkable," Beau assured his lover, nibbling a little on skin that hadn't seen a razor in several days. "If you don't shave, no one will be able to see it."

"I thought you said they had a dress code," Jacob mumbled, tilting his head to give Beau better access to his neck. It felt so good to be touched. The past few weeks had been so tense that Jacob hadn't felt like making love. The worst had come to pass, though, and all that remained was to pick up the pieces and figure out how to move forward. Making love suddenly seemed like the perfect way to start.

"No jeans, sweatshirts, or ski suits," Beau replied, sucking on the smooth patch of skin behind Jacob's ear. "They didn't say anything about being clean-shaven."

"I feel scruffy," Jacob insisted.

"You look good enough to eat."

Jacob smiled, turning in Beau's arms. "What are you waiting for?"

Beau pushed the blanket to the floor as they tussled on the couch, shoving clothes out of the way. When they were both finally naked, Beau stared down at Jacob. "I love you," he said firmly. "Nothing is going to change that, and I'll keep saying it and doing everything I can to prove it until you believe me."

"I believe you," Jacob gasped, squirming beneath Beau until he managed to part his legs, welcoming his lover into the cradle of his body.

The light from the flames limned Jacob's hair with red fire as Beau made love to him, so slowly and deliberately that Jacob felt his doubts melt away. They might come back later, but in that moment, Jacob knew himself cherished.

"Fuck," Beau muttered. "Lube and condoms are in my duffel."

"Surely you can think of other ways to get me wet," Jacob replied huskily.

"I still need a condom."

"Do you really?" Jacob asked. "I got tested after the night I slept with Melissa, and I haven't had unprotected sex since then."

"That's putting an awful lot of trust in me."

"Is it unfounded?" Jacob challenged.

"No," Beau said slowly. "I had my last blood test done at my physical a couple of months ago, just to be safe, and I haven't been with anyone but you in far longer than that."

"Then make love to me already," Jacob insisted.

Beau pushed back onto his knees. "Turn over."

Jacob rolled beneath him until his hands rested on the arm of the couch and his backside rubbed against Beau's chest. "That feels good," he purred as the hair on Beau's chest teased his skin.

"This'll feel even better," Beau assured him. He rose up on his knees so he could reach Jacob's shoulder, brushing his long hair out of the way and kissing the birthmark on his shoulder before licking his way down Jacob's back one vertebra at a time. Jacob squirmed beneath him, rubbing his ass against Beau's erection, but Beau ignored the provocation. Jacob didn't need a hard, fast, meaningless rut. He needed slow and tender. Or maybe it was Beau who needed it, but either way, Beau fully intended to make this a night—and a weekend—to remember.

When he reached the smooth cheeks of Jacob's butt, he lingered over them, kissing, licking, nipping at the lower curve until Jacob was moaning with every caress. He nudged his lover's thighs apart so he could reach the heavy balls, sucking on them lightly. Jacob let out a choked gasp, bringing a smile to Beau's face. That was what he wanted: his lover so lost in what he was doing that words were too much for him.

Working his way upward, he urged Jacob to rock back a little so his pert ass was lifted high, finally too much temptation for Beau to ignore. Even then, though, he took his time, laving Jacob's perineum and up his crease, tantalizing Jacob without touching his entrance. "Beau," Jacob begged, his voice little more than a whimper. "Please."

There was no more beautiful word in the English language in that moment, as far as Beau was concerned, unless maybe it was the sound of his name falling in broken sobs from Jacob's mouth as Beau gave him what he wanted, licking across the tight entrance, then stabbing his tongue against it.

The stress of Jacob's suspension and hearing had kept them from being in the mood to make love over the past several weeks, so Jacob's muscle was tight, fighting Beau's penetration. "Relax, baby," he cajoled, massaging Jacob's perineum lightly. "I can't get you wet if you don't let me in."

Jacob squirmed beneath the sensation, fighting to relax, but if anything, his hole clenched even more tightly.

"Turn back over," Beau said, pushing on Jacob's hip. "We'll try this a different way."

Jacob shifted obediently, his eyes wild with need when his face came into view. Beau kissed the concave planes of Jacob's belly and deliberately rubbed his chest against Jacob's cock, watching as Jacob sucked in a harsh breath at the stimulation from the rough hair. "You're too wound up," Beau said. "I need you to come for me so you can relax."

Jacob shook his head in mute protest.

"Don't worry, baby. I'm still going to make slow, sweet love to you, just like I promised," Beau said, rubbing soothing circles on Jacob's thigh. "It'll just take a little longer to get started."

He ran his palm over the tip of Jacob's cock, gathering fluid to reduce the friction before he circled the shaft with his hand, pumping desultorily. Jacob undulated restlessly beneath him, his hips pumping into Beau's grip. Beau increased the pace to match Jacob's movements, all the while nibbling on the juncture of hip and thigh. He might get splattered when Jacob finally climaxed, but it would be worth it.

When Jacob's movements grew frantic, Beau switched his attention from Jacob's inner thigh to his tightly drawn sac, tonguing the crinkled flesh until Jacob cried out and spilled his release onto his stomach, every muscle pulling tight before he collapsed bonelessly onto the couch.

Smiling, Beau lifted Jacob's legs onto his shoulders as he continued to stroke Jacob's cock. Jacob took the cue and raised his hips enough that Beau could return to his earlier occupation with Jacob's entrance, much more relaxed after his orgasm. This time when Beau pressed the tip of his tongue to the tight furl, it gave easily.

Jacob whimpered slightly but gave no other sign of needing Beau to stop, so he lingered over the preliminaries, giving Jacob the chance to recover for a second round. His own need battered his senses, but he ignored it. This afternoon was all about Jacob.

Finally the cock in his hand hardened again.

Beau scooped up the evidence of Jacob's first climax and smeared it over his cock. His whole body trembled in anticipation of sinking into Jacob's heat with nothing between them but skin. He couldn't remember the last time he'd had sex without a condom. Certainly not since Harrison was born.

"Ready?" he asked Jacob. As much as he wanted to join with his lover, he would wait if Jacob asked him to.

"God, yes," Jacob replied. "I need you."

"I love you."

Conscious of the absence of lube and the need not to hurt Jacob in any way, Beau took his time joining their bodies. The sensation of Jacob's tight heat, undulled by any barrier, stole Beau's breath and nearly his control, but he reminded himself anticipation was part of the pleasure, especially this time.

Jacob squirmed beneath him to find a better position in which to rock up into Beau's thrusts. "You feel... so good... inside me."

"You feel so good around me," Beau replied, leaning forward to kiss Jacob. "Just you and me."

"Just you and me," Jacob echoed, his body clenching so hard around Beau that he nearly climaxed on the spot.

Beau worked a hand between them, but Jacob caught it in his, holding tight. "Just you and me," he repeated. "I want to come from you inside me."

Beau nodded and pushed aside the need for release, focusing on doing everything he could to give Jacob pleasure. He kept his thrusts shallow, nudging Jacob's pleasure point repeatedly until Jacob was thrashing on the couch beneath him, curses and pleas providing an erotic soundtrack to their lovemaking.

Knowing how much Jacob enjoyed it when Beau talked to him during sex, Beau leaned forward so he could nuzzle Jacob's neck and whisper in his ear. "You are the most beautiful thing I've ever seen," he said, tracing the whorl of Jacob's ear with his tongue, "all spread out on the couch, letting me fuck you with nothing between us. I want you to come for me and then I'm going to pump you so full of spunk you'll overflow with it."

Jacob moaned, the decadent image pushing him precariously close to the edge of release. Another well-placed thrust completed the job, his climax spooling out of him and covering his stomach and Beau's chest. Beau reared back, pulling Jacob's legs to his shoulders and abandoning all control, pounding hard into Jacob's ass. "Pretty pink hole, all stretched around my cock," he crooned, running a finger along the upper curve of Jacob's entrance. "You need this, don't you?"

"Yes," Jacob cried, the new position and continued stimulation drawing out his climax even though his balls felt completely drained.

Beau's hips stuttered against Jacob's ass, fulfilling his promise as he filled Jacob's passage. His eyes stayed fixed on the place where they joined, his essence seeping from the stretched hole. "So do I, baby."

THEY showered and dressed for dinner, Jacob pulling on two pairs of long underwear beneath his pants before he would agree to make a dash for the main lodge and dinner. Beau kept tempting him with descriptions of meals he'd eaten there on previous trips, combinations that sounded amazing enough to convince Jacob to brave the cold. Even so, he went directly to the fireplace when they entered the lodge, toasting himself in front of the flames.

"Would you like something to drink before dinner?" one of the waitstaff asked. "Our drink special this evening is a Captain's Apple, which is rum, sour apple liqueur, and hot apple cider."

"That sounds wonderful," Jacob said. "I'll have one of those."

"A Grey Goose martini, dirty with a twist," Beau said when the waitress turned to him.

Jacob shivered. "No cold drinks for me."

Beau put his arm around Jacob's shoulders, pulling him close. "I'll warm you up when we get back to the cabin, I promise."

"I'll hold you to that," Jacob said. "I refuse to be cold all night long."

"There are extra blankets if you get cold during the night," Beau said, "but I'm sure I can think of ways to keep you warm."

"I'm sure you can."

The waitress returned with their drinks and invited them to take their seats at their leisure.

They lingered a few minutes more in front of the fire before moving into the dining room. Régine met them and showed them to their table, offering them the menu with the evening's choices. "We have a soup, two salads, and two entrées each night," she explained, "as well as a choice for dessert. If you have any questions about the menu, your server should be able to help you or I will be glad to answer them."

They took a few minutes to make their selections, Beau choosing the salmon and Jacob selecting the wild boar. Once they had placed their order, Jacob took a deep breath and reached for Beau's hand across the table. "I have enough in savings to cover my mortgage for about six months, but I don't know how much beyond that I can go if I don't find a new job."

Beau was surprised at the choice of subject since Jacob had been avoiding it since he had been fired, but maybe their lovemaking and Beau's promises that afternoon had finally done the trick and Jacob believed they were in this together. "Do we need two houses? There's plenty of room at my house for you and Finn, and the chances of finding a job in Prestonsburg are better than the chances of finding one in Elliot, if only because of the size of the town. Even if you end up working in Elliot or one of the other surrounding towns, you could still drive from my house to work. That would cut down on our expenses too."

"I don't want to be dependent on you," Jacob protested automatically.

"I'm not suggesting you would be," Beau replied, keeping his voice light. "I'm suggesting you sell or rent out your house and we pool our resources to cover the shared expenses of our household. We can't get married in Alabama, but that doesn't mean we shouldn't act like a committed couple intending to spend the rest of our lives together. The reasons for maintaining separate houses, separate lives, are gone. We're out. People know about us whether we want them to or not. We can do away with the pretense now."

"And if I can't find a job?" Jacob asked.

"If I weren't in the picture and you'd simply lost your job, what would you do if you couldn't find another one?" Beau asked slowly.

"Probably see if Finn and I could move back in with Mama and Dad," Jacob replied. "It would be a blow to my pride, but they'd help out until I could find something else."

"So why is that a better choice than moving in with me?" Beau asked, determined to use the skills he'd developed as a lawyer to get Jacob to see reason rather than demanding his lover stop fighting the obvious solution.

"Because....," Jacob started to answer only to realize he had no answer. He could say that his parents were family, but Beau was his lover. They had come out as Jacob had wanted all along, albeit in slightly stressed circumstances. At any other time, the invitation to move in with Beau would have delighted him as the next step in their relationship. "Because nothing, but you have to let me contribute as much as I'm able."

"I wasn't planning on anything else," Beau replied easily. "I don't want to be your sugar daddy. I want to be your partner. That means we pool our resources, whatever they are at any given time, and use them the way we both agree on. Right now, you don't have a job, but you'll find another one. And if we ever reach a point where we can move, you might find it easier to get a job than I do. They need teachers everywhere. There might come a point down the road where I'll be the one without a job, and if that happens, you'll be the one supporting me for a time. It's not about counting pennies. It's about facing things together."

"You realize it's not going to be that simple."

"Yes," Beau had to admit. "It's going to be a huge challenge for the next few months, and we may end up having to move sooner rather than later, but it's too late to go back in the closet even if we wanted to. Which I don't, by the way, just in case you were thinking I regretted any of this. The only thing I regret is how much it cost you."

"No more regrets," Jacob said. "We've had enough of those for a lifetime. Let's enjoy our meal and our weekend, and when we get back to Prestonsburg, we can start moving my stuff and getting my house ready to go on the market." He squeezed Beau's hand. "I love you."

"I love you too, baby."

Their server brought the first course then, a delicious cream of mushroom soup that warmed Jacob from the inside out. A thought struck him suddenly, leaving him feeling incredibly guilty. "You have spent the past week taking such good care of me, and I haven't even asked if you felt any backlash from coming out."

Beau shrugged. "Not as much as I expected," he said. "I honestly expected pickets outside the courthouse and lawyers demanding to be scheduled with a different judge, and I haven't had any of that. Some pinched looks in my direction, a couple of canceled appointments that could be because I'm out or simply because there was a scheduling conflict like they said there was. I'm not convinced I've seen the worst of it, but maybe it won't be as bad as I feared."

"How long until your term is up?" Jacob asked.

"Four years," Beau replied, feeling more than a little bad that Jacob had suffered so much more than he had when he had been the one so worried about the consequences, "and by then, we may not even want to stay in Prestonsburg. After the way they treated you, I wouldn't blame you if you wanted to leave as soon as we're able."

"Part of me wants to leave," Jacob admitted, "to go anywhere else just to be away from the scandal, but part of me feels like that would be admitting they were right, that there isn't a place for a gay couple in a small Alabama town, and I don't believe that. I don't want to let them be right, so for now, we'll stay and see what happens. If we leave in a year or two because we see better opportunities elsewhere, it'll be less like letting the bigots win."

"DO YOU want to wait here while I see what condition Mom's in today?" Beau asked as he stopped outside his mother's room at the Shady Oaks Nursing Home.

"Only if you'd rather talk to her alone first," Jacob said, squeezing Beau's hand. He'd been surprised when Beau asked if he'd like to meet Beau's mother. With her health precarious and the doctors advising against anything that might jar her or disrupt her environment, Jacob had not expected to get a chance to meet her, but Beau had insisted he wanted her to know the truth, that Beau had found someone to love, even if she never truly understood.

"I don't know what I'd say that I couldn't say with you there," Beau replied with a smile of relief, "but not everyone is comfortable with, well, people in her state."

"It's not about being comfortable," Jacob said. "I'm meeting your mother for the first time. I doubt that could be comfortable no matter how sharp she was, but that's not the point. I'm here with you because this is where I want to be. Maybe she won't understand consciously, but something might get through, and maybe that will comfort her on a level we can't detect."

Beau squeezed Jacob's hand, not releasing it as he led his partner into his mother's room.

"Beauregard? Is that you?"

The woman on the bed had been beautiful once. Jacob saw that immediately, even through the pasty, dry, wrinkled skin and the vacant look in the blue eyes that matched Beau's exactly. Her hair was gray now, but someone had taken the time to wash it and brush it recently, and the room had none of the antiseptic smell he had always associated with illness and nursing homes.

"Yes, Mom," Beau said, drawing Jacob with him as he perched on the edge of his mother's bed. Jacob released Beau's clasp so his lover could hold his mother's hand, but he let his own hand settle on Beau's broad shoulder, continuing the silent support. Another time, he might have teased Beau about his full name, but not now. "I brought someone to meet you."

"You always were such a considerate boy," she said. "Is this a friend from your dorm?"

"I'm not in college anymore, Mom, remember?" Beau said gently. "I graduated sixteen years ago."

"You're right," Mrs. Braedon said with a shake of her hand. "I get so confused sometimes."

"It's all right, Mom," Beau said. "We understand. This is Jacob Peters. My partner."

"Nice to meet you, Mrs. Braedon," Jacob said, his hand slipping from Beau's shoulder so he could offer it to Beau's mother. "Beau has told me so much about you."

"Don't listen to him," she said, her face contorting in a grimace. "I wasn't always like this."

"Those aren't the stories he's told me," Jacob assured her.

"Are you a lawyer also?" Mrs. Braedon asked.

"No, I'm a teacher," Jacob replied, glossing over his temporary unemployment. He had no idea if he'd be able to find another teaching job, but that wasn't a concern for the moment.

"But Beau said you were his partner," she said, obviously confused.

Beau slid his hand in Jacob's again. "Not business partner, Mom," he said gently. "Jacob is my gentleman friend."

"Oh."

The look on Mrs. Braedon's face might have been comical if the situation had not been so serious. Jacob tightened his grip on Beau's hand, bracing for the explosion to come, but Mrs. Braedon shook her head slowly. "Why didn't you say so in the first place?"

Beau slumped forward in relief. "Because I didn't know how you'd react," he admitted. "I was afraid…."

"I'm an old woman, Beau," his mother said, her voice growing feeble. "I don't have time for that nonsense. If you're happy, and I think I'm still aware enough to see that you are, that's all I need to know."

"I'm very happy, Mom," Beau said, leaning forward to kiss her cheek, "and I have Jacob and his son to thank for that. We didn't bring Finn with us today, but we could bring him back if you want to meet him."

Mrs. Braedon smiled absently. "I miss Harrison."

"We'll bring Finn next time we come," Jacob promised. "He's eight months old. He'll be thrilled with another adult to dote on him."

Mrs. Braedon nodded, her gaze clouding over.

"I think it's time to go," Beau said softly. "When she fades out like that, she doesn't make sense or remember anything for a while."

Jacob squeezed Beau's hand once more. He had resented Beau's mother for so long, but looking at her now, having her acceptance in a way he had never expected, he was beginning to understand why Beau found it so hard to think about doing anything that would make her condition worse.

"HI, BILLY."

"Where the hell have you been, Jacob?" Billy snapped. "I've been trying to call you for a week. I had a lovely conversation with your mother, but I haven't been able to reach you."

"Billy, calm down. I was with Beau," Jacob said. He'd forgotten to call Billy before he left for Canada, breaking a years-old promise, but he'd had other things on his mind. "It's been a rough couple of weeks, and he suggested we go away for a long weekend. I should have called. I'm sorry."

"Your mom said it was pretty bad down there," Billy agreed. "You want to tell me about it?"

"No," Jacob said. "I don't want to go through it again. How about I tell you what we've decided to do now?"

"We?" Billy repeated. "That sounds promising."

"It is," Jacob assured him. "It's been pretty miserable for the past couple of weeks, but some good has come out of it. Beau and I came out, and we're moving in together as quickly as we can get my house packed up. It'll take a little longer to get it ready to sell, but he's going to help me with that too."

"That's... unexpected," Billy said slowly. "After everything you said the last time we talked about him, I didn't figure he'd ever agree to come out."

"Things have changed," Jacob said softly. "A lot of things, and other than my job, I think they've changed for the better. I didn't ask him to come out, Bills. He made that decision on his own. He chose to stand with me, to defend me at the hearing, rather than to try to deny we were together. Maybe it didn't help. Maybe it even hurt my chances as far as the job was concerned, but he stood by me, and that matters more than anything else."

"I'd say it does," Billy agreed. "Send me your new address and phone number when you have a chance."

"The phone number won't change," Jacob said. "I'll keep my cell, but I'll send you Beau's address, and maybe after we're a little more settled together, you can come visit. I've met his best friend. It seems only fair he meet mine."

"I'd like that," Billy said, and Jacob could hear his smile in his voice.

"How is he?"

Beau looked over his shoulder into the kitchen, where Jacob was preparing a bottle for Finn. "Not great," Beau admitted. "He's trying to keep his chin up, but it's hard. He lost his job, he feels like he had to move in here, even if he's trying not to say it, he's not having any luck finding anything new, and he's run into some idiots in town when he's gone to the grocery and stuff. I'd hoped the relative lack of backlash against me meant he wouldn't get a lot either, but apparently people aren't nearly as shy about expressing their opinion to an out-of-work schoolteacher as they are to a local judge."

"It's only been, what, two weeks?" Sean asked.

"Four," Beau said, "from his suspension, two since the hearing, and a good part of that was spent in Canada at the Domain of Killien."

"Did he enjoy that?"

"What's not to like?" Beau asked with a laugh. "Amazing food, snow-covered lakes, a huge couch and fireplace, and no one to care if we came out of our chalet except for meals."

"And Lynn and Régine to make sure you had everything else you needed," Sean agreed. He had been the one to introduce Beau to the Canadian resort, a fact Beau was more grateful for than ever.

"Exactly. I just wish I knew what to do to help him now."

"Give him time," Sean said, "and don't let him forget you love him or think for an instant that you regret what's happened. It was never going to be easy, and coming out amid the furor of a termination hearing didn't help. You just have to wait for it to blow over, and if it doesn't get better, you can always consider other options. How's your mom?"

"I took Jacob to meet her," Beau said, smiling at the memory. "She thought he was someone from work at first. Then when I explained, she demanded to know why I hadn't brought him to see her sooner. We took Finn, Jacob's son, to see her yesterday, but she wasn't having a good day, so she kept thinking he was Harrison. She played with him some, though, which the doctors said was good, even if she was confused. I don't want to leave her, I don't want to move her, and yet I don't see that I have a choice if things don't get better for Jacob. I don't mind waiting a bit to see what happens, but I won't make him live this way forever. I can't."

"No, you can't," Sean agreed, "but make that decision with him, not for him. He's stronger than you think."

Beau had no doubt about Jacob's strength, because every time he thought he had seen the depths of Jacob's resilience, something else knocked him down and he stood right back up again, refusing to cower before the bigots or hide as if he had a reason to be ashamed. "Thanks, Sean. I appreciate everything."

"Come to dinner next weekend," Sean proposed. "Marlene has some big event planned, big enough that two more won't make a difference. It'll be good for Jacob to be in a situation where he won't be ostracized."

"You sure Marlene won't mind?" Beau asked, aware of how conscious Sean's wife could be where appearances were concerned.

"She told me to invite you."

"I'll talk to Jacob and let you know," Beau promised. "Don't add us to the guest list yet, in case he doesn't feel like dealing with the scrutiny, but I will ask."

"If not this weekend, then come in three weeks when it'll just be us and the kids."

"I think we can do that," Beau said. "Talk to you soon."

"FUCKIN' faggots! Patty, you ought to be ashamed, serving their kind in your restaurant. What's this town coming to?"

Jacob flinched, starting to rise and leave, but Patty put a hand on his shoulder. "The last time I checked, I owned Third Street Bistro, not you, Virgil Thompkins, and that means I get to decide who eats here and who doesn't. So I suggest you leave, because there's no table available and won't be for the likes of you."

Virgil huffed and threatened, but Patty crossed her arms and stared him down.

"You didn't need to do that," Jacob said when Thompkins had left. "You'll lose business if you kick out everyone who thinks like he does."

"I can't control what they're thinking, but I won't have anyone saying that nonsense about my best customers," Patty insisted. "What you do when you're alone is your business. You're still the same people you've always been."

"Now if only more people felt that way," Beau said with a sigh. His assessment of the situation while they were at the Domain of Killien had been somewhat optimistic. Things hadn't gotten as bad as his worst fears, but as news of his coming out and Jacob's change of residence had spread, they had encountered more and more people who shared Thompkins's attitude. Not everyone, but enough to make life uncomfortable at times. "I knew this would happen. It's why we decided not to tell anyone in the first place."

"Now don't you go writing off this town without giving people a chance," Patty scolded. "People are surprised, but most of 'em aren't like Virgil. Most of 'em are good, thinking people. Once they get over being surprised, they'll realize it's none of their business and everything will go back to the way it was."

Except my job, Jacob thought bitterly.

"I hope you're right," Beau said, nudging Jacob's foot with his under the table.

Jacob shook off his black thoughts and smiled up at Patty. "With you as our champion, I'm sure everything will work out. What does Mark have cooking up in the back? Anything special today?"

Patty rattled off the list of specials, giving Jacob something else to think about. They ordered their meal and returned to the discussion of where to find funding for the extra supplies they needed for the summer, doing their best to ignore the looks of the other patrons in the restaurant. No one else said anything openly derogatory, but Jacob swore he could feel eyes on the back of his head, burning into his skin with derision.

"Their world doesn't revolve around us," Beau said softly, nudging Jacob's foot again, "and our world doesn't revolve around them. Relax and enjoy your dinner."

"I'm trying," Jacob said, "but I know they're whispering about us behind their hands. They keep looking over here at us, and while I don't know those three ladies, I know their type. They're the matrons who dictate the tone of any event. You'll never manage a successful campaign appearance again if they have their way."

Beau shrugged. "My term doesn't expire for another four years. By the time I have to campaign again, I may not want to. We may not even still be here four years from now. Don't borrow trouble. We have enough trouble as it is."

"I know," Jacob said. "I've looked everywhere I can think of for a job, but I know half the places dropped my application in the trash as soon as I walked out the door, and I'm not qualified for the other half of the jobs."

"I already told you not to worry about that," Beau insisted. "You and Finn can stay with me as long as you need to, and don't bring up paying rent again. I want you to have a job that will make you happy because I know how much you hate sitting at home with nothing to do, but that's the only reason I want you to find a new job. I'm not going to suddenly decide you aren't pulling your weight and kick you out. I love you, remember?"

"I remember," Jacob said, summoning a smile. Even as depressed as he was over losing his beloved teaching job, hearing those words from Beau, openly and in public where anyone might overhear, reminded him of how lucky he was. "You aren't making me feel this way. I'm doing it to myself. I need to feel useful, and taking care of the house isn't cutting it."

Beau reached across the table and squeezed Jacob's hand. The tittering at the next table suddenly increased in volume, but Beau ignored them. "We'll find something. It's only been a couple of weeks, and job hunting is never easy around here, even when you don't have any strikes against you. In the meantime, there's still plenty to do for this summer. Try to focus on that."

"I suppose I could see if there are other things Paula needs done too," Jacob mused, not letting go of Beau's hand. "Non-profits always seem to need more hands than they have."

"And there are other volunteer organizations you could work with to get out of the house," Beau suggested. "Habitat for Humanity has a couple of new houses going up. Salvation Army has a prisoner rehabilitation program that was looking for volunteers to help with literacy and job skills. All you have to do is decide what you want to do."

The door to the restaurant opened and another of the local matrons came in. The women at the table next to Beau and Jacob waved at her to join them, but she ignored them for the moment, crossing to Beau and Jacob's table instead. "Judge Braedon," she said, her voice clear enough to carry through the entire restaurant, "it's good to see you."

"Mrs. Breckenridge," Beau said, rising and shaking her hand. "How are you?"

"Doing very well, thank you," the lady said, glancing over her shoulder at the other table before turning back to Beau. "I wanted to personally invite you to the Oaks on Saturday. Mr. Breckenridge and I are celebrating our golden wedding anniversary, and we want to share the occasion with all our friends. You will bring your gentleman friend with you as well, of course," she added with a nod for Jacob.

"We would have to see about finding a babysitter for Jacob's son," Beau demurred.

"Nonsense," Mrs. Breckenridge insisted. "This is a family celebration. My great-grandchildren will all be there. One more child will hardly be noticed. I do expect to see you, Judge, along with Mr....?"

"Peters," Beau supplied. Jacob rose at the introduction. "Jacob Peters."

"Pleased to meet you, Mr. Peters," Mrs. Breckenridge said, offering her hand. "As I said, I do expect to see you on Saturday at two o'clock."

"We would be honored to attend," Jacob said, hoping he wasn't speaking out of turn. "Love deserves to be celebrated."

"It does indeed. Now I'll leave you to your dinner. And no gifts on Saturday. The gift of your presence is all we desire."

She sailed across the restaurant before they could reply. "What just happened?" Jacob asked when she was out of earshot.

"We just got her seal of approval," Beau replied slowly. "You don't know Mrs. Breckenridge, do you?"

Jacob shook his head.

"She was Melanie Preston before she married, Preston as in Prestonsburg, and her husband's family has been here almost as long," Beau explained. "Their anniversary party will be the event of the year. She just shared her opinion of us with the entire town. I'm not saying our problems are over, but our lives just got a little easier. I never imagined…."

"I told you to give people a chance," Patty said, appearing at their table with their dinners. "There's a lot of good folks in this town, and you know none of the old biddies will stand up to Mrs. Breckenridge, so you can expect a flood of invitations, if only so they can hear all the details of the party *they* weren't invited to."

"Is she really that influential?" Jacob asked.

"Yes," Beau replied. "She doesn't throw that influence around very often, but when she does, nobody will argue with her. If she chooses to cut someone, that's the end of them as far as society is concerned."

Jacob chuckled. "There are times I love southern towns. There are times I want to beat my head against the wall, but there are times I'm glad of their antiquated traditions."

"Don't let Mrs. Breckenridge hear you call her antiquated," Beau said with a laugh. "I don't know why she decided to take our side in all this, but we certainly don't want her to change her mind."

"I didn't say she was antiquated," Jacob replied, truly smiling for the first time in days. "I said the society that gives her so much influence is antiquated. She's anything but, given her attitude toward us."

"Excuse me, Judge Braedon."

Jacob and Beau looked up to see the ladies from the table next to them. "Mrs. Palmer, Mrs. Nicholson, Mrs. Waters," Beau acknowledged.

"We haven't met your… friend," one of them said. "We were hoping you'd introduce us."

Beau glanced at Jacob, trying to hide his smirk. "Of course. Jacob, I'd like you to meet Beth Palmer, Blythe Nicholson, and Katharine Waters. Ladies, my partner, Jacob Peters."

Jacob rose and offered his hand, his most charming smile on his face. "So nice to meet you, ladies." He might hate their hypocrisy in snubbing Beau and him until after Mrs. Breckenridge's intervention, but he wasn't about to squander the opportunity she had offered them. "Mrs.

Nicholson, I believe I've met your husband as well. Isn't that who we met, Beau?"

Beau nodded in amusement as he watched Jacob charm the three women. He'd known Jacob's charm would be an asset. He just hadn't expected him to get to use it. It would seem he had been wrong.

"Who won the tennis match, Mrs. Waters? Your husband or Mr. Dickerson?"

"You know about that silly old rivalry?" Mrs. Waters asked.

"Mr. Nicholson mentioned it," Jacob explained. "We weren't able to attend the match, but I'm sure it was a sight to see."

"Aaron won," Mrs. Waters said. "You really should have been there."

"Perhaps next time," Jacob said smoothly. "I'm sure they'll play again."

"As soon as the weather warms up enough for them to be on the courts," Mrs. Waters said with an indulgent shake of her head. "In the meantime, we're organizing a charity ball for the Prestonsburg Woman's Club. We work with local schools to stock classrooms with supplies for children who can't afford what they need."

"An admirable project," Jacob said, "and one dear to my heart. I came to the area with Teach For America."

"Then you'll attend?" Mrs. Palmer asked.

"When is it?" Jacob asked. "I have a young son, so we'll have to make sure we can find a babysitter for him before we commit to anything."

"Oh, that's easy as punch," Mrs. Nicholson said. "My daughter babysits. I'll tell her to mark the date on her calendar. She'll be happy to watch him for you."

Once again, the hypocrisy of the whole situation struck Jacob, but he smiled anyway. "The date?"

"Oh, so sorry. It's March twenty-third, three weeks from now," Mrs. Nicholson replied.

"We'll let you know if we can't find a sitter," Jacob said.

"How wonderful!" Mrs. Nicholson gushed. "Thank you for letting us interrupt your meal. Have a good evening, now, Mr. Peters, Judge Braedon."

The three women bustled out of the restaurant. The moment the door closed behind them, Beau burst out laughing. "Oh, God, never in my life did I imagine that would happen! You've just charmed the three biggest gossips in town. Not that I doubted your ability to be charming. I just never expected them to give you the chance."

"They only said something to us because of Mrs. Breckenridge," Jacob reminded Beau. "They'd probably prefer we were anywhere other than here."

"Maybe," Beau had to agree, "but you still charmed them. Their faces weren't nearly as pinched when they left as when they first came up to the table. You might have been right after all."

"Right about what?" Jacob asked.

"You told me change required a catalyst, and I dismissed it as wishful thinking," Beau said. "You might have been right. Change might come more easily than I thought."

"I'm not sure I'd call losing my job 'easy'," Jacob said, the events of the evening not enough to erase all his anger.

"I didn't mean it that way," Beau said, "but I really expected the whole town to react the way Thompkins did. I didn't expect to be able to stay if we came out. Instead it looks like it'll be a question of simply weathering the storm. And we will weather it, and you'll find another job, and we'll be able to stay after all. If we want to, that is."

Jacob wasn't quite ready to go that far, but he was more hopeful than he had been in weeks.

[10]

BEAU, Jacob, and Finn arrived at the Prestonsburg Oaks Country Club at precisely two o'clock to find the line of guests already out the door. They joined the receiving line, nodding politely at the others waiting with them. No one said anything directly, but Jacob thought he caught a few surprised looks at their presence. He refused to cower, though. Mrs. Breckenridge had invited them, and that gave them as much right to be there as anyone.

"Smile," Beau murmured at his side. "We're celebrating today."

Jacob summoned a smile for his lover and kept it in place as they advanced through the line. "Judge Braedon, Mr. Peters," Mrs. Breckenridge said as they reached her. "So good of you to join us. Mr. Peters, I don't believe you've met my husband, Walter Breckenridge."

Mr. Breckenridge offered his hand to Jacob. "I heard about that business in Elliot. It's a shame, I tell you, kicking you out of the classroom when the children obviously benefited from you being there. I've had a word with their board of directors, for all the good it did. Sorry bunch of hypocrites. I know enough about every one of them to get them fired if they had to abide by the same contract they require of their teachers."

"Walter, we are not at a board meeting," Mrs. Breckenridge scolded. "You can discuss business with Mr. Peters another time. For now, we have other guests to greet."

"Yes, Melanie," Mr. Breckenridge said meekly.

"Congratulations on your anniversary," Jacob said, smiling at the exchange. "Any advice on staying married so long?"

"Yes," Mr. Breckenridge said. "She's always right."

Jacob laughed. "I'm not sure that will help me, but thank you, and again, congratulations."

"So I'm not always right?" Beau asked as they moved deeper into the reception area.

"Only if you're willing to be my 'wife'," Jacob teased.

Beau squeezed his shoulder. "We can discuss our respective roles later. For now, let's enjoy the party."

"Excuse me, Mr. Peters," a girl Jacob didn't know said, approaching them. "My grandmother said I should tell you there's a nursery where you can leave your son during the party if you want. You're welcome to keep him with you, of course, but if he gets sleepy, there are beds and a quiet room prepared and someone to watch him."

"Thank you, Patricia," Beau said. "We'll keep that in mind when he gets tired."

"Another Breckenridge?" Jacob asked when the teenager walked away.

"The Breckenridges had three boys and a girl," Beau explained. "Patricia is the daughter of the youngest son, who is quite a bit younger than the other three, so she's caught between generations. Her cousins are all either your age or Finn's age."

"Poor kid," Jacob said, looking around the crowded room. "So how many of the guests are family?"

"About half," Beau guessed. "Maybe a little more, but that includes second and third cousins and other shirttail kin."

"The whole 'husband's cousin's husband's cousin' kind of family?" Jacob asked.

"Exactly."

Jacob chuckled. "All the more reason to let you introduce me around. I'll never keep track of everyone."

"I'm not entirely sure I know everyone," Beau said, "but I'll do my best."

By the time all the guests had arrived and the receiving line gave way to the buffet line, Jacob was completely overwhelmed with names and faces. It seemed Beau's prediction about the Breckenridges' approval had been correct. While not everyone at the party seemed glad to see them there, no one snubbed them directly or made any comments the slightest bit out of line, and several other family members greeted them quite warmly, making it clear that, for whatever reason, Mrs.

Breckenridge had ordered the family to close the ranks in their support of Jacob and Beau.

"A moment of your time, Mr. Peters," Mr. Breckenridge said, catching Jacob's attention as he finished filling his plate. "Melanie will fuss if we linger, but I'm hoping you'll come by my office one day next week. I want to take a look at your résumé. I'm always in need of competent people who aren't afraid to stand up for what's right. I can't make any promises, mind you, but I'd like the chance to undo some of the damage my so-called friends did when they fired you."

"My schedule is pretty open at the moment," Jacob admitted. "Tell me when and I'll be there."

"Tuesday at ten o'clock, then," Mr. Breckenridge decided. "I look forward to the chance to talk business with you."

"What was that all about?" Beau asked when Jacob joined him and Finn at a table.

"He wants me to come by his office on Tuesday so he can look at my résumé," Jacob said. "He doesn't even know me."

"He probably knows quite a bit by now," Beau said. "He's not just a wealthy socialite. He's a very shrewd businessman. If he wants to talk to you, it's because he thinks you can help him at least as much as he can help you."

"Doing what?" Jacob asked. "I'm an elementary school teacher."

"You're a teacher who chose to start your career with Teach For America," Beau reminded him. "That says something about your character right there. You didn't choose some rich suburban school where everything would be easy. You chose to work in an underserved area, and you chose to stay there, albeit at another school, even after you finished your Teach For America contract. For all I know, Mr. Breckenridge wants to open a charter school with you at its helm."

Jacob snorted incredulously. "Sure, like that's going to happen."

"Okay, probably not," Beau agreed, "but he has his fingers in so many pies that I wouldn't be surprised if he has a place for you. Just keep an open mind when you go to talk to him."

"It's not like I have anything to lose by seeing what he has to say," Jacob said, taking a deep breath and trying to relax. "Are you sure you don't want me to hold Finn so you can get a plate?"

"Eat," Beau insisted. "I'll get something when you're done. He's almost asleep, and if I give him to you, he'll wake back up again. Once he's asleep, we can put him in the nursery and enjoy the dancing."

"You don't really mean...." Jacob froze, his fork halfway to his mouth.

"Why not?" Beau asked. "The Breckenridges invited us as a couple. Very pointedly, I might add. I'm not going to make a big scene, but surely we can share one dance while Finn naps."

"Because there's being here and then there's being obvious?" Jacob replied.

Beau shook his head. "Finn's asleep. Finish eating while I put him in the nursery and get something for myself. We'll talk about it some more after we're done eating."

Jacob watched his lover walk off with his son, his emotions in turmoil. It always thrilled him to see Beau taking care of Finn as if Finn were his son as well, not something they would be able to make legal in Alabama at the moment, but maybe that would change in the future. On the other hand, the thought of dancing with Beau under the disapproving eyes of society made his head hurt. It wasn't the dancing itself. They had danced on their cruise and in Key West, but they had been anonymous strangers there, two faces in a crowd of hundreds. Here in Prestonsburg, they were well known, notorious even because of their relationship, and even with the support of the Breckenridges, he could feel the eyes on them. No one would say anything to their faces or where the Breckenridges could hear, but that wouldn't stop them from talking later, when they were assured of being with others who shared their opinion. If they were discreet, doing nothing to call attention to themselves, the gossips would find something else to talk about, but if they acted outside the norm, it would make matters worse.

"I don't know what has you frowning when we're supposed to be celebrating, but you'll upset my mother if you aren't careful," a woman Jacob didn't know said, sitting down at the table. "And you really don't want to upset my mother. Constance MacAllister."

"Jacob Peters," Jacob said, offering his hand. "You must be another Breckenridge."

"Yes," Constance said. "Mother told me she'd invited you and Judge Braedon. My husband and I live in Houston—we just came home for the party. I told her it was about time someone forced this town into the modern age."

"I don't know why your mother supports us, but we really appreciate it," Jacob said.

"Then smile instead of looking like you're at someone's funeral," Constance scolded.

"Beau—Judge Braedon—wants to dance," Jacob admitted. "I don't want to make a scene."

Constance smiled. "Dance with him. I'll make sure no one says anything."

"How?" Jacob asked.

"Trust me," Constance said. "I learned all there is to know about managing the gossips at my mother's knee. My parents will start the dancing in a few minutes. After all the family dances, go ahead whenever you're ready."

"If you're sure," Jacob said.

"I'm sure."

Beau returned then. "Sure about what?"

"Sure the two of you should enjoy a dance together," Constance said. "Good to see you again, Beau."

"You're looking lovely as ever, Constance. How's Houston?"

"Same as always," Constance replied. "The DJ is getting ready to start the dancing. I have to go now, but remember what I said."

"I will," Jacob said.

"What did she say?" Beau asked.

"That she would take care of the gossips," Jacob said.

"Then let's go applaud the happy couple and join them when it's time," Beau said.

"You didn't eat," Jacob protested weakly.

"I'd rather dance with you."

Jacob had no argument for that, so he took Beau's hand and walked with him to the dance floor where Mr. Breckenridge was leaning in to whisper something that made Mrs. Breckenridge blush like a schoolgirl.

"I hope we're still that much in love when we've been together fifty years," Beau said softly.

The sentiment squeezed Jacob's heart. He and Beau had talked about a future, but everything had been so unsettled that Jacob hadn't let himself dwell on it. To hear Beau speak of it so casually, with such certainty, stole Jacob's breath and left him trembling with the need to show Beau he was as committed to their future as Beau was. The DJ announced the dance, and the Breckenridges waltzed around the dance floor to the same tune they had danced to at their wedding fifty years ago.

When they had finished, the DJ invited the family to join them, the music changing from slow and sentimental to "We Are Family," which brought laughter to the crowd. When that song ended, the DJ opened the dance floor to all the guests.

"You ready for this?" Beau asked.

"Not really," Jacob admitted, "but waiting isn't going to change that."

Beau led him onto the dance floor. "Look at me. Not at anyone else. They don't matter. They don't even exist. It's just you and me."

Jacob nodded. "Just you and me."

The music started, and Jacob turned his hand in Beau's grip, his other hand going to his lover's shoulder so they mimicked the pose of the other dancers swaying together or twirling more pointedly. Jacob saw surprise on some of the faces over Beau's shoulder, but before he could tense, Beau squeezed his hand. "Look at me, baby."

Jacob did, staring into the beautiful blue eyes that had captivated him from the first time they met, even before he knew Beau was gay and interested in him. Then, he had told himself it was simple fascination with the strikingly deep color. The color continued to intrigue him, but it was the expression in them that kept him rapt now. They had softened, so warm and tender that Jacob felt his heart beat faster. To be loved this way… nothing else mattered in the face of that overwhelming epiphany. Beau really was here to stay.

"I love you," Jacob murmured, wishing he dared kiss Beau there on the dance floor.

"I love you too," Beau said, resting his forehead against Jacob's as they danced. The music changed, but they didn't separate or change position, continuing to dance like no one else mattered.

When the second song ended, a much faster one taking its place, Jacob finally took a step back. "Think we shocked them all?"

Beau shook his head. "No, I think we showed them love comes in all different forms."

Jacob smiled, squeezing Beau's hand as they left the dance floor.

Constance appeared at their side a moment later. "I was going to dance with one of you when you were done to show everyone we approved, but you don't need me. Every single person in this room saw how right you are for each other."

"I only hope they remember it an hour from now," Jacob said.

"They will," Constance assured them. "I don't remember when I last saw such a beautiful dance."

"We didn't do anything special," Jacob protested.

Constance smiled. "Yes, you did. You looked at each other. Enjoy the rest of the party."

THEY drove back to Beau's house after the party ended and they dropped Finn off with Melissa for the rest of the weekend, high on each other and happiness and the sheer joy of being accepted as they were in a place they had never dreamed could do so. Jacob was pretty sure it was the perfect moment. Until they turned onto Beau's street and saw the police cars in front of his house.

"What's going on?" Jacob asked as they pulled to a stop behind one of the cruisers.

"I have no idea," Beau said, parking the car and jumping out. "Officers," he called, "is there a problem?"

"Is that your house, Judge Braedon?" Officer Jenkins, a stout black policeman Beau recognized from court, asked.

"Yes, that's my house. Why? What happened?"

"Your neighbors called us, reporting hearing strange noises. When we came to investigate, we found some smashed windows, some nasty graffiti, and a big ol' mess of plants," Officer Jenkins explained. "I've got people interviewing your neighbors, trying to figure out what happened and when and who mighta been responsible."

Jacob winced at the callous description of the destruction. The officer obviously knew Beau on sight but not well enough to realize what any kind of damage to his garden would do to the man. He slipped his hand into Beau's in silent support. The officer's face tightened a little, seeing him, but he nodded at Jacob politely.

"Can I see what they did?" Beau asked, his voice hoarse.

"If that's what you want, Judge," Jenkins said, "but you can't cross the crime tape. The team is still looking for footprints or any other evidence. We'd love to find a paint can because then we might get fingerprints, but we haven't yet."

Beau nodded numbly and stepped closer to the line of police tape surrounding his yard. Jacob followed closely, but Officer Jenkins stopped him. "I'm sorry, sir, but I can't let you go with him."

"I live here too," Jacob said, realizing he could be exposing Beau to all kinds of problems, but he couldn't leave his lover to face this alone. "You seemed to know him, maybe even respect him—"

"He's one of the fairest judges we got," Jenkins interrupted. "I heard... well, it don't matter what I heard. You're here with him, and you obviously care about what happens to him. Just don't cross the yellow tape."

"Thank you," Jacob said, hurrying after Beau.

When Jacob reached Beau's side, he flinched. In the fading evening light, he could see the broken window into the living room and the wood on the porch rail that looked like someone had taken an ax to it. He wondered how that could happen without the neighbors noticing, but Jenkins said someone had indeed called the police, so maybe they had stayed inside for fear of their own safety. The words "faggot" and "sodomite" were spray-painted onto the wood siding, but a fresh coat of paint would hide those. It was the damage to the plants that would be the hardest to undo. The flowers had been pulled up by their roots, the bushes had been chopped off, probably by the same ax, and the beautiful dogwoods in the front yard had been decimated, branches hanging askew.

"Whoever done this, they sure hate you, Judge," Jenkins said. "I talked to some of the other guys. You've always done right by us from the bench. We'll do right by you here on the street."

"Thank you, Officer Jenkins," Jacob said, speaking for Beau, who stared forlornly at his garden. "We both appreciate it. I know we're a bit of a shock to the system, being together and all, but we don't want to cause problems."

"From where I'm standing, you and the judge ain't caused nothing," Jenkins said. "I know what hatred looks like. I've stared it in the face since I was old enough to know what I was looking at. It wasn't right when they hated me because I was black. It ain't right that they're hating you because you're gay."

"You won't catch the ones who did this," Beau said slowly. "I've seen cases like this. Unless they did something incredibly stupid or brag about it later, there's no way to prove who was responsible."

"You never know," Jenkins said. "At least one of your neighbors was concerned enough to call us. One of them might have seen something. I gotta ask a couple of questions, if you don't mind. Where were you when all this happened?"

"At the Prestonsburg Oaks," Beau said, visibly pulling himself together. Jacob's chest swelled with pride as Beau turned his back on the decimation wrought on his house and did his best to give the policeman concise, helpful answers. "Mrs. Breckenridge invited us to her anniversary party."

"Nice," Jenkins said with a low whistle. "I heard half the town was beggin' for invitations. Your friend was with you?"

"Yes. I'm sorry I didn't introduce you. Jacob Peters, my partner. Jacob, this is Officer Jenkins from the sheriff's office in town."

"Nice to meet you, Officer," Jacob said, sharing a smile with the man.

"Either of you had any run-ins with anyone? Anyone threatening you?"

"I lost my job in Elliot a few weeks ago," Jacob said, "and there were a lot of irate parents because I'd been teaching their children and who knows what kind of perversions they'd learned from me, but it seemed to die down after I was fired. None of them has contacted me or anything."

"What about you, Judge?"

"I'm a county judge," Beau said. "People threaten things every time I decide against them in court, but nothing like this. Nothing about Jacob and me."

"What about outside of court?"

"There was that one guy Patty ran out of Third Street Bistro," Jacob recalled, "the same night Mrs. Breckenridge invited us to her party. I don't know his name."

"Judge?" Jenkins prompted.

"Virgil Thompkins," Beau said, "but he was just making noise."

"That ain't for you to decide," Jenkins said. "What did he say?"

"Something about Patty serving 'our kind' and what was this town coming to," Jacob replied. "I don't remember exactly. Patty kicked him out, and then Mrs. Breckenridge showed up out of the blue, and the rest of the evening is kind of a blur."

"She does have that effect on people," Jenkins agreed. "I'll have someone talk to Virgil and see where he was this afternoon. Maybe he was just talking smack, but maybe he decided to do something about it, or maybe he knows who did."

"How soon can we go in?" Beau asked. "If I get the flowers back in the ground, some of them might survive."

"Give us a few more minutes," Jenkins said, "but you shouldn't stay here tonight, Judge. With that window broken, it ain't safe. I don't think the guys who did this will come back, but you never know. Is there somewhere else you can go?"

"We can go to my house in Elliot," Jacob said. "We'll have to get a change of clothes, but we can stay there tonight. It's on the market and mostly empty, but as far as I know, there aren't any broken windows."

"Give me the address," Jenkins said. "I'll call the sheriff in Elliot and have him send a car by to check and make sure. If you're livin' here, there ain't much reason for them to hit your house down there, but you never know with some people. No point in you drivin' all the way home if you can't stay there either."

Jacob shivered. The thought of someone breaking into the house, maybe intending to harm him or Beau or, even worse, Finn, chilled him to the bone. He recited the address to Officer Jenkins, giving in to the need to stand closer to Beau. He hoped his presence comforted Beau as much as Beau's nearness comforted him.

Officer Jenkins placed the call, nodding a couple of times before hanging up. "The dispatcher is going to send someone to check on your place, Mr. Peters. They'll give us a call back in a few minutes." He looked up at a call from one of the officers inside the crime tape. "In the meantime, you can go inside and pack a bag for a night or two. They've finished what they can do as far as gathering evidence. Do you have a cell number where I can call you if we find anything or if we need more information? In case you aren't at home."

Beau gave the officer his number in a mechanical voice, the complete lack of emotion as worrisome to Jacob as the damage to the house. When the officer thanked them again and headed toward his patrol car, Jacob took Beau's elbow, guiding him around to the back of the house. The fence had sustained some damage, but the vandals had not gone into the backyard, leaving that space untouched and flowering in the early spring evening.

Making sure the gate was shut behind them to ensure their privacy, Jacob pulled Beau to the porch and then into his arms. "I'm sorry," he whispered, his lips brushing Beau's cheek as he spoke. "They wanted to hurt you and they knew exactly how to do it. I'm *so* sorry."

"They're plants," Beau said, although the pain in his voice belied his words. "They can be replanted."

"Yes, they can be, and we will replant them," Jacob agreed, "but that's not the point. This wasn't some natural disaster, a flood or a tornado or a hurricane that damaged the yard, something you couldn't control and simply have to recover from. This was an attack on you. It's not about the plants at all."

"I know that," Beau snapped, pulling away. "It's about us being gay."

"No, it's about them being intolerant bigots with nothing better to do than make trouble," Jacob retorted. He held out his hand. "Dance with me."

Beau looked at him like he'd lost his mind.

Jacob pulled out his iPhone and started some music playing. "Dance with me," he repeated. "Just like this afternoon. You and me and nothing else matters."

"This won't solve anything," Beau said, but he stepped forward and took Jacob's hand.

"There's nothing to solve," Jacob insisted. "This is their problem, not ours."

"They made it our problem when they vandalized my house," Beau said.

"No, they made it Officer Jenkins's problem," Jacob replied. "It's only our problem if we let it get between us." He pulled Beau closer, leading where earlier he had followed. "You and me and nothing else, okay?"

Beau took a deep breath, warring with his need to control and his inability to do so at the moment. He let it out and relaxed into Jacob's arms. "Okay."

Jacob waltzed them slowly around the porch. He could feel the decrease in Beau's tension, but it was not completely gone. When the music changed, he kept them dancing, letting his body brush Beau's.

That seemed to do what his words could not, the remaining tension seeping slowly from beneath Jacob's hands until Beau leaned against him fully. Jacob entertained the notion of dancing Beau inside and making slow, sweet love to him. Beau had grown more comfortable with Jacob taking charge after their weekend in Key West and especially after their visit to Domain of Killien, when Beau had encouraged Jacob to top on more than one occasion, as if he'd realized Jacob needed one area of his life he could still control, but Jacob was not sure tonight was the right time to test that newfound ease. He would bide his time and see what mood Beau was in when they got to Elliot.

"Judge Braedon, Mr. Peters?"

Jacob stopped dancing, but he didn't pull away from Beau. He would leave that up to Beau.

"We're on the porch," Beau called, moving to Jacob's side but leaving his arm around his lover's waist.

"I heard back from the sheriff's office in Elliot. No damage at Mr. Peters's house. They're going to send a car by occasionally to make sure it stays that way during the night."

"Thank you," Jacob said. "We'll get our things and head that way."

"You're welcome. Y'all have a good night."

It wouldn't be the night Jacob had been looking forward to, the two of them alone in Beau's bed with no baby in the next room and no reason to wake up early the next morning, but he echoed the sentiment nonetheless. "Come on," he said. "Let's get what we need for tonight. We can deal with the rest tomorrow."

Beau followed Jacob silently into the house and up the stairs to their bedroom. They gathered toiletries, a change of clothing, and clean towels. Jacob still had his furniture at his house for show, but he'd brought everything else to Beau's house already. "Ready?" Jacob asked after a moment.

"No," Beau admitted. "It feels like we're running away."

Jacob set down the bag he'd packed. "Okay. What do you want to do?"

"I want to go to Home Depot and get some lumber to board up the window, and then I want to see what I can salvage of the flowers," Beau said. "I want to start painting over the graffiti and reclaim our house."

"Then that's what we'll do," Jacob said. "Even if we decide to sleep in Elliot, we don't have to go right now."

"Thank you," Beau said, giving Jacob a quick kiss.

Jacob pulled him back, kissing him more deeply. "There's nothing to thank me for. This is my home too. They attacked us both with their nasty words and their violence. We'll just have to show them we're above that. Home Depot doesn't close until nine. Let's see what we can do for the flowers first. Like you said, the longer we wait to get them back in the ground, the less likely they are to make it."

They changed out of the suits they'd worn to the anniversary party and into jeans and T-shirts they wouldn't mind getting dirty. Traipsing down to the outlying shed, Jacob said, "Why don't you see what can be done for the bushes? I can dig holes for the flowers, but anything more complicated than that is beyond me."

Beau nodded, handing Jacob a hand trowel. "I doubt there's anything to do but replace the bushes," Beau said. "They might come back from the roots, but I can't mend broken branches."

"Then we'll have to water them and fertilize them and see if we can't convince them to give us another chance," Jacob proposed.

Beau smiled, albeit a little weakly. "We'll make a gardener out of you yet."

Jacob suspected Beau could convince him to become almost anything if it would bring a smile to his face.

They worked in the front yard until nearly dark, clearing away the broken limbs, replanting the flowers that could be saved, and trimming the remaining bushes into something resembling a healthy shape. Jacob could see the progress, but it bore no resemblance to Beau's usually immaculate yard. There were holes where plants had been too damaged to save, and even those that remained were scraggly rather than perfectly groomed. "It'll take time," Jacob said, wrapping his arms around Beau's waist, "but we'll get it back in shape. We fixed all the shit that was wrong between us. Compared to that, this will be easy."

"You have a point when you put it that way," Beau said with a chuckle. "Let's get some plywood so we can cover the broken window and some paint so we can start on the graffiti tomorrow."

[11]

BY THE time they finished putting the plywood over the broken windows and sanding the wood that would need to be repainted after the graffiti, they were covered in sweat and dust and grime, but the house was secure and the vile slogans were much fainter than before. "What do you want to do now?" Jacob asked as they walked inside. "Shall we shower here or in Elliot?"

"I'm too dirty to get in a car," Beau said, "but more than that, I don't want to leave tonight. This is our home, damn it, and they shouldn't be able to drive us out of it with their hatred and abuse and destruction."

"Now that we've blocked the window, I suppose there's no reason to go," Jacob agreed, suddenly unsure what mood Beau was in. He had been grim but determined to hide it as they worked on the house and yard, but the false cheer had suddenly disappeared. "It would certainly be easier not to have to lug everything we'd need down to Elliot. Even the fridge is empty. And then we'd have to get it ready to show again before we left."

"That's not the point," Beau said, his eyes hard as he herded Jacob down the hallway to the downstairs bathroom. "This is our house. Our home. They don't get to run us off. They don't get to weaken us that way."

Jacob nodded, letting Beau push him into the bathroom and strip him down. Beau's clothes landed on the floor on top of them. Steam filled the room, ghosting between them in the tense silence. "We just got our lives back on track," Beau growled after a moment. "They don't get to derail that."

"Nothing's derailed," Jacob promised. "I'm right here with you, and I'm not going anywhere."

"You sure as hell aren't," Beau agreed, crowding against Jacob as they stepped into the glass enclosure. "You're mine, and they don't get a say in that."

Jacob had never seen Beau in quite this mood, but while he hated the circumstances that had created it, he wasn't at all averse to the results. "No say at all," he replied, leaning against the back wall quiescently. He had a feeling doing anything else would be poking the sleeping tiger, and he wasn't sure that was such a good idea. Given the wild gleam in Beau's eyes, their lovemaking would be fierce and raw enough without adding to it.

Beau's heart pounded wildly as he pressed against Jacob, fear, anger, and lust riding him hard. As angry as he had been when Jacob lost his job, that was external, an attack on Jacob, not on him. Even the occasional encounter with people like Thompkins had been external, and he'd found it easy to take the high road, to ignore them and move on, but the vandalism of his house had struck a deep nerve, leaving him feeling exposed and vulnerable.

He didn't like it.

He attacked Jacob's mouth, relief surging through him as the sweet lips parted beneath his in eager welcome. The vandals might have ruined his garden, defaced his house, and broken his windows, but they hadn't shaken Beau's foundation. Not if Jacob could still kiss him so sweetly and love him so fully.

With that relief came the need to prove they were still together, stronger than the external forces trying to separate them.

"I need you," he said bluntly. "I need to fuck you so hard and so long that I'll know nothing will ever come between us."

Jacob nodded, sucking on Beau's tongue one last time before turning and pressing his buttocks against Beau's erection. So much for taking charge tonight, but if this was what Beau needed, Jacob would give it to him.

The submissive posture enflamed Beau, igniting needs he didn't know he had, to fuck, to mark, to claim until even a blind man could see that Jacob was his and they belonged together regardless of the bigotry that surrounded them. Grabbing the conditioner that kept Jacob's long hair tamed, Beau squirted some on his fingers as he rocked against Jacob's ass. He might intend to give Jacob the ride of his life, but he did not intend to hurt his lover while doing it, not when Jacob breathed more life into his soul than his garden had ever done.

At the first touch of Beau's hand, Jacob spread his legs wider, reaching behind himself with one hand to part his cheeks in silent offering. The sight took Beau to his knees, his face pressing into the dark crease. He could taste sweat, not yet washed away by the water that fell mostly on his own back, and smell the musk of Jacob's desire, the combination only adding to his need.

Jacob mewled a little, the needy sound another goad to Beau's passions. He licked furiously over the tight furl, tantalizing it until the muscle relaxed and he could press inside, but it wasn't hard enough, deep enough, fast enough. Pushing to his feet again, he stabbed his fingers into Jacob's heat, stretching as quickly as he dared, probing for the nub that would offset the burn of his rushed entry.

Jacob thrashed against the wall, bracing himself with both hands as Beau's fingers fucked him. "God, fuck, now, Beau!"

The babble was music to Beau's ears, proof that Jacob was as desperate as Beau was. Pulling his fingers free, he pressed in, more slowly than he had before, knowing that even with preparation, his cock would stretch Jacob more widely and deeply.

Jacob was having none of it, pushing back hard against Beau, impaling himself completely on Beau's erection. "I thought you said you were going to fuck me hard," Jacob goaded.

Beau's control shattered, his body moving without any conscious thought. His hips pistoned against Jacob's ass, fucking him against the wall with all his might. Jacob met him thrust for thrust, cursing and begging and moaning until Beau thought he'd go mad with need.

His orgasm blindsided him, leaving him gasping for breath, his vision graying out and his balance deserting him. He slumped against Jacob's back, only dimly aware from the tension in the slim shoulders that Jacob had not climaxed.

Trying to gather his wits, he slid to his knees, urging Jacob to turn. He licked across the tip of Jacob's cock before sliding his lips down the long shaft.

Jacob took the cue, beginning to move. "Put your fingers in me," he ordered.

Beau did as Jacob directed, sliding his fingers into the seed-slick passage, fucking Jacob with them as Jacob fucked his mouth. His other hand cradled Jacob's balls, massaging them in time with the rest of their movements. It only took a few moments before Beau felt them draw up in his hand in prelude to Jacob's climax. He thrust harder with his fingers, pressing down on Jacob's prostate. With a long, low moan, Jacob shuddered, his release filling Beau's mouth.

Beau kept right on sucking and licking and thrusting until Jacob whimpered. "Too much."

Beau nodded, giving the tip of Jacob's cock one last lick as he pulled away and slid his fingers free.

"That was…. damn, Beau, I think you broke my brain."

"As long as I don't break anything important," Beau teased, rising to his feet and pausing to kiss the two tawny nipples he had neglected in his earlier frenzy.

Jacob swatted at him playfully. Beau caught the offending limb and brought it to his lips, kissing Jacob's fingers tenderly. "Thank you for your help today."

"I'm sorry it had to be done," Jacob said, "but I was happy to help. I know how much your garden means to you."

"I think it's our garden now," Beau replied. "You worked as hard on it as I did."

Jacob smiled. "Our garden. I like the sound of that."

THEY slept late the next morning, neither of them interested in going to church, where the sermon was probably about the perils of sodomy and the necessity of driving it out of their midst. Beau knew that was unfair the minute he said it, but he was still feeling a little raw from the attack on the house the day before.

"I'm not exactly devout," Jacob reminded him. "We'll have a lazy morning and work on the yard some more after lunch, when no one will stare at us for working in the yard instead of being at church."

They made a big breakfast, pancakes and bacon, scrambled eggs, and a gallon of coffee, and ate on the back porch, the chill still lingering in the air as the sun rose and burned off the slight fog. When they had eaten and were sipping their third cup of coffee each, Beau reached across the space between them and took Jacob's hand. His gaze didn't waver from the back of the yard. "We could put a swing set beneath that elm tree in a couple of years," he said. "Finn would love it."

"I'm sure he would," Jacob agreed. "It'll break up the line of sight for the fountain in the back, though."

Beau shrugged. "We can move the fountain, or we can move where the furniture is on the porch. Or we can not worry about it. Finn needs a place to play. It's going to be hard for him, growing up here with two dads instead of a dad and a mom."

"He has a mom too," Jacob replied, "but I know what you mean. We'll just have to help him understand that families come in all different varieties and that there's nothing to be ashamed of with ours."

"That's easier said than done if people keep attacking us the way they did yesterday," Beau said.

"So what are you saying?" Jacob asked. "That we should turn tail and run? That wasn't what you said last night."

"Last night I wasn't thinking about Finn," Beau said. "He's a baby. He can't defend himself, and it would kill me if something happened to either of you."

"Nothing's going to happen to us," Jacob said. "People are still getting over the shock of finding out about us. Everyone at the party yesterday was as kind as could be."

"It wasn't the local gentry who tore up the house."

"No, it wasn't," Jacob agreed, "but other than in court, the majority of the people we have to deal with on a regular basis are going to be people who were at the party or whose opinions are swayed by people at the party. We don't deal with the Virgil Thompkinses very often. I don't mean that to sound snobbish, but it's the truth."

"That doesn't mean we won't run into people like him," Beau said. "If it were just us, I wouldn't worry so much, but if Thompkins decided to start something while we had Finn with us, he could get hurt accidentally."

"So you want to move? What about your mother?"

"I don't know," Beau said with a sigh. "It's all a muddle in my head. I think I see the right path to take and then something else occurs to me and it all gets confused again."

"We'll figure it out," Jacob said. "We don't have to decide today." He glanced down at his watch. "It's late enough to get started in the yard. Let's do that. It'll make you feel better to have dirt on your hands."

Beau summoned a smile and swallowed the last of his coffee. They put the dishes inside to clean up later and went to the shed for their tools. As they walked around the front of the house, Lisa Matthews, their neighbor across the street, drove into her driveway and hopped out. "Oh, good, you're home, Beau!" she called across the street. "You can help me with this."

Beau handed Jacob his shovel with a grimace he hid before crossing the road to see what his neighbor needed help with. She opened the back of her SUV and pointed to a huge potted azalea. "I can't possibly carry that."

"Where do you want it?" he asked, manhandling the bush out of the car.

"Oh, that's up to you," she said. "You know your yard better than I do."

"What?" Beau asked, sure he'd misunderstood.

"I wasn't home when those miscreants tore up your yard or I'd have gone after them with a shovel," Lisa said. "I saw what happened when I got home last night. I can't change what they did, but I can help you get things back in order. So you decide where that bush will grow best, and just remember that whoever did all that damage, it wasn't someone from around here. We may not understand, but that doesn't make what happened right."

"Thank you, Lisa," Beau said, his throat tight. "We're going to get this in the ground now. If you'd like, you could come over later for something to drink. Maybe around five?"

"I'd like that," Lisa said. "I've seen your... I don't even know what to call him."

"Partner," Beau suggested.

"I've seen your partner coming and going from the house, but I haven't actually met him yet, and if he's going to be our neighbor, too, then I'd better get on that. Do you mind if the children come?"

"The more the merrier," Beau said, hefting the pot in his arms. "We'll see you at five."

"See you then."

Beau carried the azalea back to his yard. "Can you believe it?" he asked, setting it down next to a hole where one of his bushes had been totally ripped up. "She bought this for us."

Jacob smiled. "I've pretty much decided there's nothing this town could do that would surprise me anymore. Between Mrs. Breckenridge and the vandals, they've got the whole spectrum covered. Shall we get this planted?"

They spent the next hour expanding the hole to fit the larger bush and getting it settled in the ground. They had moved on to the annuals Beau had bought the night before along with the plywood when a car of teenagers drove by. One of them shouted an insult out the window. Beau flinched but didn't look up. He didn't want to know which of his neighbors' kids—and by extension, his neighbors—felt that way. The car stopped, a door slammed, and it sped off. Then Beau heard a different voice, scolding this time.

"But Ma, I wasn't the one that said it."

"I don't care. One of your friends did, and you'll apologize to Judge Braedon right now for being a part of that kind of nonsense."

Beau looked up to see Jessica Spencer, the neighbor from three doors down, standing at the edge of her yard with her adolescent son. "Go on," she urged.

"I'm sorry, Judge Braedon," the boy mumbled.

His mother smacked the back of his head. "A proper apology, Joel William, or you'll be eating dinner standing up for a week."

"I'm sorry, Judge Braedon," the boy repeated. "My friends were out of line for what they said."

"I'm sure they're just repeating what they hear at home," Beau said.

"Maybe," Joel replied, "but Ma's right. That doesn't give me any excuse."

"We appreciate the apology," Beau said, including Jacob with a gesture of his hand. "I'd hate to think someone who knew us could feel that way about us."

"Can we go now, Ma?" Joel asked, obviously not comfortable with the situation.

"No," his mother replied. "The judge needs help cleaning up this mess. Go put on some old clothes. You're good with a paintbrush. You can start getting rid of that nastiness on his porch."

"But Ma—"

"But nothing. Now git!"

Joel slunk down the sidewalk. "He doesn't have to do that, Jessica," Beau said.

"Yes, he does," Jessica insisted. "Those friends of his are no good. He needs to learn to stand up for what's right. Maybe spending the afternoon with you will help remind him of what that is."

"Lisa Matthews is coming over around five for drinks. Why don't you and Bill join us too?" Beau suggested.

"Bill will probably still be on the golf course," Jessica said with a roll of her eyes, "but I'd love to come down. I've got some fresh lemonade made. I'll bring a pitcher of that because with two men living here, you probably don't have anything but beer in the house."

"That's not true," Beau protested. "I have a fully stocked liquor cabinet."

Jessica smirked at him. "When was the last time you opened any of it?"

Beau had to stop to think.

"I rest my case," Jessica said with a laugh. "I'll bring the lemonade. Lisa's kids and Joel can drink it, if nothing else."

"What's this about drinks?" Jacob asked when Jessica had left.

"Lisa mentioned not having met you," Beau explained, "and she bought us the plant, and now Jessica made her son apologize and insisted he come help us, and it just seemed like the thing to do."

"I think it's a great idea," Jacob said. "I just wanted to know what you were planning."

"Nothing really," Beau replied. "It wasn't a plan as much as an impulse."

Jacob chuckled. "I have no idea if we have snacks, but I suppose it doesn't matter. It's about spending time with the neighbors, not about putting on a show."

"Hey, Judge Braedon!"

They turned to see a boy on a bike.

"Hello, Tommy," Beau said, recognizing one of the kids from the summer program where he and Jacob had met. "How are you today?"

"Doing okay. Mom said I could come see if you needed any help. I heard what they did to your house, and well, after all the time you and Mr. Jacob spent helping us two summers ago, I figured I could come help you now."

"I think we could find something for you to do," Beau said. "How are you with a paintbrush?"

"Not great," Tommy said, "but I help my dad with his construction business in the summer. I could clean out that broken window and get it ready to be replaced."

"That would be great," Beau said. "We boarded it up, but I was going to have to call someone to get it fixed."

"I'll get it prepped for you," Tommy said, "and then maybe Dad can squeeze it in before or after work tomorrow. One window doesn't take all that long to install."

"If he can, we'd really appreciate it," Beau said, "but you make sure to tell him we'll pay him for his time, just like we'll pay you for yours. We appreciate everyone's help, but honest work deserves honest pay."

"I won't say no to that," Tommy replied with a grin. "I'm saving up for a car. Can't go impressing people—" He took a deep breath, glanced between the two men, and started again. "Can't go impressing guys on a bike, now can I?"

"No, I don't suppose you can," Beau said with a laugh. "Come on, Tommy. I'll show you where the tools are."

They came back a few minutes later, Tommy going up onto the porch and beginning to take down the plywood while Beau came back to where Jacob was standing, putting his arm around his lover's waist. "I'll be damned. You know what Tommy told me? He said that since we came out, a group of kids at the local high school have started a GSA chapter, and they have fifteen members already. That school only has three hundred kids total."

"Change requires a catalyst," Jacob said. "I told you that months ago."

"And I didn't believe we'd survive being that catalyst. I may not be an expert in chemistry, but I remember enough to know that nothing comes out of a chemical reaction the way it went in."

"We haven't come out the way we went in either," Jacob reminded him. "Personally I like the way we've turned out."

"We still have to find you a job."

"We'll find one," Jacob said. "It may not be in education, although I'd miss the kids if it isn't, but we'll find something. And in the meantime, we have the Autism Society monthly meeting next week.

That's what I need to work on tomorrow while you're at the courthouse. We haven't made much progress this month."

"We've had a few other things going on," Beau replied dryly.

"The kids don't care about that. They just want to have something fun and structured to do this summer, and it's our responsibility to make sure they do."

"It can be your job if you want it to be."

They turned around at the sound of another voice. "Paula?"

"Sorry to sneak up on you like that," Paula Hodges said. "I couldn't help overhearing. I just got word from the national Autism Society that they've funded the position for a full-time educational director for the local chapter. Of course the salary is commensurate with a non-profit job rather than with a teaching position, but I thought of you as soon as I read the e-mail."

"Are you sure you want me in that kind of position?" Jacob asked. "I mean, I heard some pretty nasty things from the parents in Elliot. I'd hate for that to come back on you and the fundraising efforts you have to do to finance all your programs."

"We won't find anyone more qualified for the job," Paula replied, "and while I know you'll be up to your elbows in the day-to-day running of the summer camp because that's the way you are, your job description includes the planning as much as the implementation. If people comment on it, we'll focus on that and show the faces of the volunteers carrying out your plans. They don't need to know that you were the one taking the pictures."

Beau laughed. "I like the way you think."

"What do you say?" Paula asked. "Want to come work for the Autism Society?"

Jacob felt his smile widening until he swore it took up his entire face. "Yes. I... I don't even know what to say. I was just telling Beau I didn't expect to be able to work in education anymore. I know this isn't traditional education, but... I don't know how to thank you."

"Oh, I'm sure you won't be thanking me when you see your first paycheck," Paula said with a short laugh, "but we really would be thrilled to have you aboard."

"It's more than I'm making now," Jacob pointed out, "and it's not about the money as much as it is about feeling like I'm contributing. I've felt so useless since they suspended me."

Paula nodded sympathetically. "There's nothing worse than feeling unwanted. Believe me, you're wanted at the Autism Society. I discussed it with the local board last week, when we got word the national board was reviewing our proposal. There were a few people who took some convincing, but the final vote was unanimous. If the money came through, we would offer you the job."

"Do you have a paintbrush, Judge?" Joel interrupted.

"Excuse me a minute," Beau said to Paula. "Joel is going to help fix up the mess someone made of our house last night."

"I see that," Paula said, frowning at the damage. "And I see he isn't the only help you have. I'll let you get back to work. Jacob, we'll need a few more days to process all the paperwork from the national headquarters, but you can start a week from Monday. We'll make the official announcement at the monthly meeting on Wednesday."

"Thank you, Paula. Some of the neighbors are coming over around five for drinks if you and Jim would like to join us."

Paula smiled. "You know how Jim is in unfamiliar social settings, but I'll ask him. Given that it's you and Beau, he might be willing to give it a try."

"We'd love to see you if you can make it, and if you can't, we understand," Jacob said. "And we'll see you Wednesday night for sure."

Beau came back as Paula was leaving. "I guess I don't have to worry about a job after all," Jacob said.

"It looks like we've got quite a bit to celebrate tonight," Beau agreed, kissing Jacob quickly. He looked at the bush Lisa had given him, up at the two teens on the porch, and back at Jacob. "We might actually make this work."

Jacob shook his head. "We *will* make this work. If it turns out not to be here, well, that's a problem for another day, but this"—he gestured back and forth between Beau and himself—"is here to stay."

ARIEL TACHNA lives outside of Houston with her husband, her daughter and son, and their cat. Before moving there, she traveled all over the world, having fallen in love with both France, where she found her husband, and India, where she dreams of retiring some day. She's bilingual with snippets of four other languages to her credit and is as in love with languages as she is with writing.

Visit Ariel's website at http://www.arieltachna.com/ and her blog at http://arieltachna.livejournal.com/.

Contemporary Romance by ARIEL TACHNA

http://www.dreamspinnerpress.com

Also by ARIEL TACHNA

http://www.dreamspinnerpress.com

Historical Romance by ARIEL TACHNA

http://www.dreamspinnerpress.com

From NICKI BENNETT & ARIEL TACHNA

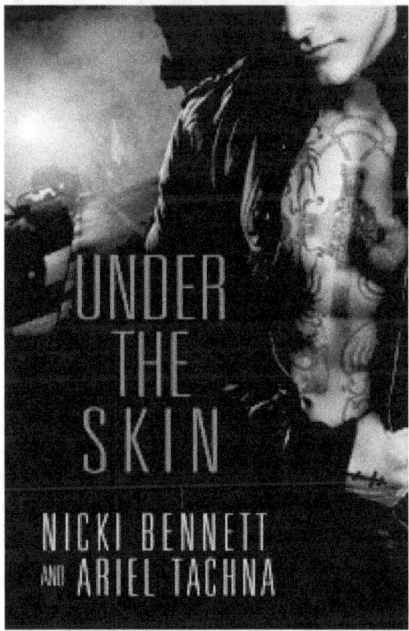

http://www.dreamspinnerpress.com

www.ingramcontent.com/pod-product-compliance
Lightning Source LLC
Chambersburg PA
CBHW070010260626
47159CB00005B/1742